ONE
TRUE
MATE · 1
Shifter's Sacrifice

LISA LADEW

Book cover by The Final Wrap *waves* Hi Rebecca!!

Cover model: Burton Hughes

Photographer: Eric Battershell

Special editorial assistance by The Blurb Diva and Savan Robbins. Without you, I would be lost, and much less interesting. Thank you.

Thank you to Kristine Piiparinen for all of your help with everything, again, as always <3

Thank you beta readers, arc readers, babes, and all of my readers. Goodness you make writing worth doing and so much easier and fun.

I also want to thank Fay Reid, Sandra McAulay and John McAulay for being my Scottish language and culture consultants.

Thank you Carin Borland for your evil help ;)

And special thank you to Amanda Quiles, my Shifter Guru.

GLOSSARY

Bearen – bear shifters. Almost always work as firefighters.

Citlali – Spiritual leaders of all *Shiften*. They are able to communicate with the deities telepathically, and sometimes bring back prophecies from these communications.

Deae – goddess.

Dragen – dragon shifter. Rare.

Echo – an animal with the same markings of a *shiften*. Usually seen as a harbinger of bad things, but could also be a messenger from the Light.

Felen – big cat shifters. Almost always work as mercenaries. They are also the protectors of Rhen's physical body and a specially-trained group of them can track Khain when he comes into the *Ula*.

Foxen – the *Foxen* were created when Khain forcibly mated with female *wolfen*.

Haven, The – final resting place of all *shiften*. Where The Light resides.

Impot – a *shiften* that cannot shift because of a genetic defect caused by mating too close to their own bloodline. Trent and Troy are not thought to be *impots* because they were born during a *klukwana*.

Khain – also known as the Divided Demon, the Great Destroyer, and the Matchitehew. The hunter of humans and the main nemesis of all *shiften*.

Klukwana – a ceremony where a full–blooded *shiften* who mates another *shiften* does so with both in animal form, then the mother stays in animal form during the entire pregnancy. The young in the litter are always born as their animal. *Wolven* from a *klukwana* always come in at least 4 to 7 young. *Bearen* are always two cubs, and *felen* are unpredictable, sometimes only one. *Shiften* born from a *klukwana* are almost always more powerful, bigger, and stronger than regular *shiften*, but many parents don't try it because of the inherent risks to the mother during the (shorter) pregnancy and the risk that the *shiften* young may choose not to shift into human form. A lesser known possibility is that the *shiften* young will have a harder time learning to shift into human form, especially if no one shifts near them in the first few days after birth.

KSRT – Kilo Special Response Team, or Khain Special Response team. A group of *wolven* police whose primary goal is to hunt down and kill Khain, if that can be done.

Light, The – The creator of the *Ula*, humans, Rhen, Khain, and the angels.

Moonstruck – Insane. *Shiften* who spend too long indoors or too long in human form can become *moonstruck* slowly and not even realize it.

Pravus – Khain's home. A fiery, desolate dimension that sits alongside ours.

Pumaii – a small group of specialized *felen* tasked with tracking Khain when he crosses over into our dimension.

Renqua – a discoloration in a *shiften's* fur which is also seen as a birthmark in human form. Every *renqua* is different. The original *renquas* were pieces of Rhen she put inside the wolves, bears, and big cats to create the *shiften*. Every pure-blooded shifter born since has also had a *renqua*. Half-breeds may or may not have one. Some *foxen* acquired weak *renquas* when they mated with *shiften*. Also called the mark of life.

Rhen – the creator of all *shiften*. A female deity.

Ruhi – the art of speaking telepathically. No humans are known to possess the power to do this. Not all *shiften* are able to do it. It is the preferred form of speaking for the *dragen*.

Shiften – Shifter-kind.

Ula – earth, in the current dimension and time. The home of the *shiften*.

Vahiy – end of the world.

Wolfen – a wolf shifter. Almost always works as a police officer.

Wolven – wolf shifters, plural.

Zyanya – When a *wolfen* dies, the funeral is for the benefit of humans, but the important ceremony is the *zyanya*. The pack mates of the fallen *wolfen* run in wolf form through the forest, heading north to show the spirit the way to the Haven. When they reach a body of water, they all jump in and swim to the other side, then emerge in human form.

CHAPTER 1

The three wolves raced through the forest at top speed in the waning moonlight, the large one in the lead urging the others to go faster, harder, push themselves to their limit. But even his perseverance couldn't hold the other two for long. As they neared the clearing, the two black wolves slowed, panting and grinning and jostling each other with their hips, the one with the brush of white on the very tip of his tail snapping playfully at a pocket gopher who chose that moment to push his head out of his hole to see what the noise was.

The black and gray wolf in the lead, with the boomerang-shaped patch of white on his left shoulder, didn't slow. He pushed himself harder, driven from somewhere deep inside to give everything he had until the very last second, like always.

He felt the danger coming from his left a split second

before it reached him, but there was nothing he could do. It was coming too fast. The large animal hit him on his left flank and they both tumbled together, a mass of fur and limbs, over the forest floor, their teeth snapping, their mouths frothing, as they snarled and tore into each other, their bodies only stopping when they slammed into a tree.

The wolves separated, rolling away from each other. As they rolled, they both shifted into human form, fur disappearing, legs lengthening, thickening, hips changing shape, muzzles shortening, claws retracting and reforming, eye color changing. Both males scrambled to their feet in fighting stances, naked, but still ready to throw down.

"What is your problem, Mac?" Trevor Burbank, a tall, Mack-truck of a man, shouted, but before his second-in-command could answer, the other two wolves caught up to them, both launching their black-furred bodies at Mac and knocking him to the ground. "Fuck," Trevor swore, running forward to get into the fray before his brothers tore Mac to pieces.

Trevor elbowed his way past the furiously shaking bodies of his brothers, one at Mac's thigh, and one at Mac's throat.

"Get your *mutts* off me," Mac snarled, fighting back, but no match against the two massive wolves.

Aw, hell no. He didn't just say that. Trevor clamped his hands around the jaws of the wolf at Mac's throat and pulled the opposite way of the bite-down, knowing Mac could heal his own leg by shifting, but if his throat was torn open, he could bleed out before he ever had a chance to recover. "Trent, Troy, he's not worth it, let him go," he forced out, all of his energy focused on keeping Trent from killing Mac right then and there.

Mac screamed and Trevor knew that Troy was grinding

into his leg, maybe all the way to the bone. "Troy, stop!" Trevor demanded. He aimed a few kicks at Troy's flank while still cranking Trent's jaws apart. Blood flowed down his fingers and across Mac's neck, the iron tang of it infusing Trevor's nostrils. Minimal pain in his hands told him only some of that blood was his, and as he looked closer, he could see several of Trent's teeth violating Mac's skin.

"Trent! Lay off! You're gonna fucking kill him! He's an asshole, but you can't kill *wolven* for being assholes, the *Citlali* will fry you!" *Citlali* were the spiritual leaders of all *wolven*, beings who could transform from wolf to human form at will, who almost always worked as police officers. The *Citlali* acted as judge and jury in all matters that weren't covered by human courts.

Finally, Trent eased slightly. "Let him go," Trevor continued, his voice taking on a soothing quality. "Even *dogs* like him have their uses. He doesn't have to like me."

Trevor ignored the growl that came from Mac's throat and caught his brother's projected thought like it was a ball launched at his face.

He does *have to respect you.*

Trevor grinned sourly. *We can't force him to,* he sent back.

We can let Troy bite his balls off though.

Trevor laughed out loud, relieved to see Trent letting go of Mac's throat, even if it was reluctantly. He turned to look at Troy who had also let go, but Mac's thigh was a mess of dirty hamburger. *Too bad, so sad.*

As soon as Mac was free he scrambled to his feet and limped away, leaving Trevor and his brothers on the cold forest floor to watch the blood drip from Mac's body, staining the foliage beneath him.

"The Chief wants you in the office in thirty minutes," Mac threw over his shoulder, just before he shifted and loped off.

Trevor watched him go, admiring the fierce strength of Mac's pure white animal, even as he disliked the male. Trevor wanted to like Mac, it would make his working environment much easier, but with as much as Mac hated him, Trevor had no choice but to feel the same. He didn't blame Mac though.

Mac thought Trevor was a fraud, and Trevor agreed.

CHAPTER 2

What little was left of Ella Carmi's past lay spread out in front of her in the large attic, packed into boxes or sitting in random spots, as if left there by a busy toddler. Ella eyed it, knowing she shouldn't go through anything, she should just allow the resale shop to come in and take everything, but she was feeling grumpy that it had to happen at all. She *knew* there was nothing valuable in the boxes, but she still felt obligated to check. God helps those who get off their asses, and all that.

If she didn't come up with fourteen thousand dollars in the next two weeks, she would lose her aunt's house, and she had no idea if that would be a blessing or a curse. So her ass would be in motion until she figured something out.

Turning her attention back to the dark and dusty room, she tried to mentally divide it into the most likely spots to search, but was distracted by a soft rubbing against her leg.

She looked down to see Chelsea, a black and orange harlequin cat, twisting its body around her ankle and she smiled, bending to pet the feline on the head, the cat's silky fur calming her. Her aunt's other cat, all-black except for a bit of white on the tip of his tail, rubbed against her too, then looked up at her with sad, golden eyes and meowed once.

Her smile vanished. "I know, Smokey. You miss her," she told the cat softly, her voice echoing in the large attic.

Ella couldn't say the same, but she wouldn't tell Smokey that, not that Smokey didn't already know. Ella snorted, then bit her lip. "Sorry," she whispered to no one in particular. Now that she had no other humans to talk to, having conversations with the cats seemed normal, but she knew it wasn't. She feared it was just one more reason to believe she was going insane.

The cats looked at her as if to ask if she was going to stay up in the drafty, dusty attic and Ella nodded before she could catch herself. The cats meandered away and she watched them, until Chelsea carefully picked her way down the attic steps and Smokey dropped to the floor and began to clean his paws.

Ella's phone chimed in her pocket, startling her. No one knew her number except her mom and her aunt, and both were dead. She had no friends, her mom had made sure of that. *Except Accalia. Online friends count.*

Ella pursed her lips and wondered if in fact they did, really, but Accalia didn't have her number, so it didn't matter anyway.

She looked at her phone. The text had no name with it, but she knew immediately it was Shay. The words were too vicious to be anyone else.

So you finally did it. You killed them both. I want what's coming to me you fucking bitch. You better not have spent all the estate yet.

Ella's hands trembled as she muted the conversation and put the phone away. The only question now was, how long would it take her sister to show up at the house where she would not be so easily muted? Was she in town, or on her way?

Ella turned back around to the boxes, desperately trying to distract herself. She could do nothing else. The van from the resale shop had taken all the furniture, the china, the hutches, and her aunt's and mom's clothes the day before. Today was all the miscellaneous things left downstairs and everything in the attic, and she needed to get to work.

She ran her fingers over a trunk to her left, then opened it and peeked inside. Clothes. Old clothes. She eyed a standing mirror and wondered if it was worth anything, but a quick check with Google told her no. She pushed her long, black hair out of her eyes and made a face at herself in the mirror, choosing not to look at her wide hips and the pooch forming in her belly, like maybe she was two months pregnant. She stress-ate, always had, and no matter how much she exercised, it didn't seem to matter. Maybe now her stress would back down a bit and she could try to get a handle on her life and the way she looked.

Ella moved away from the mirror, moving moth-eaten blankets and kicking through a pile of platform shoes, feeling completely hopeless. There was nothing good up here, she should just turn around and—

A crashing noise called her attention and she whirled around to see Smokey leaping through the air away from a tipping pile of boxes. The top one had already hit the floor and spilled its contents everywhere.

Ella watched the cat stare hard at her. The cat wanted her to look in that box. She was sure of it. Ella walked forward slowly, then shook her head and swore softly. The cat didn't want anything and she was a fool to think so. Hadn't her mother told her that a thousand times?

She shooed the cat away from the mess and straightened up the closed boxes that had fallen, then knelt down to gather the contents of the open one. Mostly cheap jewelry. Fake pearls. Rhinestone earrings. Beaded bracelets. Ella didn't know a lot about jewelry, but she knew this stuff was junk. Probably her mother's. Aunt Patricia had never worn jewelry, and when she saw Ella's mother wear it, she would shake her head, press her lips together and mutter something under her breath. Ella couldn't remember it exactly, but it started with *Neither love the world nor the things in the world...*

"How about your cats, Aunt Patricia, were they of the world?" Ella said absently as she shoved the jewelry back into the box, the metal upon metal clinking musically. "Were you allowed to love them?"

Without warning, her thoughts repeated, then doubled on top of each other, causing a dizzy sensation that rocked her until she couldn't remember if it was her mother's jewelry and her aunt who hated it, or her aunt's jewelry and her mother hated it. She shook her head, disliking the queer sensation that had been happening so frequently lately. Her mother had liked jewelry. Of course. She knew that.

She shoved the last necklace back in the box then froze as a shiny gold pendant caught her eye. She pulled a knot of fake stuff away from the pendant, her eyes glued to it, as she felt suddenly transfixed. Had she seen it before? She couldn't remember but a feeling of *déjà vu* hit her hard, like maybe she'd had this experience before.

Which made no sense.

The pendant was an inch and a half tall, and in the shape of an angel, its head bent, a small gem that looked like a too-large crystal ball between its hands. She hooked the delicate gold chain of the pendant and raised it out of the box, taking a step back with her prize in her hands. The gold piece dangled at the end of the chain and twisted, revealing its back. Which wasn't the back of an angel, like Ella expected.

It was a snarling wolf with honey-colored eyes.

Ella stared at the wolf, loving everything about it, even as she felt a worm of worry or fear thread through her. She ignored it and reached in her pockets for her phone. Had she left it downstairs? No, no. She shook her head again, chastising herself for forgetting that she'd just received a text from Accalia. She shouldn't forget something like that. She shook her head again. No, it was *Shay*, she'd gotten the text from. She tried to concentrate, hating the way her mind was slipping, like she was eighty years old instead of twenty-five.

She found the phone and drew it out, wanting to take a picture of the wolf so she could send it to Accalia who would, no doubt, appreciate it as much as she did.

She held her hand out below the slowly-twirling pendant to catch it, then brought it towards her face, as her thumb lovingly caressed the detail of the wolf's body.

The wolf's eyes glowed and the room flooded in bright light, making Ella squint against the glare.

The glare that felt achingly familiar.

Ella gasped and dropped the pendant, her eyes tracking it as she immediately regretted the act. What if the pendant were broken?

But the floor beneath her was gone, replaced by green grass. She looked at her feet, surprised to see they were too small and clad in a pair of pink and white sneakers, one of them streaked with grains of golden sand.

A boy laughed and she looked up, amazed to find herself in a playground, with black swings to her left, a sandbox to her right, a large red building blocking most of her view of the road, and four sneering boys surrounding her. Ella pinched her leg hard, dismayed to discover that the leg pinch happened in what could only be some sort of a hallucination.

Except it had actually happened.

"I said give me your bag," the largest one who stood right in front of her snarled. She remembered his name, it was Chad. He was well-known in the school as a bully and a future criminal.

"No," she spat out at him, unable to help doing exactly what she had done fifteen years before. Her head swiveled, looking for her mother, but her mother had forgotten to pick her up again, drunk and passed out on the couch maybe, and all the teachers had gone home. She was on her own.

"I love it when they fight," Chad said to the boy next to him and they both laughed. Ella heard something evil in that laugh, something that she didn't quite understand, but something she instinctively knew was very dangerous to her. These boys were older than her by several years. Thirteen, or fourteen, maybe.

"She needs a lesson," a sly but somehow awful voice said, and Ella's head whipped to the left. Another boy was sitting on a swing, but he hadn't been there a second ago. She barely had time to wonder who he was when he stood up and approached Chad. He was big, and even older than these boys, with long dark hair and eye-arresting eyebrows. He wore faded blue jeans and a sweatshirt that said Wolves Drool with a cartoon rendition of a wolf on its back, its tongue hanging out and its

legs in the air. He held a cigar between the thumb and index finger of his left hand. A puff of wind brought the scent to her. Sweeter than a cigarette could ever dream of being.

Before Ella could work out what any of it meant, her attention was forced back to Chad, who backed up and curled his hands into fists, his face mistrustful. "We weren't doing nothing," he spit at the new boy.

"Indeed," the boy said, and Ella forced down the gorge that rose in her throat at the sound of his voice. Something about it was just so ... wrong. He must not attend her school. She knew she would remember that voice. The way it crawled through the air and fastened itself to her like ticks in the forest.

She crouched slightly and threw a glance behind her. She was fast. If she could slip between two of the boys, maybe she could escape. Her house was more than three miles away, but she could walk it, she had many times before. A pang of sadness that her mother wouldn't let her ride the bus hit her, but she ignored it. Not the time.

Chad looked like he might break and run. Maybe this would all be over before it started. Ella felt a fierce hope stir in her chest.

But no, the boy with the wolf shirt held up his hands, the cigar leaving a trail of wispy smoke. "I mean it. I know you aren't doing anything wrong. I thought you might need help." Ella felt like falling to the ground at the voice. Giving up. Permanently. The boy's eyes met hers and she saw them flash yellow, but only for an instant.

Chad snorted, but relaxed. "I don't need help."

The boy backed up and dropped into a swing. "Ok, I'll just watch then," he said, with a sick smile, as his eyes found Ella's. When the connection was made she felt a strange stirring in her body, like a car engine turning over. It was pleasant and terrifying at the same time. It made her feel powerful and very strange. But it didn't erase the danger of the situation.

Ella hitched her bag up on her shoulders and backed up as Chad signaled to his crew and the boys began to close in on her. She could hand over her backpack, there was nothing in there but books and assignments and maybe some loose change left over from lunch, but she knew the bag wasn't really what these boys wanted. They wanted something ... more than that from her. Maybe just to make her cry. But maybe not.

Without warning, the boy behind her lunged and caught her by the hair. She made a high keening sound and tried to pull away as the other boys laughed. Chad pushed up against her and looked straight in her eyes, his face only inches from hers. This was it. She knew she was going to get beat up or something worse.

Movement to her left made her shoot her gaze that way. The boy from the swings was up, his grin feral and dangerous, his cigar pitched into the sand. He reached Chad and pushed him out of the way, knocking him backwards easily. But his eyes were on Ella. His attention was only for her.

She shrunk backwards, against the boy who had ahold of her from behind, whimpering. She didn't want to be touched by the boy with the horrid voice. His hand raised, heading for her, the fingers mere inches from her midriff.

He covered the distance in an instant and she felt tears drip down her face. It was going to be so bad...

The moment he touched her that engine inside her kicked over again, pushing a foreign power outwards in a pulse, and a scream erupted from deep inside her. The face of the boy contorted in surprise, and then, not fear, but utter and absolute disbelief, before he was catapulted twenty feet in the *air, like he'd been pulled backwards by a rope tied around his middle, the other end fastened to an airplane.*

She watched his face, even as she screamed, even as she didn't believe it either. He landed hard, staring at her with a malevolence she'd never experienced, then winked out of existence, disappearing before her eyes, as if he had never been.

Ella's mouth dropped closed, cutting off her scream. She put a hand to the back of her head, noting the throbbing there. The boy who had ahold of her hair had disappeared. She turned in a circle. The two boys who had been at her sides were backing away slowly, like she was a bomb. She flipped back around to face front and saw Chad had the same look in his eyes.

"She's a ... a witch!" one of the boys yelled, and they were all up and running away in an instant.

The sound of the pendant hitting the floor as it fell jolted Ella back to her aunt's attic. The necklace lay between her feet, the angel side of it facing up.

Ella hadn't thought about that incident in years. That had been what had caused her mother to start homeschooling her, and although being home with her mother all day hadn't been as bad as being in school, it had still been pretty bad. But she hadn't been able to go back. Not after what had happened to the boy who had his fingers twisted in her hair.

Her eyes traced the contours of the golden jewelry as her mind tried to make sense of what had just happened. It had been too detailed to be a memory—it had been like she was there. She had even felt the pain in her head.

Ella's hand drifted to the back of her head as she noted with something like terror that she still had a faint throb there. She really was going crazy. She backed away from the pendant, clear across the room to where a broom and dustpan stood. She picked them up and walked back to the pendant, her eyes glued to it, like it might animate and start talking to her. She had no idea what had happened, but she did know she wasn't touching that thing again.

She bent and pushed the pendant into the dustpan with the broom, turning it over as she did so. The wolf snarled at her, making her hesitate. She loved everything about it. The wildness. The duality. But no. She forced herself to dump it into the box, where it thudded dully. Something was wrong with that thing. And she never wanted to replay that incident again. The nightmares had lasted for months after it had actually happened. Years, maybe.

Ella closed the box and sealed it with tape. Even if most of the jewelry was worth nothing, that pendant had to be worth a few dollars at least. She pushed the box towards the stairs, then tackled the rest of the attic, thankful to lose her thoughts in her work.

CHAPTER 3

*T*revor pushed his red Silverado work truck to its limit, not wanting to be late. Wade abhorred lateness, and since he was not only one of the deputy chiefs of their all-wolf-shifter police department, but also the *Citlali* for the entire region, he had a lot of authority. Plus Trevor respected the hell out of him.

Citlali were the spiritual and judicial leaders of the *shiften*. The *shiften* were a group of beings who could shift into their inner animal at will, which consisted of *wolven* (wolf-shifters), *bearen* (bear-shifters), *felen* (big-cat shifters, like cougars and puma), and *foxen* (fox shifters).

Citlali were given the leadership position at birth because of their star-shaped *renqua*, a variably-shaped mark on their left shoulder that all proper *shiften* had, but only *Citlali's renqua* were shaped like stars. *Citlali* earned greater power with their first prophecy, and as far as Trevor knew, none had ever been fired or found wrong.

Trent, sitting on his haunches in the passenger seat with his nose out the window, and Troy, lying in the back, sprawled in a wolf's curious resting pose, whined at the same time. Trevor looked out his side window, knowing what he would see.

The green and white sign that read 'Welcome to Serenity' with the large stone statue of a bear marking it.

Trevor locked eyes with the bear as he always did, feeling the cool autumn air hit him in the face. He locked eyes with the wolf and the mountain lion on the other roads into Serenity when he passed their statues, too. He told himself it was the respect he paid to the guardians of the little town that had become his home, but in reality, the statues creeped him out, and his brothers, too.

He shushed them and put a comforting hand on Trent's flank. At one hundred and seventy-five pounds, Trent was the smaller of the two *wolfen*, and the more sensitive.

Trevor cranked his neck out the window and looked up, way up to the water tower behind the sign, seeing graffiti there. He frowned and craned his neck to read it.

They walk among us. Werewolves are real!

Trevor's frown deepened. Someone was trying to spread rumors in Serenity? And where the hell had the *felen* who was supposed to be guarding the water tower been when that graffiti had been placed?

Fifteen minutes later, Trevor pulled into the police department parking lot and got out with the *wolves*—dogs, his mind corrected. He had to think of them as dogs when they were at the station. He couldn't afford to slip up and say wolf or even *wolfen*, which was the singular form of *wolven*, to a member of the public. The Czechoslovakian Wolfdog cover story could only hold the K9 unit for so long if some human heard a cop refer to them as actual wolves.

Trevor lifted his nose, sorting the different *wolven* scents out of the air. Mac's arrogant scent lingered, but was already starting to drift. He'd gone inside only a minute or two ago. Trevor walked faster, then started to jog to keep up with his brothers.

They strode in the back door and ran into Mac almost immediately, fully healed, and ready to continue their battle. Trevor met him head on, knowing he'd calm down eventually if Trevor let him get it all out.

"Finally." Macalister Niles' eyes were cold and his sneer showed his long canine teeth. "You know if you got laid every once in a while, you wouldn't need to hide out in the woods so often."

Trevor kept his expression neutral, with effort. "Getting laid doesn't protect you from going *moonstruck*." He dropped a hand to Troy's head to try to quell the growl that was co-alescing in his throat.

Mac snorted. "*Moonstruck.* Yeah, that's why you were out there." He turned on his heel and strode away. Trevor heard him mutter, "Nice try," under his breath.

Trevor and Troy watched Mac go, while Trent sat down on his haunches in the hallway, seemingly bored with the situation. *Let me bite his ass,* Trevor caught from Troy. *If I take a big enough hunk out of it, maybe we'll be able to see his personality.*

Trevor nodded hi to a patrol officer passing them in the hallway, then rubbed the scruff growing on his chin and rolled his eyes heavenward. "We've already discussed this. Now both of you, head to the K9 center. See what's been going on overnight. I'll come get you when my meeting is over." He watched long enough to make sure they obeyed him, then jogged down the other hall after Mac, catching up to him just before he entered the deputy chief's office.

It was empty. Wade would be waiting for them in the underground meeting room. With a frown on his face.

Mac passed Wade's cluttered desk, the flag in the corner, the plaques on the wall, then brushed aside the poncho hanging on a hook on the wall and leaned his head forward to stare directly at what looked like a slight imperfection in the paint there.

Trevor tensed like he always did when someone used the retinal scanner, but he jogged inside to be right behind Mac, that way the door that would open in the wall wouldn't have a chance to close before he got through it, making him have to shove his eye right up close to the damn thing. He hated looking in it. It creeped him out in the same way the statues did.

Mac's eyes passed muster and the wall slid open, letting them into the dark, musty-smelling staircase that would lead them to the underground tunnels, filled with meeting and storage rooms. They descended, the door closing behind them. The passage was narrow, too dark for an ordinary pair of eyes, but not theirs. They went down the corridor quickly, their footfalls making little noise on the meticulously painted concrete. They picked their way through the maze of tunnels, Trevor slightly behind Mac. Neither spoke a word, even when they found the correct door.

Mac turned the knob. The door opened up into a large room, at least the size of a high school gymnasium. Their footfalls echoed strangely under the high ceiling as they entered. Mac headed straight for the monster conference table that was easily as big as a back yard, but Trevor wound his way along the inner wall, unable to help staring at the masses of news stories tacked up there. *Shiften* were forbidden from recording their history any way other than orally, spoken from generation to generation, but that didn't stop them from collecting any human written history that pertained to the core purpose of the *shiften* race.

The humans wrote off the actions of the *shiften's* sworn enemy as accident, coincidence, terrorists, or just evil conduct of a select few, but the *shiften* knew differently.

Trevor's gaze ran over the headlines, even as he curled his fingers into his palms to avoid his impulse to touch anything. The cool air and lack of light in the tunnels preserved the newspapers and magazines, but still thousands of them were yellowing and cracking with age.

FIRE KILLS 12

FREAK EXPLOSION LEVELS CITY BLOCK, 20 MISSING, PRESUMED DEAD

EARTHQUAKE! SAN FRANCISCO IS OBLITERATED. 300,000 ARE HOMELESS

EVERY PERSON IN SMALL TOWN DISAPPEARS: SUPPER STILL ON TABLE IN MOST RESIDENCES

NEW, PLAGUE-LIKE DISEASE EMERGING

SARS EPIDEMIC FEARED

SWINE FLU PANDEMIC SPREADING

CHOLERA OUTBREAK SPREADS FEAR

EXPLOSIVES FOUND IN TOY, PROMPTING
MASSIVE RECALL

BATTERY PLANT EXPLODES, ENTIRE CITY
EVACUATED

COUNTRY'S WATER FOUND TO CONTAIN
HIGH LEVELS OF WOLF'S BANE AND CUMIN.
OFFICIALS STUMPED

WORLDWIDE WATER SUPPLY FOUND
TAINTED WITH XYLITOL, CUMIN, AND
WOLF'S BANE. MILLIONS OF PETS DIE

TERRORISTS BLAMED FOR EXPLOSION THAT
BROUGHT DOWN CHICAGO SKYSCRAPER

POISONED CITY: FLINT WATER CRISIS GROWS
DEADLY

TWO PLANES COLLIDE IN MIDAIR –
WITNESSES REPORT BRIGHT FLASH IN THE
SKY JUST BEFORE

Trevor let his eyes wander over the monstrous room. Every available surface was covered with these stories. He didn't know who put them up. Whose vigil this was. He thought it was a fitting way to remember why they were all doing this job. The headlines in this room alone signified millions dead at the hand of their nemesis. All of whom would someday receive vengeance. He swore it. He would find a way to make it happen, no matter how much of a fraud he was. Determination and hard work could make up for personal failings.

The sight of the tragedies was enough to make his fists clench, enough to make a lump form in his throat even as his body became battle-ready.

Someone cleared their throat, drawing Trevor's attention to the center of the room. He shook his muscles, rather in the manner that a dog shakes off water, trying to rid himself of the tension. There was nothing to fight there.

Deputy Chief Wade Lombard sat at the end of the conference table, his hands tucked under his chin as he perused files, a police radio on near him with the volume low. He was, by appearances, a male close to sixty with silver hair, although Trevor knew he was much older. Bastard still had a mate, which would keep him young for a good two hundred years, unlike the rest of them. Sometimes when he came to work, Trevor could smell Wade's mate's scent on him, and it always made Trevor turn away, emptiness eating at him. Trevor drew close to the table, but slowed before he got to it, sensing something off in Wade.

"Wade," Mac drew close to the table and greeted him first. "I…"

Wade held up a hand. "Before either of you say anything, let me speak. You need to know we've got a transfer coming in from Scotland. He'll be here tomorrow."

"Scotland?" Trevor's dark eyebrows furrowed. He knew nothing about *wolven* in Scotland. Nothing about how they ran their enterprises. Nothing about their loyalties.

"He's got some special abilities, and so he'll be coming in to help the KSRT. You said you needed new bodies."

"Wait, what? I'm the head of the KSRT. I should have been consulted about this."

Wade raised his eyebrows and cocked his head. "It wasn't my call."

Trevor pulled back. No one told Wade what to do… except Rhen, not even the Chief of Police. If Rhen was involved, no amount of complaining would change anything. "What kind of abilities?"

"A way to track Khain. Maybe a way to reach him wherever he goes when he leaves our world."

Trevor stalked to the table and leaned over it, a cold shiver at the thought passing through him. He had to at least let his objections be known. "How do we even know what he's saying is true? Or that he's not being controlled by—?"

"Yeah," Mac said. "He could lead us straight into a trap."

Trevor pointed at Mac, appreciating the support for once. He focused on Wade again. "Hell, no. All of us in the KSRT trust each other. We can't bring in a stranger. Not now." Trevor winced at the lie, but pressed on, daring Wade or Mac to call him on it.

Wade stayed calm. Unflappable. "Trevor, you need all the help you can get. We haven't seen any sort of progress in years."

Trevor's jaw clenched. "We are doing everything we can. If the *Citlali* are not satisfied, then they're free to replace me. I never signed up for this anyway."

The Deputy Chief sighed and steepled his fingers together. "I'm not trying to accuse you of anything, Trevor. In fact, I'm trying to help you. At the very least, you should meet him and see what he can do for you. Surely, there's no harm in that."

Trevor said nothing. Who was to say there was no harm in welcoming a stranger? Even if he was *wolfen*, that didn't mean he was trustworthy enough to be on the task force working directly on Khain's trail.

Wade fixed him with a hard stare. "Relax, Trevor."

"I'll relax when it's all over," Trevor said.

Wade nodded. "I would expect nothing less from you, son."

Trevor said nothing. Wade didn't know that Trevor didn't believe what everyone else believed about him.

Wade sat back in his chair and shifted his gaze to Mac. "Good. Now that that's settled, care to tell us why you called the meeting?"

Trevor narrowed his eyes at his second-in-command. "You requested this meeting?"

Mac nodded.

Trevor sighed and he rubbed his forehead. "Had I known, I would have taken a shower."

"I'll be sure to tell you next time," Mac snarled, his expression reminding Trevor exactly how bad he smelled.

The Deputy Chief cleared his throat.

Mac's voice went all-business, and totally determined, like he already knew he would meet with opposition. He faced the Deputy Chief and spit it out. "The males need a rut... a real one. We have to make it happen for them or we're going to be in deep shit soon."

Trevor's eyes shot to Mac. Out of all the things Mac could have said, that was the last thing Trevor would ever have imagined was going to come out of his mouth.

A rut. With no female shifters left, how would they ever manage that?

CHAPTER 4

*E*lla climbed carefully down the attic stairs, finally done, checking the time.

7:09.

Mrs. White had told her to drop off the items before the store opened, which happened in less than an hour.

"Crud." She grabbed a jacket from the hallway closet and headed out, the heavy box full of what little she could find of value, including the angel/wolf pendant, in her arms.

She could have made the trip from her aunt's house in the older, but still-nice, subdivision to downtown Serenity with her eyes closed, that's how often she had walked it. She noticed as soon as she stepped off her front porch that the empty house three blocks to the right of her had a moving van in front of it. Someone was finally moving in. The real estate sign had come down months ago, but the house had stayed empty. Until now.

Ella had always loved that house. It was twice the size of hers, with a ton of history. The entire back of it was built with a lovely sandstone that always drew her eye, every time she passed. She'd often wondered at the history of the house, but never had the time to look into it. Until now. Now she had more time than she knew what to do with.

As Ella passed the truck, she kept her eyes on the ground, not wanting to deal with anyone.

A loud bang ricocheted off the inside of the truck and Ella looked up, startled. A refrigerator of a man appeared at the back of the truck, wiping his brow, sweating even in the crisp, late-autumn air.

The man saw her and raised a hand, his eyes traveling up and down her body in a way that made Ella shiver.

She focused on her box and moved on, even as she could feel he wanted her to stop and talk.

She ignored the feeling and stepped off a curb, looked both ways, and jaywalked across the street, then followed the sidewalk two miles straight into town, the traffic and businesses both increasing in density as she walked.

She found the tiny red-brick building with the sign proclaiming, *You Need It*, over the incredibly cute red and white door. She tested the door and, finding it unlocked, pushed inside, her eyes flying to the counter, hoping Mrs. White would be the one working.

She was. Ella blew out a breath and headed over, dropping the box heavily on the glass display case that served as a counter.

"Dear," Mrs. White said. "You made it. I was starting to wonder if you found anything at all."

Ella stared at the woman, unable to respond. Mrs. White was probably in her eighties, with a heavily lined face and a kind smile. She always dressed up, wearing costume jewelry and elaborate outfits. But today, she'd done the unthinkable, in Ella's mind.

Her hat was fine. An orange felt hat with a velvet bow. Her jacket was fine. Wool maybe. But the thing draped over her shoulders made Ella's heart beat faster and her palms sweat.

Mrs. White, not noticing Ella's discomfort, smiled at her and opened the box, taking out an item at a time. "Oh, this is nice. I can give you a hundred up front for this. All this jewelry here, it's not worth much separately, but as a lot, maybe, let's say, fifty dollars. This set won't sell here, but you can try Lucy's consignment shop, two doors down." Her voice dropped as she dug farther into the box and her breath hitched. "Whatever is this?" she said, and Ella, even in her state, could hear the wonderment there.

Ella's eyes traced the fur and tail and eyes and teeth of the thing Mrs. White had draped over her shoulders. *Old? Or new?* Because that made a difference. Ella thought old.

From the corner of her eye, Ella could see Mrs. White examining the pendant and she tried to pay attention. It was the only thing in the box she thought might have any real value.

"Gorgeous," Mrs. White breathed, holding the pendant approximately two inches from her eyes. "Is it real gold?" she asked. "It has to be real gold." She dropped it to her arm and rubbed, then triumphantly showed Ella the black mark. "It is, it's real gold. And the eyes of the wolf? Yellow diamond? No. Too bright. Maybe yellow sphene. Or tourmaline." She clicked her tongue and hurried to the wall behind her, holding the pendant tight in her hand, then returning with a jeweler's loupe and holding it to her eye. When she looked back at Ella, an excited smile crossed her face. "What is the story behind this piece?"

Ella shook her head. "No story. I found it in the attic. I don't know."

"How much?" Mrs. White said, her eyes suddenly shrewd.

Ella's gaze flopped down to the full fox stole around Mrs. White's shoulders. "I-I don't know. What is it worth?" she asked in a much smaller voice than she had intended.

"I'll give you two thousand for it," Mrs. White said, her lips tight, her voice cold for the first time. She moved to the register and pressed a button. "Cash. Actually, I'll give you three thousand for everything in the box."

Ella couldn't think. She knew she shouldn't take it. Should investigate more. But the fox stole had distracted her. Stolen her right mind. Besides, she didn't want that pendant anyway. Didn't want to have to take it away from here if she struck a hard bargain and lost.

"I'll take it."

"Good." Mrs. White counted out thirty one-hundred dollar bills and put them in Ella's hand, then made the box and the pendant disappear. "A pleasure, dear. Do come back if you find anything else you think I might like. I'll pay you a good price." Her voice was warm again.

Ella nodded, shoved the money deep in her pocket and turned to go, but her heart wouldn't let her. She turned back. "Sorry, ah, Mrs. White, ah, I wanted to ask you about your fox."

The older woman's hands went to the decorative item and caressed its head right between its tiny, silky ears. "Yes, dear?"

"Do you, regularly, ah, buy fur?"

Mrs. White's eyes narrowed and Ella saw her go defensive. Ella held up her hands and spoke in a rush, her heart beating fast in her chest, her muscles tight as if for battle. "Look, Mrs. White, I don't want to offend you, and I can see that stole is probably an heirloom, something you've had for years. It's beautiful and I can understand why you would want to wear it. But when you wear fur, you support the fur industry, even if this piece was killed for food and cleaned by your own two hands. If someone in your shop sees it and thinks it's gorgeous, do you think they are going to go out and humanely kill an animal, use it as food, and make a stole themselves? No, they are going to go to a store and buy a fur. That's what we do these days."

Ella made the mistake of taking a breath and Mrs. White launched her defensive that suddenly seemed more like an offensive. Like she had the vitriol stored up and had never liked Ella in the first place. "That certainly isn't my problem, Fern Gabriela Carmi." She nodded harshly as Ella took a step backwards, surprise showing on her face. "That's right, your aunt told me all about you. Your real name. Your liberal beliefs. That you stay up all night finding petitions to sign on the internet. The way you never learned to drive and didn't finish college. How your own mother thought you were a freak! How dare you come in here and tell me what to do? Just because you think our woods should be full of dangerous animals like wolves and cougars and bears doesn't mean you're right. Animals like that were driven from the area for a reason!"

Ella wanted to ask how dangerous fox were to people, but she knew there was no point. Mrs. White had already formed all her opinions and wasn't open to learning anything new. She pressed her lips together and forced her hands to relax, unable to help a final, couched jab. "I'm sorry. I see you have made up your mind. I had hoped to share some facts with you about the cruelty of the industry and some very simple ways it could be changed, but if you don't care about animal welfare, I won't bother."

She turned quickly, forcing herself not to run out the door, but instead taking slow, deliberate steps and allowing Mrs. White to throw insults at her back without response. As she pushed the door open, an eerie thought seemed to force itself into her mind in a way she'd never felt before, even with how crazy she'd felt for the last year.

She's close. I can feel it.

Ella faltered at the intrusion and her feet tangled together, spilling her forward and jamming her shoulder into the door, hard, as shame spread through her.

She *had* to get out of there before Mrs. White saw her have one of her episodes. Even if she blacked out on the street or stood there like an idiot with her brain elsewhere, that was ok as long as Mrs. White didn't have a front-row seat to it.

CHAPTER 5

Trevor shook his head in utter disbelief. "You don't schedule a rut, they just happen."

Mac pulled out a chair and sat opposite the deputy chief, refusing to look Trevor in the eye. His voice was haughty, hostile still. "They *used* to just happen. But with no females, that's impossible now. We can't sit around and pretend the males don't need it. Things are getting dangerous. You know what happened last full moon."

Finally, Mac snatched a look at Trevor, but Trevor could only shake his head. He knew...?

Mac snorted, disgusted and looked away. "Of course you don't know. Some fucking leader."

Trevor sank into a chair at the end of the table and looked to Wade for help.

"Harlan almost killed someone. A patrol officer. The patrol officer said something flippant about mates."

Trevor dropped his head onto his hands, elbows on the table and spoke, almost to himself. "Harlan? But he's our most level-headed guy. Our most—"

Mac cut in. "He shifted, then tore Pickett's throat open and ate some of his ear. Poor guy was knocked unconscious immediately. Couldn't shift. We had to send him to surgery. *Surgery* for shit's sake! And then four of the guys pulling Harlan off got into a fight. It was a fucking mess and it's not going to get any better unless we have a rut. The males need it."

Trevor looked to the ceiling, as if hoping to find the answers there, then back down. "And Harlan?"

Wade nodded slowly. "No punishment. I dealt with him myself. Looked into his heart. Consulted with Rhen. She holds him blameless and agrees with Mac that a rut is needed. *Shiften* were made to breed regularly. To have mates. The full moon is a tricky time, the drive to have sex so strong in order to ensure many pups. Without pups, we die. Without females to mate with to make those pups, you are adrift. No anchor. No calming presence. Nothing to hold us together as *shiften*. You can fight and punish and raise hell all day, but you have forgotten how to love. Harlan is only an example."

Trevor eyed the Deputy Chief sourly, noting his change of pronouns during his speech. He was one of only a few *shiften* in the world who did have a mate. So he still knew how to love, apparently.

Mac spun his chair towards the door. "I don't know why we even have to tell *him* about it. It's not like he's going to fucking show up."

Trevor bit his anger back. "Because I'm the fucking leader of the KSRT, that's why. One step below Wade himself. I'm in charge here and you need to remember that."

Mac swung to face him, his smile evil. "Yes Your Pupness. I'll remember that, Your Great Mongrel Highness. Even when you act more like a little kitten rolling over to show your belly to Khain."

Trevor growled, the noise building in his throat and echoing throughout the room.

Mac laughed. "What are you gonna do without your brothers to hide behind?"

Trevor stood up and faced Mac offensively. Mac wanted to go? They were gonna go. Trevor couldn't take one more second of his shit. He popped the civilized balloon in his head that kept him in human form and felt his claws elongate, his nose turn to muzzle, his—

It all stopped. Mid-shift. Trevor struggled against the bind but could do nothing. His bones screamed in protest, caught half-way between human and wolf. He rolled his eyes to Mac, burning when he saw him silently smirking, enjoying the show.

Wade stood up out of his chair and walked to Trevor slowly, each step a vibrating brand to Trevor's eardrums and lungs. Wade stood straight in front of him and commanded his eye. Trevor felt his partial-shift reverse itself until he stood in human form again, but still unable to move, speak, or even breathe. If Wade didn't release him soon, he would die. He knew that now, even though he hadn't been bound for this long since he'd been a pup.

Trevor gave up. He was ready to die. Ready for this shitty excuse of a life to be over. No mother. No sisters. No females. No mates. No softness. No anything that made life good or worth living for. Nothing but the relentless pursuit of a demon who could not be caught. Could not be stopped.

Revenge just wasn't enough anymore.

But as soon as Trevor relaxed, Wade released him, spilling him into his chair.

Wade stared down at him, disappointment written on his face. "You're the leader for a reason, Trevor, and it's not because you are the strongest or the smartest. You have a destiny, and you will not fulfill it by taking Mac's bait."

Trevor sagged in his chair. He didn't have words to respond. All he had left was void. Nothingness. The terror of the bind then the surrender had washed away even his desire to find his One True Mate, if he had one. All he wanted was to jump off a bridge. Be done with it all. Let Mac have the command he wanted so badly. He might even do a better job. Maybe Mac was right, maybe Trevor was the kink in the system. Trevor had never believed he was the *shiften* mentioned in the *Savior* or the *Demon Death* prophecy. That disbelief had haunted him his entire life, even when the *Citlali* directly opposed his disbelief, he still felt like a fraud every moment he worked with the KSRT, every moment he hunted Khain. He would never be allowed to step down, but if he was gone… Well, they'd have to take a closer look at those prophecies, wouldn't they?

But first he had to get out of this room.

He heard the robotic tone in his voice and hoped no one knew what it meant. He spoke first to Wade, who was pacing behind him. "Sorry, Deputy Chief. You're right. A rut. Let's schedule it. You work out the details, Mac."

Wade patted Trevor's shoulder, then his eyes widened, and he stared at Trevor for several moments, before taking a few steps away.

Mac didn't say anything for a long time, just stared. Finally he spoke. "You don't even want to know where we are going to get the females?"

Trevor spoke without thinking. "Hookers?"

Mac nodded, seeming surprised. "Among others. I thought you'd have a problem with a bunch of cops hiring hookers."

That same blank nothingness swirled through Trevor, removing any stray desire to care ever again what any member of the Serenity PD did.

"Yeah, but if it's our only choice, it's our only choice."

Mac stared at him again. Trevor avoided his eye, trying to think of where and how he would do it. A bridge? His service revolver? The end of a rope? He didn't allow himself to think about what would happen after. He would return to The Light. That was all. He hoped.

"You don't have any complaints at all?" Mac wheedled. "You don't want to lecture me on the dangers of half-breeds or tell me how we should be looking for One True Mates, not hookers?"

Trevor sucked in a breath. Mac knew him well. Knew exactly what he would be thinking. He waved his hand. "You know as well as I do it's hard for us to get humans pregnant. And half-breeds aren't dangerous, just… unpredictable. Like humans." He sighed, knowing he needed to admit it. "What do I know about the One True Mates? No more than anyone. Maybe you'll find some among the hookers."

Mac laughed long and hard at that. "You giving up, Trev-Trev? I almost like you better with a little spunk in you. Almost."

Wade returned to his seat and glared at Mac. "Enough, meow-mix-for-brains. Keep a lid on your disrespect or I will let Trevor have at you next time. The Light knows you deserve it after all you've been pulling lately."

Mac half growled-, half-whined deep in his throat, his

version of an apology, but it did Trevor no good to hear it. Mac was a non-issue to him. All he cared about was Wade releasing them. Getting out of there.

The police radio on the table crackled, a distorted male voice sending out instructions.

All units, respond to the area of 15th and Terrace Drive. Multiple reports of an explosion outside a store.

Wade held his hand up and turned up the volume. They all knew who made explosions happen. Trevor tried to care, tried to start the strategic side of his brain, but he couldn't.

Until his best friend's voice crackled over the radio.

"Unit 632 here, Central," he heard Blake say, his voice excited, his breath coming in pants like he was running. "I'm right around the corner. I heard the explosion. It's him, it's Khain, I know it is. I can feel him. *I can hear him*!"

Mac swore and stood, and so did Wade. "Fucker isn't supposed to say that name on the radio and he knows it!" Mac yelled, even as Wade snatched up the radio and bellowed into it. "632, backup, you wait for backup! Who's close by?"

Trevor stood, his desire for self-destruction suddenly replaced by his need to help his friend. But more than that, he finally had his chance. If he got out there quickly enough, he could finally see Khain face to face. Finally prove that he was the subject of the prophecies… or prove that he wasn't. He'd been preparing for this his entire life.

That is, if Blake was right. If Khain had resurfaced for the first time since he'd murdered Trevor's own mother, stealing her from his life. Since he'd murdered almost every female shifter on the planet, robbing the very future of all the *shiften*.

Trevor shook his head, a growl building deep in his chest, his teeth and claws growing of their own accord. He stood and sprinted toward the door, not hearing Wade's frantic words to him as he ran.

He couldn't stop, no matter what they were.

CHAPTER 6

*E*lla pushed outside into the sunshine, feeling the bite of the autumn wind touch her face. Instead of the cold clearing her head, the intrusive thoughts immediately got worse, making her sag against the building. They weren't painful, at least not physically, but mentally they were like nails on the chalkboard of her mind.

The Promised. I can smell her. She's scared.

The vision or hallucination she had seen earlier in her attic screamed into her mind, the face of the boy on the swing set with the strange shirt filling her range of view, making her momentarily blind. She tried to take a step, but faltered. She blinked her eyes again and again, until the face cleared.

Ella looked around, feeling frantic pulses of fear pulling at her. She hated the feeling, but was helpless to stop it at the same time. Somehow she knew that this was no panic attack. This was not more evidence that her mind was falling apart.

This was something much, much worse, and she had to run, had to hide, had to get away from whatever was coming.

She swung her head left, then right, crouching slightly, ready to run as soon as she knew what she was running away from. The street looked normal. A mother pushing a baby carriage toward her from her left. A shopkeeper sweeping off the street to her right, a loud group of Girl Scouts, moms in tow, heading into the ice cream shop across the street.

To her right, one block away, a man appeared, turning the corner. A huge man with muscles that had to make women stare, and an exotically handsome face, all harsh lines and dark eyebrows framed by long dark hair. To Ella, he looked like a Polynesian warrior from another time, but also like death. He wore hip-hugging jeans and a black t-shirt with a cartoon rendition of three pink pigs in champion's poses, holding up their fists in triumph. At first glance, the man seemed normal, but Ella knew immediately he was what she should be running from. It was his thoughts she had overheard, his intentions she was reading and reeling from.

His eyes found hers and she hugged the wall next to her in fright, making small noises of fear and hating herself for doing so. She had no way of knowing the color of his eyes from this far away, but she knew they flashed yellow all the same. He lifted his left hand to his mouth and puffed on a cigar and she felt her fear ramp up inside her. She whimpered again, the noise getting her going finally. Her feet moved on their own, pulling her away from him, anywhere but where he was. He passed the shopkeeper, who didn't look up, but took a step backwards as if sensing something he didn't want to deal with.

Ella kept backing up, until she heard a baby's cry behind

her. She threw a glance over her shoulder and saw the mother with the stroller had stopped in the middle of the sidewalk, the stroller sideways, blocking most of the way past. Ella pushed away from the wall and stepped off the curb. She couldn't lead this man towards the mother and baby. He might hurt them. She didn't know how she knew it, but she did, as sure as she knew her own name.

A laugh from the direction she was traveling in caught her frantic attention and she whipped her head towards the sound. Some Girl Scouts, ten or twelve of them, walked aimlessly down the sidewalk in groups of twos and threes, all with ice cream cones in their hands, giggling.

She couldn't retreat behind her. She couldn't draw the monster—she was sure that's what he had to be—across the street. And there was no way she would head toward him. That left only one choice. Back into Mrs. White's store. She had to have a back door somewhere.

Ella forced herself back to the door, hating how the action took her closer to the direction she didn't want to move in, even as the man grinned knowingly at her. He was close now, within twenty feet of her. She could see his eyes were actually blue, not yellow. Not that it mattered. The fat, pink pigs on his shirt seemed to dance obscenely and for the first time she saw the words on the shirt.

The Three Little Pigs are Heroes

Ella whimpered again, then slipped inside and slammed and locked the door.

"You, girl!" Mrs. White said from behind her. "Get out of here! We've done our business! All sales are final. You can't have your things back."

Ella blinked against the darkness of the shop and hurried into the center of the room, throwing glances behind her.

"Mrs. White, we have to get out of here. Someone is coming. He means to hurt—"

"Now you listen here, girly." Mrs. White ducked behind the counter with surprising ease. When she reappeared she had a shotgun in her hands, pointing straight at Ella. "I'm not going anywhere, but you most certainly *are*. I've asked you to leave, I won't tell you again."

Ella froze at the sight of the gun, then looked back at the doorway. If *he* came, maybe the gun would dissuade him.

The four square windows were still clear, a bit of cold blue sky showing. She looked back at Mrs. White, her inexplicable fear still palpable, but somehow more controlled now. "You know, you really shouldn't pull a gun on people unless you are willing to use it."

Mrs. White scoffed and socked the gun into her shoulder. "Try me, honey, I've shot two husbands and a tax collector. It won't bother me for a second to shoot you, too."

Before Ella could even blink at that, a darkening in the room made her palms sweat. She turned slowly, knowing what she was going to see.

The face at the window made her suck in a breath and think she must have misjudged the man's age before. She would have put him at twenty-five, but now he looked older. A hearty and terrifying fifty. As she backed away, his features shifted slightly, wrinkles disappearing before her eyes, and now the man was a wise and menacing thirty. Still unbelievably tall, with biceps like beams of sculpted steel.

She knew what she was seeing was not who this man really was. She also knew she'd been waiting to meet him her entire life. Something wound his fate with hers, something dark and rancid that she didn't want to face.

She'd dreamed of him.

The door opened slowly, appearing to float open at some mental command.

"Oh God," Ella breathed, her legs shaking. She turned her body so her back was to Mrs. White and she took several unsteady steps backwards until she felt the counter dig into her butt.

"What in the hell are you doing, girl?" Mrs. White hissed at her, then in a normal voice, she spoke to the man who was walking through the doorway, a satisfied smile on his face. "Hello there, what may I help you find?"

Ella saw the gun was gone. "Mrs. White, your gun, get it. Get it now."

The man smiled, as if the two of them were being naughty girls, hoping for a punishment. *"Promised. Come here."*

Ella shrank against the counter, whimpering again at the voice. It wasn't human. It couldn't be. It sounded like death moaning at your windows to be let in, and it made her skin crawl with the sensation of a thousand spider feet. Her hands snuck to cover her ears. She snaked her way around the counter, meeting Mrs. White there.

Mrs. White's face had gone gray, and her eyes moved between the man who had just entered and Ella. "What's going on here? Some sort of a crazy sex game between you two? I won't have that licentiousness in here, you understand?" She reached under the counter again. Ella would have rejoiced if she didn't feel sick to her very core.

The man raised his right hand and passed it in front of him, almost lazily, even as his left hand flicked ashes on Mrs. White's floor.

Mrs. White began to shriek as her fox stole came to life, let go of its own tail, and sank its teeth into her shoulder.

Eyes wide, stomach constricting, Ella raised her hands

and went for Mrs. White, unsure of what she could do, but wanting to help.

"No!" Mrs. White shrieked, as she fought with the fox, her wrinkled hands wrapped around its midsection. "Stay away from me! How did you do that? Oh, you hateful little bitch!"

Ella shrank away, running into the back wall of the place. Her fumbling, grasping hands found a doorknob. The back door! She had to run, had to get away. She turned around, grasping the door knob and twisting but she knew immediately she wasn't going to make it.

He'd somehow crossed the room in an instant and was right behind her. She could feel his presence, like a wall of stiff fabric pressing into her from behind.

His hand grasped her shoulder. Ella screamed at the touch, and at the strange sensation that filled her when it happened.

Fireworks consumed her vision and her body took over, but her mind was gone.

CHAPTER 7

Trevor yanked the wheel and slammed on the brakes to avoid running through the yellow crime tape. He threw the truck in park and twisted the keys violently, even as he opened his door and jumped out. Trent and Troy had already leaped out the window and were racing into the heart of the scene, causing people to jump back in fright from the two large black *dogs*.

Unorthodox behavior, but this was an unorthodox situation. Damage control could come later.

Within moments, Trevor stood in front of a burned-out storefront, having picked his way over blackened bricks the entire way. Fire was on scene standing by, but nothing seemed to be burning anymore. Trevor sniffed the air and under the smoke, he smelled only lingering scents he would sort through later, including one enticing sweet smell that made his blood pound. Khain was long gone. Trevor's shoulders sagged.

This wasn't his moment after all.

He could see his brothers inside, working, scenting, both as disappointed as he that Khain had come and gone.

A woman in an ambulance parked nearby swore and screamed, one hand clamped to her shoulder, blood running freely under it. The paramedics tried vainly to get her to calm down and let them treat her, but she kept screaming and baring her teeth at them. Behind another ambulance, twenty girls dressed in Girl Scout uniforms clustered together, throwing scared glances toward the screaming woman.

"Lieutenant," a voice called, and Trevor turned towards his friend, relief filling him.

"Blake, damn it, you almost gave me a heart attack. Did you see him? Was he really here?"

Blake stepped close and looked around before he spoke. "The baby-killer? Yeah, that fucker was here alright. I didn't see him, but I knew it was him before I even got here."

"How?"

Blake looked up at Trevor and shook his head, slowly. "I could feel him. Like nothing I've ever felt in my life. Like I was a magnet and he was a big-ass piece of steel. I couldn't have waited for backup even if I wanted to. It was like I was born just to hunt that fucker down."

Trevor shook his head and grasped Blake's arm. "That's exactly what you were born for, what we all were born for. You know that, but you still have to wait for backup. You can't fight him alone."

Blake waved it away. "I know, I know, but, Trev-man, I could feel him. And I could hear him talk in my mind. I swear I know the exact second he popped into existence here, and the exact second he popped out."

"Is that because you were so close to him?"

"I don't know. Maybe."

"What did you hear him say?"

"First he said, '*she's close, I can feel it.*' Then a minute later he said '*The Promised. I can smell her. She's scared.*' A minute or two after that he said, '*Promised. Come here.*' But that last one was different somehow." He shook his head and held up a hand. "Don't ask me how. I don't understand it. I don't get any of it. I just know it was different."

He pointed to the end of the storefronts where a road t-boned into the one they were standing on. "I was giving a speech at the middle school two blocks down Crescent St. when I first heard him. It was like a humming in my mind. I left the classroom, just walked out. I couldn't have stopped myself from coming this way even if I wanted to, even though I didn't know why. As soon as I heard him say *The Promised. I can smell her,* I knew it was him. I was still running up that road there when I heard the last thing he said. I couldn't see him, but I could still tell where he was, or at least where my body wanted to go. Then I heard the explosion. By the time I came around that corner, this whole wall was gone, and so was Khain."

"What did he sound like?"

Blake grimaced. "Bad intent. Like if an Anaconda talked to you while he was squeezing the life out of you."

Trevor eyed the hole in the red brick in front of them. It really wasn't Khain's style. "Those sound like thoughts. At least the first two things he said. I've never heard of any *shiften* being able to hear his exact thoughts before, not even the *Pumaii*, and it's their job to track him when he comes over here. No one's seen him on this side for over two decades, but I've studied all the past interactions with him. No one's ever said they could hear him like that."

Blake shrugged his wide shoulders. "I know." He looked hard at Trevor. "Someone beat me here. He saw Khain."

Trevor leaned forward and grasped Blake's arm in a pincer grip, causing the other male to wince. "Who? Where is he? I must talk to him!"

Blake pulled his arm away and nodded at the dirty sidewalk just to the left of the gaping hole in the building. He took a step that way and pointed at what looked like a pile of ash. "There's a twisted piece of black metal in there that is probably a gun, and another gold lump that certainly used to be a badge."

"Ah fuck," Trevor breathed, pushing a hand through his hair. "Do we know who it is?"

"My guess is Pickett. I heard him on the radio just before the explosion, he said he was next door. I told him to wait for me, but…"

The two males stared at the pile of ash heavily. Trevor had heard of Khain doing something like this before, but he'd never seen it.

Blake cleared his throat, his voice strained. "Poor bastard. It was his first day back to work since he got hurt."

Trevor shook his head, unable to say anything. He had never wished so hard to be the *wolfen* everyone thought he was before. To be the one who finally brought the murdering bastard down would be the greatest victory available to his kind.

Someone pushed past him. Trevor looked up and saw Mac heading into the shell of a building. Trevor growled at his back.

"Back at you, mangy mutt," Mac said, then stood in the center of the room, hands on hips, head high, turning in a circle.

Trevor heard a new vehicle pull up to the scene and stop behind him. He stepped backwards to look past Blake. The rest of his team was arriving.

Harlan stepped out of the driver's seat of the KSRT's work truck and raised a hand to Trevor. Trevor watched him go into investigatory mode immediately, taking in the scene as a whole, his nostrils flaring. Beckett and Crew also got out of the car. Strong warriors, all of them, and Trevor was glad to have them on his side even if none of them particularly cared for him. Except Harlan. Harlan was the only member of the KSRT who hadn't immediately seen Trevor's placement as the new boss two years ago, usurping Mac, as an act of war. Harlan was the oldest member of the KSRT, and possibly the one who'd lost the most at the hands of Khain. He'd lost his mother just like all the rest of them had, but having been older already, he hadn't grown up in the war camps. He'd been mated before all the females had been lost. For almost a full day. Harlan would never rest until Khain was stopped, and he never let his ego get in the way of that.

There were four other members of the KSRT, but Trevor hadn't expected to see any of them. They didn't get out of the tunnels much.

Trevor tipped a hand to Harlan, then turned back to his friend, a weariness settling in his bones that he hadn't ever felt before, now that his adrenaline was waning.

The woman in the back of the ambulance let out a loud shriek, pulling Trevor's attention that way. "What's her story?" he asked Blake.

"This is her shop."

"Did she see him?"

"Maybe. If she did, it might have driven her mad. All she will say is that some bitch assaulted her and stole her stole."

"What?"

Blake pulled out his notebook and showed Trevor a page. "I asked her to spell it. Stole her stole."

"Who assaulted her?"

"I never saw anyone but her and all the girl scouts and their leaders, plus a few other witnesses. None of them were seriously hurt, and all their stories are a bit different but there might be one woman unaccounted for. I just hope she wasn't fried, like Pickett." He dropped his voice and leaned towards Trevor. "The paramedics say her only injury is a bite mark to her shoulder."

Trevor's eyes widened? "A bite mark?"

Blake nodded. "I smelled it. Fox."

Trevor looked around, this new information burning his brain. "But there are no reports of *foxen* being on the scene?"

"None."

"What about *Pumaii*?"

"Yeah, there was a *Pumaii* here, but he took off. Said he had to report to Kalista."

"You didn't stop him?"

Blake shook his head, his lips pressed together. "You know we have no jurisdiction over the *Pumaii*. He could have bitten me himself and I would have had to stand aside and let him go."

Trevor growled, knowing that was true, but hating everything about it.

This was big, the biggest event to happen in his career, and he wasn't going to wait very long to hear from the leader of the *Pumaii*, the team of all-*felen* mercenaries who tracked Khain when he moved into the real world.

If he couldn't hunt Khain down, he would settle for hunting down Kalista.

CHAPTER 8

Trevor physically held himself in place, trying to decide what his top priority was, but the sound of a new vehicle pulling up to the edge of the crime scene caught his attention. He wouldn't have to hunt Kalista down after all. Her car, an obscene silver Bugatti Chiron, purred in the same way Trevor knew its driver did.

"Fuck," he said on a huff of air, wishing the Chief would show up so he wouldn't have to be the one to *talk* to Kalista.

The car door opened and a six-inch white heel dropped into view. Trevor snatched his gaze away, looking straight ahead.

"The Light save the baby Jesus," Blake breathed. "Who is that?"

"You never met a *felen* before?"

"No."

"Can't you just see her animal in the way she moves? All slink and stalk like a jungle cat?"

Blake didn't answer for a moment, and Trevor could see his brain working overtime until he got himself together again. "I thought they lost all their females too," Blake rasped, rubbing a hand over his mouth.

"They did, but Kalista is one tough female. She got sick. Almost died. She's fought Khain directly a few times, some people think that gave her more strength than most of the females somehow."

"How old is she?" Blake's voice was lowered, and his eyes were on the approaching female.

"Not sure. Over a hundred and fifty, I've heard."

"So she's mated."

Trevor knocked Blake in the back of the head. "Yeah, she's mated. The *felen* don't mate like we do, but they do mate, and they do live longer when they are mated, just like us. I heard her mate is a healer and that might have been what saved her."

"She's still so..." Blake ran out of words and his tongue poked out of his mouth. Trevor couldn't blame him, but he could make fun of him.

He popped his friend on the back of the head again. "Get it together, Romeo, the *felen* are all like that. Even the males. Walking, talking sex and it won't be any better once she gets here."

Blake tried to look away but he couldn't do it. A goofy grin spread over his face. Trevor still didn't look, but he could imagine Kalista looking back boldly, giving him a half-smile, possibly biting her lip or running her hand up her neck into her hair.

She strode up to them and stopped. "Lieutenant," she said, her voice thick and sultry, reverberating in the back of her throat and making him think of lips closing around his dick. The velvety softness of tongue and mouth…

He steeled himself and turned to her, ignoring Blake's sappy smile. She was curvy and tall. Six feet he guessed, which put her seven inches shorter than him, but with those heels, she could easily look him in the eye. She wore a white, one piece bodysuit that separated into straps just above her breasts and crossed around her neck. Her dark, dappled hair was twisted up into a bun, her feline eyes watching him shrewdly, invitingly.

"Kalista," he barked, not meaning to sound so harsh, but unwilling to follow in Blake's idiot footsteps either, and the roughness seemed to be the only way to make sure he didn't. Too bad he was positive Kalista liked it rough. She'd made that clear the only other time they'd ever spoken. "Where did your male go? We need a full report. And why weren't we notified that Khain was on the move?"

"Relax, Lieutenant," the female said, her lips pursing slightly on the words. "I've got your report. You were notified. Your dispatch was told immediately." She raised her perfect eyebrows and barely cocked her right hip. "Are you saying they never called you?"

Trevor shook his head.

Kalista tsked her tongue, her facial expression barely changing. "Naughty dispatch. Then again, they didn't have much time between when we called and the big explosion. That and we haven't called them in years. Maybe some policy needs revising?" She turned her head and smiled at Blake, then turned her knowing eyes back on Trevor, dropping the cute act. "Something big is coming."

Trevor sighed in relief at her change in attitude. "Why do you say that?"

Kalista motioned to the building. "He popped into our dimensionality about two blocks that way, went straight into this building, and popped out of our dimensionality shortly after. Plus he was trying to jam us, which he's never done before. He had this planned, and the purpose of it was not to kill humans. In my opinion, he hasn't finished coming after *shiften* yet, and this is part of it."

"Jam you?"

Kalista sighed and rolled her eyes before she explained. "Normally *felen* can read Khain easily. We can roughly tell where he is even in the *Pravus*. We don't know what the *Pravus* looks like or how it corresponds to our dimension, so roughly, I'd say we can tell if he's still near Illinois or not. When he pops into our dimension we can hone in on him, figure out exactly where he is, but it takes some doing. We have to move around to feel exactly where the pull is. And we can read him. Not his exact thoughts, but his intent. But this time when he came over he was repelling and jamming us. I felt him immediately, like a constant scream in the night, but I was too far away to tell exactly where he was. Nalan was in the area, and he said that from this close, it felt like he and Khain were two like poles of the magnet that repelled, instead of two unlike poles, like it used to be. Like Khain had been messing with whatever he has inside him that lets us track him."

Trevor nodded, then lifted his chin at Blake. "Meet your new like pole."

Kalista's eyes fastened on Blake and she drew closer to him. "Really? You were attracted to him?"

Blake blubbered for a moment, staring up at the *felen* before he managed to speak. "I-I knew where he was yes, and I felt him come here. I could hear him too."

Kalista took his arm and purred into his ear. "How fascinating. I really must talk to you more. Figure this mystery out." She led Blake away but before she had gone more than a few steps she turned back. "Lieutenant?" She nodded at the building. "The explosion? He didn't do it."

Trevor stared hard at the building, the surrounding storefronts, his crew and the patrol officers investigating and cataloguing everything.

If Khain didn't cause the explosion, then who did? How? Why?

Trevor gritted his teeth and felt them ache to grow long, his body itch to shift.

His wolf wanted out very badly.

***

Trevor headed back to the station, leaving his brothers and his crew at the scene to finish the investigation. He'd told Mac where to find him and that he wanted a full report the second the investigation was done. He'd told Blake to head to dispatch when he left and review the procedures when any *felen* called in with a location on Khain, and he'd given Kalista his cell, telling her he wanted a heads up the instant any *felen* so much as got a hint of Khain being on this side.

As he drove, he thought about the mysterious female that may or may not have been on the scene. One witness had described her as tall, with dark black hair and paper-white skin. No one else had seen her at all, and the lady who'd been bitten by the fox only screamed when asked about her.

Trevor fiddled with the buttons on his tactical pants, hoping she hadn't ended up another pile of ash, or worse yet, been working with Khain. He knew Khain had supporters, but he'd never heard of a human being one of them.

Trevor pulled up to the station and parked his truck, then headed to an unobtrusive door on the side of the building. He stood in front of the lock and waited for it to read his retina and open, resisting the urge to blink, to pull back, to run screaming through the parking lot. He hated that eye-scanner thing.

The door opened only long enough for him to slip inside the dark hallway. He pulled his arms and legs in quickly, before the door slammed on them. Only one person could pass at a time unless it was two moving quickly, that was one of the heightened security features of the outside door.

Trevor walked fast, his footfalls echoing in the cool chamber. The hallway slanted down, taking him straight where he wanted to go, the underground tunnels. He twisted left, then right, then around, until he found the room he was looking for.

He pushed open the wooden door, noting by the smells that came at him that Wade had been the last one in here, two, maybe two and a half weeks ago.

The only history the *shiften* were allowed to record were all in this room. Three hundred and eighty four thousand and two prophecies, most taken down centuries ago. Only a few had been recorded in the last thirty years, but that was the section Trevor headed for. He needed to hear the One True Mate prophecy again, see if there was any reference to them being called The Promised.

He knew there wasn't. He had the prophecy memorized, but he would not trust something so important to his memory. If Khain were hunting down the One True Mates meant for the *shiften*, that would change everything.

Trevor pulled out the DVD recording he was looking for and stuck it in the DVD player over the small TV in the corner, then turned everything on and sank into the overstuffed lounge chair, his mind spinning.

An older *wolfen* appeared on the screen, sitting in an easy chair, his head back, his eyes closed, his hands soft and relaxed on the arms of the chair.

"Hi, Dad," Trevor whispered, feeling sorrow gnaw at his chest and throat. He should have had so much time with his parents still, but his father had been older than his mother, and when she had been murdered, his father had only been able to hang on for three more years. This was the last prophecy he had ever received. He'd died of old age or a broken heart four days later. To *shiften*, they were the same thing.

Trevor had been five when his father had died and he'd gone to live permanently in the war camps, but he still had a few memories of the man. Of his mother, he only had impressions. Softness, a smile, a scent of warmth and love.

Trevor shot to his feet, unable to stand the warring emotions within him. He stalked across the room, hearing growling coming from himself, but unable to hold it back. He surrendered into a violent shift, dropping onto all fours, his clothes and gun falling onto the floor as his powerful body changed into the big black, silver, and gray wolf with the white boomerang on its left shoulder.

The wolf snarled wildly and hit the door at a run. He needed to bite, to fight, to claw and kill. But his only blood enemy, the demon known as Khain, was nowhere to be found, so he ran, ran through the cool, dark tunnels at top speed, ran for miles, body stretching to the limit with each extension and flexion. Each time he came to a dead end, where a *wolfen's* family home was, he turned around and went back the way he came to take a different shaft, his claws on the concrete and the sound of his tearing breath echoing back to him.

When he finally returned to the prophecy room, it was at a slow walk, his head and tail drooping. He had met no one during his departure from sophistication, and that was probably a very good thing.

Trevor shifted wearily back into human form, anticipating needing to open the door with human hands, but Wade was already there holding it open for him, the expression on his face saying he knew exactly what Trevor had been doing and why.

"Thanks," Trevor said dully.

Wade shoved Trevor's clothes at him. "Get dressed. We have a problem."

CHAPTER 9

*E*lla stumbled over her own feet again, walking swiftly around and around her neighborhood, as the late afternoon sun began to drop behind the houses to her west. She steadied herself, looked over her shoulder, then slunk off into the grass to one side of the sidewalk. Her legs were aching. She'd probably walked twelve miles since escaping from Mrs. White's shop.

The cool grass welcomed her as she sank into it with her back against a tall white oak tree, glad to take her weight off her legs, but terrified to not be on the move. She couldn't go home though. What if someone was following her? What if *he* was following her?

"No," she said under her breath. "No one followed me. There was no one to follow me."

She took a deep breath and looked around, hoping the stillness and saneness of the cool day would reassure her that she was right. What she remembered could not have happened. A fox stole could not have come to life and bitten Mrs. White. She could not have caused a man who touched her in Mrs. White's shop to shoot backwards twenty feet through the store with enough force that when he hit the front wall, he destroyed it all. Even if that was what it had felt like.

She had to have imagined all of that, right? Maybe she should go to the hospital. Check herself in. Maybe her sister was right, and she *was* crazy. Maybe her mother had always been right, and she was dangerous too.

Ella held her head and moaned deep in her throat. If she had imagined what happened today, had the man been real? Had she done something crazy in front of people? Had she torn through Mrs. White's store and left by the back door? Why couldn't she remember that part very clearly? Had Mrs. White really pulled a gun on her? Maybe the police were looking for her right now, for… for trespassing or something.

A small part of her mind tried to get her to think about the incident fifteen years ago. The one she'd somehow relived earlier that day, but she refused to do it. She refused to go there. Refused to consider the fact that the boy on the swings and the man in the shop had been the same person. Even though she knew they had been. *That voice.*

Ella squeezed her eyes shut, trying to will her brain to stop working. She stood and looked hard at the winding path that led to the small park near her house. *No one was following her!*

She stepped onto the path and walked briskly home, refusing to let herself look over her shoulder, trying not to cry.

***

Trevor checked his uniform for rips. Finding none, because of the velcro pull-aways in prime spots all their uniforms had, he pulled the pants and shirt on quickly, secured his gun and badge, and looked to Wade expectantly. He was ready to head back out as soon as he heard what was going on. "What problem? Is he back?"

Wade dropped into an office chair near the small desk to the left of the door and held up a hand. "Relax, son. He's not back. I need to know when the last time you were bound was."

Trevor stopped in the act of lacing and tying a boot. "Bound? What? Why?"

"When I bound you earlier, what happened, after I let you go, I mean?"

"That's when the building exploded downtown and I ran over there."

Wade shook his head. "No, son. What happened to you? What did you feel? What-what kind of thoughts did you have?"

The desire to eat a bullet came flooding back to Trevor and he grimaced. "I don't…" he mumbled, trailing off.

Wade stood and waited for him to finish tying his boot, then straighten. "May I?" he asked, holding out his hand. Trevor just stared. Wade waited him out. Finally, Trevor's hand floated up on its own.

Wade took it with both of his hands and closed his eyes, drawing something from Trevor. Trevor was only too happy to let whatever it was go. The drawing felt good, soothing. Wade's hands were warm and dry, with latent strength pulsing in them.

When Wade opened his eyes and dropped Trevor's hand, Trevor did not like the expression he saw on Wade's face. A combination of pity and sadness. Trevor waited though, a deep exhaustion settling in him. He knew there was no running from this.

"Grey abused you," Wade stated, his voice flat, emotionless.

Trevor startled at the name. He hadn't thought of that crazy *wolfen* in fifteen years, not since he'd escaped the camps and gone rogue until he was old enough to join the force. He walked away from Wade in the small room. "Yeah, he was a tough, crazy, old fucker. But he abused everyone."

"Most of them got to go home when their fathers weren't working though. Not you. You were at his mercy. He never should have treated you the way I am afraid he did."

Trevor looked up sharply. He had no real memories to sort through of his time in the camp. He had buried all of that years ago, with such animosity his mind never went there.

Wade followed him. "How many times did Grey bind you?"

Trevor shook his head. "I don't remember."

"What did he say to you when you were bound?"

Trevor stopped pacing and stared the old *shiften* down. "I don't remember!"

Wade held up his hands. "I'm sorry. I know you have a lot going on right now. I'll deal with this. We can talk later after I find Grey, get the story out of him. But I want you to know that I will be sending word out to the *Citlali* that you are not to be bound. I should not have done it to you earlier. I sincerely apologize." Wade hung his head and whined deep in his throat.

Trevor backed up, his mind spinning. "No, Wade, no, I deserved it. You were right to do it." He hated Wade offering him supplication. It wasn't right. Wade was a great and strong male who had taken Trevor in when he got here, been the one *wolfen* who believed fully in Trevor. Even if that belief was wrong or misplaced, Trevor still held Wade in the same esteem he held his own father.

Wade stepped after Trevor and grabbed him by the back of the throat, pulling him in for a hug. "You're too hard on yourself," he whispered. "If I find out Grey was behind any of that, the wolf will pay. I promise you."

Trevor hugged Wade back, hard. After a few moments, Wade let him go. Trevor turned to the only thing in the room that could take his mind away from all of the stuff he didn't want to think about. Work.

He snatched up the remote for the DVD and turned it back on. "You want to watch this with me? I'm afraid I might know what Khain wanted today."

Wade pulled up a chair and the two males sat down. Trevor pressed the button. His father reappeared and began speaking, his eyes still closed. The words came out slowly, but clearly, as if he were being fed them by an unseen source.

In twenty-five years, half-angel, half-human mates will be discovered living among you.

This is how you will rebuild.

Warriors, all, with names like flora.

Save them from themselves, for they will not know their foreordination.

They will not be bound by shiften law, but their destinies entwine so strongly with their fated mates, that any not mated by their 30th year will be moonstruck. Those who are lost may be dangerous.

A pledged female will have free will that shiften know not. Never forget this or it will cause grave trouble.

Her body may respond to any, until she is mated in a ceremony of her choosing, then she will acknowledge only one male, as he becomes her one true mate, and she, his one true mate. He shall be sworn to her in her life's purpose, to rebuild the shiften race, so that they may fight the evil Matchitehew and protect the humans from him, until the day he draws his last breath.

Trevor stopped the DVD and faced Wade. "The word *pledged* bothers me. Today, Khain said something about *the promised.* I knew we never referred to the one true mates as the promised, but pledged is almost the same thing." Trevor leaned close to Wade, his expression scared and deadly at the same time. "You don't think Khain is trying to kill our one true mates, do you?"

Wade took a deep breath and stared at the image of Trevor's father on the screen. "Maybe he's trying to do something worse."

"What could be worse than killing them?"

"Mating with them."

Trevor pulled back and hissed between his teeth, holding his animal back with considerable force of will. "That *is* worse." He stood, pacing again. "Do you think that's possible?"

Wade sighed heavily. "There are rumors of Khain mating with our females a few times, by force or by trickery."

Trevor stopped still, his entire body on pause. "I've never heard such a rumor."

"Until today, such a word has not been breathed outside of the great hall. I only tell you because that prophecy was spoken twenty-five years ago today."

Trevor's eyes shot to the date on the DVD case. Wade was right. How had he missed that? Did it mean anything? Were the one true mates now *available* to be found? He clutched at Wade's arm, excitement filling him. "How are we going to find them? To know them?"

Wade cocked his head. "Calm down, son. No one knows."

"You talk to Rhen! Ask her."

"Rhen had nothing to do with the one true mates. After Khain's slaughter of our females, Rhen knew she had to do something or we would die, but her physical body has never recovered from the Act of Creation."

Wade ran a hand through his hair and looked around the room, then back at Trevor. "How much of this story do you know, son?"

Trevor clenched a fist to his chest. "Tell me all of it. Like I know nothing. I can't know what's rumor and fact out of what I have heard."

Wade nodded. "All right. I'll tell you what I know, but I don't think it's going to appease you."

Trevor paced again, unable to sit or stand still. Finally, for the first time, this information he'd begged for, longed for, dreamed of, would be shared with him, a non-*citlali*.

He nodded at Wade. "Tell me."

CHAPTER 10

*E*lla passed the lovely sandstone house on her way to her own, walking quickly, watching the house out of the corner of her eye. The moving truck was gone and no lights shone out of the bare windows.

She moved on, her eyes on her own house. A splash of white paint against the blue backdrop next to the front kitchen window caught her eye and sent a shiver of shame through her, triggering a memory from two weeks ago.

She'd been standing at her aunt's funeral, expecting no one to show up but her and the priest, when men had started to trickle in. All older police officers, all in uniform, several in dress uniform. The sight of all those uniforms had stirred something in Ella, something she didn't understand, and had no one to ask. She had wanted to know why they were there! Her aunt had always seemed to have no friends, no lovers, no acquaintances, and had been house-bound during her later years. No one had visited her in the hospital, but Ella counted thirty-four police officers attending her funeral.

As the priest had closed his statements and addressed her, they all slipped away, her chance to ask one of them how he knew her aunt gone. Not that she would have been able to work up the courage, anyway. She'd always been shy, but the way her mind had been slipping had made her more shy than ever. She was forever afraid of having an episode when she talked to a stranger. Especially a police officer stranger. She'd probably end up in a mental hospital.

Ella had walked home, feeling curiously empty, and wondering exactly how she should be feeling. Free, maybe. She'd been taking care of her mom or her aunt almost full-time for ten years, but now that they were both gone she had no one to take care of but herself. Problem was, she didn't know how to do that. Her former life had made her unable to think about herself.

She'd walked in the door, turned on a P90X video, and followed the video for the full hour three times, till she was dripping with sweat and dropping with exhaustion. She'd showered, eaten something, watched a little TV, and fallen into bed.

Ella remembered a lovely dream of following the moon, picking her way carefully through a forest while the moon's light shone on the path in front of her. Animals had surrounded her. Large animals, who were dangerous to everyone but her. Her, they'd not seen as prey, but as someone to be protected. Her feet had been bare, the dirt silky against her soles, the night air sweet with the scent of heavy flowers, and filled with the sound of crickets and other animals. But the moon, the moon had held all of her attention. Calling her, urging her on, speaking to her in a way she could almost understand…

A sharp pain in her foot brought her out of the dream and she woke up in the yard in front of the house with a can of white paint in one hand and a dripping paintbrush in the other. The moon shone directly overhead, large and heavy, and she guessed the time to be between midnight and three in the morning. In front of her, an arc of white paint had been applied to the blue of the house.

Ella had looked at the paint and brush in her hand and known immediately what she had been trying to paint on the front of her dead aunt's house.

The moon.

***

Wade sat and invited Trevor to do the same. He looked around the room as if trying to decide where to start. Finally, his gaze settled on Trevor. "You've heard the prophecy. It came from your own father. You know what Khain did to our females. But what you may not know is that Rhen is much weaker than anyone has ever let on. She may never recover. We don't know if she can die, just as we don't know if Khain can die, but she may never be able to return to her physical body."

Trevor rubbed the hair growing in on his chin. How long had it been since he'd shaved? Or slept? This revelation would be giving him nightmares for sure. The creator of all *shiften* too weak to ever recover? Was Khain stronger than her? What would happen to them if Rhen did die? Could the *shiften* continue to hold Khain at bay or would he wipe them out with a stroke of his hand?

Wade leveled him with a stare. "You know that no one has heard from The Light in millennia. Not even Rhen. Not even the angels."

"Is The Light dead?"

Wade sighed. "We believe that if The Light were to die, all of us would stop existing, so no, we don't think so. We think he's still up there, in The Haven, resting maybe. What seems like a long time to us may only be like a day to him. One of your own prophecies says that when you come into your power and fell the demon, The Light will return again."

Trevor winced. "If. It says if, not when."

Wade stared at him for a long time. "Son, I believe in you. There is no if in my mind."

Trevor shook his head and stared at the floor. "Prophecies only spell out one possible future, you've told me that yourself."

Wade didn't speak for several moments, sizing Trevor up. Finally, he pushed on, choosing to ignore Trevor's statement. "History gets fuzzy as to exactly when The Light disappeared and what might have happened to cause it, but you can be sure it had something to do with Khain. You know The Light has always existed. You know The Light used pieces of himself to create companions and gave them the earth as a home. Something happened, of which even Rhen is not sure, some sort of a war among The Light's companions, until all of them were gone but Rhen and Khain and a few angels, who never have had a permanent physical body or been able to come to earth for long. Khain disappeared. Rhen stayed with The Light but he was restless and created more companions, this time giving them only the smallest piece of himself, so they had no powers, no ability to rise up against him if one of them chose to do so. They were soft and weak, these humans, but he loved them. He gave them the entire earth as their domain, filling it with other creatures also, though none quite captured his heart in the way the humans did, possibly because of their good conversation and ability to create offspring that are pleasing to the eye. If there's one thing humans are good at, it's making and taking care of more humans."

Wade stopped for a moment and wiped his mouth with the back of his hand, then took a few deep breaths before continuing, as if he were getting tired. Trevor hated to see the signs of his age. "But the humans started getting hurt, and sick, and disappearing. When his favorite human didn't come to him for forty days, The Light sent Rhen to earth to see what was going on. Rhen found Khain, traveling from village to village, destroying them all with fire and explosions, or sickness and madness. Rhen didn't understand it. She loved the humans as much as The Light did and she questioned Khain as to why he would destroy them. He said they were unhappy, miserable creatures who could barely take care of themselves, and all he had ever met wanted to die, wanted to not exist on earth anymore."

Trevor snorted. He'd never heard this version of Khain's motives before. "A regular humanitarian."

Wade nodded. "That's how he played it off, like he was doing them a favor. Rhen said Khain had gathered a band of humans to travel with him and do his bidding. Wash him, feed him, kill other humans for fun. Rhen said Khain made her watch one such escapade and it turned her stomach. Khain's human was large and strong and Khain sent him after a much smaller man. Rhen stepped in, not allowing the first human to finish his hunt. She and Khain battled fiercely, and she managed to drive Khain off. She said she was lucky, because she and Khain seemed to be exactly matched, and for every power she has, he has an equal and opposing power. They fought for months, burning the earth in their wake. The Light sent the angels down to help Rhen, but some of them went to Khain's side, whether by trickery or will, no one knows. The Light called these renegade angels back to him, merging them with him, but each time he did, he seemed to weaken. Rhen said she called out to The Light many times, but he would never take direct action against Khain. To do so would upset the balance, was all he would say on the matter."

"Just when Rhen thought the battle could never end, the moon became heavy in the sky and their fighting crossed through the territory of a pack of timber wolves who were out hunting. Rhen called out to the wolves for help and they responded, surrounding and attacking Khain. The distraction was what she needed to gain the advantage and she struck Khain a finishing blow. He retreated, wounded, disappearing into the *Pravus* for centuries."

Wade stopped, eyeing Trevor, seeing if he was keeping up. Trevor nodded at him. He'd heard much of this in songs and nursery rhymes and bed-time stories, but never with this kind of surety and detail.

Wade half-smiled. "Rhen was wounded herself, tired and aching from battle, but she did not retreat. She went to the alpha of the clan and thanked him and his wolves deeply for their courage and fierceness, then offered him the only thing she had to give. A piece of herself which would provide strength and power to his descendants forever after. You know the rest of this part of the story, I'm sure."

Trevor smiled. "Of course." He felt pride pulse through him at the actions of his brave ancestors, a thick swath of tingles and emotion marching from his breastbone to the top of his head. He touched his left shoulder with his right hand, running his fingers over the *renqua* there, causing it to prickle. Wade ran his fingers over his own *renqua*, a source of pride and honor for all *shiften*, and a reminder of their purpose and connection to the *deae* Rhen.

Wade bobbed his head, looking more tired. "Every piece of herself that Rhen gave out that night weakened her even more, until she finally had to retreat also. The *felen* have watched over her body for centuries, just as we have guarded the humans, our constant battle with Khain evolving every century. When he emerged from the *Pravus* to find us millions strong and completely organized, he knew he couldn't beat us, and that is why he came up with the plan to kill our females. The half-breeds we make with humans just aren't strong enough to defeat him, nor do they have the protection drive that we do. Killing our females devastated us, and for three years, most of the first three years of your life, we thought we were ruined. Those were dark times, son, and your generation paid the price for them. We *Citlali* appealed to Rhen, but she did not know what she could do for us. She could not fight. Her body was not substantial enough to create more *shiften*, and The Light had retreated to some corner of the Haven that no one could follow him to. There was no help to be found."

Wade looked off at the wall covered with shelves stuffed full of prophecies, the light from the TV playing over his face. "That's what we thought, anyway, until your father spoke his final prophecy." Wade motioned to the TV where the image of Trevor's father sat still, paused. "He told us of the One True Mates and we immediately sat session, the only all-*shiften* session in history." He turned a bold eye to Trevor. "Except the *foxen*. They have no *Citlali*, so of course we did not include them."

"Smart," Trevor said. "Who knows what they would have done with the information."

Wade nodded sharply. "Never trust a *shiften* with a weak *renqua*, Trevor." He watched Trevor's face carefully, then went back to his story. "It took too many hours for all the *Citlali* to calm themselves enough to cross over. By the time we all were there, it was a full day later. Rhen had been told what we were after by the first to cross, so she had done her own crossing, into the Haven. We had to wait another day for her to return. When she did, she had astounding news. The few remaining angels had always refused to get involved in human matters, but one had taken pity on Rhen. Her constant mourning had touched his heart. From the way she speaks of him, I might surmise he is in love with her, and if so, all the better for us. He came to earth over the course of forty nights and mated with thousands of human women all around the world, with an intention of creating females strong enough to be our mates, to make offspring that would have a chance at fighting Khain. He hadn't told her because he was waiting to see how the babies developed, what sort of identifying characteristics they would have, what kind of powers and abilities."

Trevor leaned forward eagerly. This is what he had been wanting, needing to hear!

Wade held up a hand. "Don't get too excited. Rhen got that information second-hand from another angel. Her angel, Azerbaizan, had disappeared."

Trevor stood, pacing again. "Disappeared? How? Can angels die?"

Wade shook his head. "No one knows. He hasn't been heard from in twenty-five years. We think the prophecy your father received was sent to him by Azerbaizan. Your father said it came through disjointed and hard to read, and definitely not from Rhen, but from a powerful being."

Trevor curled a hand into a fist and looked for something to hit. There was nothing, unless he wanted to pound on a chair or the floor like a child. "Khain killed him. Or took him."

Wade nodded. "He may have. Which is why I accepted our transfer from Scotland without a second thought. We can't afford to be ignorant about the *Pravus* any longer."

Trevor sighed. "So all that, and we still have no way of knowing who the One True Mates are."

Wade stood also. "We must carry on like always, son. They may be looking for us. We may be revealed to each other over the next few days or weeks or months. We have three clues, four really." He held up his hand and ticked off the clues on his fingers. "One, they are warriors, whatever that means." Trevor grimaced and Wade laughed lightly as if he knew Trevor was wondering if he was going to be mated to a female who looked like Mac, or maybe Blake for the rest of his life. He popped up a second finger, "Two, they don't have fathers, and three, they are named like flora."

He paused and Trevor finished for him. "Four, they are twenty-five years old." He shook his head. "That's not much to go on."

Wade clapped him on the shoulder. "You're a cop, son, this is what you do best."

CHAPTER 11

*E*lla stalked into her driveway, trying to keep herself together. She hated the state of her mind and thoughts lately. Painting in her sleep was just one more reminder of her recent failings.

Ella dug her keys out of her pocket, her eyes glued to the arc of white paint on the front of the house. She would paint over that mistake tonight. Now. She didn't want to have to look at it anymore.

Before Ella could step up onto her porch, a small animal shot out of the bushes on the side of the house and ran for her like it wanted to attack her. Ella almost screamed until she realized it was Smokey. He put his two paws around her ankle and aggressively smelled up and down her leg as far as he could reach. She could hear the sniffs of breath he took in and out of his nose.

"Smokey, what?"

He looked up at her and yowled, a mournful, sad sound that confused her.

She reached down and tried to pick the cat up, but he evaded her hands and shot out of her reach. He looked at her one last time, then prowled to the center of the driveway and sat on his haunches, looking very little like a cat and much more like a guard dog. Ella watched him for a moment, then shook her head and stepped up to the house. He had a cat door. He could get in whenever he wanted.

By the time she was inside, his strange behavior weighed on her more heavily. What if the man from Mrs. White's shop had been here? What if he was in her house right now? Ella had never been much of a cat person until she and her mother had moved in with Aunt Patricia, so she didn't know a ton about them, but it stood to reason that they would be good at sniffing out bad people. What if Smokey had been trying to tell her something?

Ella dropped her keys in the bowl next to the door, her eyes wide, attempting to take in the entire house at once. She snapped on the light, then walked through the front room and kitchen slowly, barely breathing, placing her feet lightly, trying to hear noises from the house. It felt empty to her, but did that mean anything?

Ella took the three thousand dollars out of her pocket and put it in the fake can of soup in the kitchen pantry where her aunt had always kept cash. She changed the cats' water dish and filled their perpetual feeder. Then she began a thorough investigation of the house.

She swept through all the bedrooms, looking under beds, in closets, and behind things. She checked each bathroom and shower, then pulled down the attic stairs and checked up there. She didn't know what she would do if she found someone, but she knew she wouldn't be able to sleep if she didn't at least look.

Finally, most of the house clear, she stood at the top of the basement stairs, looking down the too-steep steps. Her mind ran free, imagining many different kinds of monsters down there waiting for her. But the only other option was to leave the house. She had to look.

The stairs creaked as she walked down them, each one making a different sound. Ella tensed more with each stuttering descent, until she finally reached the bottom, mostly because the closer she got to the bottom, the more her legs were exposed to the rest of the basement.

But when she got all the way down, the basement sat completely empty, which she had expected since she'd already given away or sold everything that had been in the large, open room. What she didn't expect was how safe she felt down there. Sounds were dampened, making her able to hear her own blood rushing in her ears. The heavy concrete walls pressed in from all sides, making her feel like she was undetectable. Ella shook her head. What a strange thought.

She purposely took a deep breath, her first of the day, and wished for a chair to sink into. She felt the tension retreat from her muscles and she smiled, another first.

The basement was one large room, mostly unfinished, except for a custom shelf and entertainment center built against the far wall, a semi-circle of carpet jutting out in front of it. Ella had always found the combination incredibly strange. Who leaves the basement unfinished, but only puts in some shelves and a sliver of carpet?

She walked to the carpet and lowered herself onto it, cross-legged, happy that it was there. She would go upstairs later, but for now, she just wanted to relax for a bit, shake off some of the day.

She listened to the tiny noises of the old house and thought about the money she had put in the fake soup can upstairs. She only needed eleven thousand more and she could pay off the back taxes on the house and keep the city from taking it from her. If she wanted to do that. Maybe she should let them have the house, take that money, and move somewhere else.

As Ella thought of moving, a deep resistance filled her that she didn't understand. She had nothing in Serenity. No friends. No real family. If Shay came back to town that would be a reason *to* leave, not a reason not to leave. She could get a bus or plane ticket and go anywhere with that much money. France, even, or Australia.

Ella tried to think of somewhere she would want to go and couldn't do it. Every part of her had begun to think of Serenity as her home.

Another thought struck her, rocking her. What if there was some sort of a warrant of arrest out for her? She had to go see if she had really done what she remembered doing. Tomorrow, she decided. Tomorrow she would go back and see what the place looked like. Maybe peek in on Mrs. White. Prove to herself that Mrs. White was fine and her shop was still intact. That everything Ella thought had happened had really been a... a hallucination.

Great. Just what she needed. To add having vivid, violent hallucinations to the list of things that were wrong with her.

Ella laid there, stroking the soft carpet with one hand, forming a pillow for her head with the other. She tried to make herself get up and get paint out of the shed to paint over the would-be moon on the front of the house, but as she argued with herself about doing it, she closed her eyes, just for a moment.

She fell asleep.

***

Trevor sat in the overstuffed chair and stared absently at the wall, his eyes running over the recorded prophecies, but not seeing them. Wade had left hours ago. His brothers had checked in and said they were heading home through the tunnels.

Let loose, Trevor's mind wandered, occasionally touching on everything that had happened that day, but mostly, it circled around and around the One True Mates. There were many who believed they didn't exist, but Trevor knew they did. They had to. His soul longed for a mate, not just any mate, but one born for him. One who would understand him, who would support him, be there for him no matter what, help him raise his young. He appreciated humans, had been born with a fierce drive to protect them, but he'd never met a human woman who had created a desire in him to mate with her. Maybe it was because he wanted full *shiften* pups. Maybe it was a biological or chemical thing. But at thirty years old, he felt the pull to be mated stronger than he ever had in his life. It was a physical pain that mixed with his hatred for Khain and weighed him down in everything he did.

He thought about the upcoming rut he had agreed to. A band-aid. A chance for his pack mates to scratch a sexual itch like they'd done in the old days. Not that Trevor considered anyone but Trent and Troy and maybe Blake and Wade his true pack mates. He and his brothers were transplants from New York, transferred to Serenity two years ago, when Wade had decided both the *Demon Death* and the *Savior prophecy* referred to Trevor. There were many *Citlali* that disagreed, but Wade held a favored position, as the leader of the region where Rhen's physical body was housed, and the region where Khain was said to reside within the *Pravus*.

So Trevor was pulled from duty as a Sergeant in his local police station, transferred to Serenity, Illinois, promoted, and put in charge of the Khain Special Response Team, an unlikely collection of *wolven* who all had been named in prophecies, but Trevor was the only one who was named in two of them. He also was the only one with a *Citlali* for a father, but many had said that Crew could be a *Citlali* if he were fit for the job, so Trevor didn't think that part mattered.

Trevor sighed, missing the old days, when packs were small enough that they were made up of only family and mates. His own father had been born into a pack at the turn of the last century that only had eighteen *wolven* in it. His father had shared many stories of pranks and jokes played on his brothers and sisters, the smile on his face revealing how close they had all been, how much they had loved each other.

But today, with the way the job of the *wolven* had grown with the populace of the country, there was no such thing as a small pack anymore. Alpha leaders had been replaced by Chiefs and Lieutenants and Sergeants of sprawling police forces, and that just didn't work as well. Some families still tried to keep pack alliances strong within the family, but when a working *wolven's* first loyalty had to be to his chain of command, there were conflicts.

Serenity PD had two hundred and ninety sworn police officers, all *wolven*. That was no simple pack. Truth be told, Trevor thought the lack of one clear alpha that every *wolfen* worked with on a daily basis created many of the problems that Mac thought a rut was going to fix. He would see. After the rut, he would check the temperament of the KSRT and see if anything had changed. He doubted it. The KSRT was a boiling pot of nine alphas, all trying to live together and do the same job, without killing each other. It barely worked. So far, most of them tolerated him, but none of them accepted him as leader, and he didn't think they ever would. According to Wade, when Mac had been leader they hadn't accepted him either. Too much aggression, drive, and testosterone crashing around, but then, their aggression and drive were reasons why each of them had been chosen for the job.

Trevor thought about going home, but decided against it. If Khain had crossed over once, he might do it again. Trevor wanted to be ready. He wanted to be close.

He crossed his arms over his chest and relaxed in the mildly-comfortable chair, but with no place to put his legs. Sleep tried to come quickly, as he was exhausted from not having slept the night before, but the chair was not made for sleeping.

Desperate for just a few hours of shut-eye, Trevor slid to the area rug on the cold ground, laid his head on the pillow of his arms and fell asleep immediately with his boots still on.

He dreamed of his One True Mate. Sleeping somewhere close by. Needing him. Wanting him.

Made just for him.

CHAPTER 12

*E*lla's eyes snapped open and she shifted uncomfortably, her body stiff from sleeping on the basement floor. She groaned and wondered how long she'd been there. She forced herself to her feet and stretched her back, turning in a circle towards the window, staring for a long time at the early morning sunshine. Had she really slept all night? The sun, barely skimming the tops of the trees from the east, said she had.

No wonder she felt stiff. She used the tiny unfinished bathroom in the corner of the basement, not bothering to check her hair or face. She knew she looked awful. Her mind began spinning almost immediately with what she needed to do that day. Paint over the white splash on the front of the house, then head downtown and check out Mrs. White's shop. Assure herself it had all been a—what's a nice word for a hallucination? A fantasy maybe, or a mirage? Ella snorted then laughed at herself for snorting and walked to the stairs. As she ascended, holding onto the hand rail with her left hand, looking at nothing in particular, something caught her attention on one of the shelves built into the wall. She stopped and stared at it. It was flat, but colorful.

She stepped backwards down the stairs and made her way to the shelf, reaching above her head and feeling around where she had seen whatever it was. Her fingers found it, but as she drew it off the shelf, the shelf moved smoothly toward her, about a half an inch.

Ella gasped and stepped back, pulling the piece of paper with her. She could see immediately what it was, a bumper sticker of a police badge with the badge number K27 on it. Above the badge was written, *Remember Forever*. Ella frowned. She hadn't known her aunt supported the police. She hadn't known much at all about her aunt, even after she and her mom had moved in with her. Her mother had always seemed to discourage her and her aunt from talking, and after her mother had died, her aunt had gotten sick, so there had been no talk then either. But maybe this explained the police officers at Aunt Patricia's funeral?

Ella put the sticker back on the shelf and dropped her fingers to the wood. She pulled, experimentally and the entire shelf swung out easily, as if on oiled hinges. Ella blinked at the small room that lay beyond, her heart beating hard in her chest. She took a step forward without meaning to, then another, and another, until she was inside. It was colder back there, as if the heat didn't reach the area. The room was small, only about six foot by six foot, lined in concrete like the rest of the basement. The light was dim, but she could still see well enough. To her right were six large boxes with lids, piled as tall as she was. To her left was a door.

Ella looked at the boxes, then looked at the door. She turned and approached the door, slowly. It looked heavy. All metal, steel maybe. She grasped the knob and twisted, then pulled, but the door didn't budge. Ella let her fingers fall away, glad that it hadn't. She felt suddenly like she was at a pivotal moment in her life, like everything hinged on the next moment, and if she had managed to get inside the door, her life would have changed forever.

She slumped to the side wall and tried to calm her nerves. "Calm down, jeez. It's just a door."

Her voice didn't soothe her at all. Electricity jumped and buzzed through her nerves. She noticed, built into the wall at eye-level, a small brown, plastic contraption. She lifted her hand and ran her fingers over it. Smooth. Secure. She bent forward to stare right at it. A light played over her eye, startling her, and the plastic contraption beeped, making her back up.

The door opened as if on hydraulics, but only for a moment. Then it slammed shut, making Ella glad she hadn't tried to step inside but she didn't think about that for long. Instead, she tried to puzzle out what she had seen. A wide concrete tunnel stretching into darkness. She had no way of knowing, but her sense was that the tunnel was long, maybe miles long.

Ella backed up, trying to figure out the puzzle. Life had been so boring for so long, only an endless procession of bed care and hospital visits, punctuated only by death and awkwardness. She felt bad for thinking of her mother's last years as boring, but her mother had never liked her, had never spoken a kind word to her that she could remember. Her aunt hadn't seemed to dislike her, but she'd never talked much either. The lung issues that had stolen her last years had stolen her breath and energy also.

The door could be what? A—

Ella's thoughts were interrupted by a strange sense that something in the house had changed. She cocked an ear towards upstairs. Hearing nothing, she stepped outside the tiny room and looked at the ceiling over her head. Footsteps. Big, booming footsteps sounded over the corner, the area she knew to be just under the front door. Ella's throat constricted and suddenly she couldn't get enough air. A realization dropped into her chest, freezing her in place. Him. She knew it was him. She knew everything she'd hoped she imagined the day before had really happened and she was in more danger than she'd ever faced in her life. Too bad she couldn't move. Too bad she was going to die here, because—

Movement on the stairs caught her eye and she almost screamed. Smokey, practically flying down the stairs, ran at her and jumped from six feet away, forcing her to break her paralysis to catch him.

She turned him in her arms so she could see his face. "Smokey, where's Chelsea?" she whispered, knowing he couldn't answer. A word still entered her mind, and it was enough for her.

Safe.

She stared at the cat's yellow eyes. Had she really just read the mind of an animal? Smokey turned in her hands and bit down on her thumb, as if telling her to hurry, hurry!

Ella sucked in a breath. Upstairs, the footsteps continued into the kitchen where they stopped.

"Promised."

She didn't know if she had heard that awful word out loud, or in her head, but when she realized she had heard the horrid voice before, she had her confirmation. It was him.

Ella ran to the east window on legs that felt unable to

hold her. She slid the glass open, wincing at the slight noise the window made in its frame, then pushed the screen out. She put Smokey in the well outside. "Go," she hissed at him, but he grabbed her thumb again with his teeth and pulled. "Ouch," she moaned, fear eating at her insides. She couldn't explain the terror, but she couldn't stop it either.

She boosted herself onto the windowsill and stepped out into the well, never so glad for the egress window. The sides had indentations, like a ladder for her feet and she hauled herself up and out onto the grass, her fingers sliding in the frost there.

Smokey picked his way up the side of the well and joined her on the grass, then yowled once, softly, and took off running toward the street. Ella followed, pulling her phone from her pocket, wishing harder than she'd ever wished for anything in her life, for battery.

Twelve percent. Enough to do what she had to do. She dialed 911, still running to the street, throwing terrified looks over her shoulder. She knew whoever was in her house already could tell she had left. She could practically see him through the walls, swinging around, tracking her easily. She didn't know what he was, but she didn't think he was human. The thought terrified her, and she wondered if the police could even stop him.

"911, what is your emergency?"

Ella stopped running so she could talk. She was on the sidewalk several houses away from her house. It looked quiet, normal, like nothing dangerous ever could or would happen there.

"Sorry, yes. There's someone in my house. Someone… dangerous."

"Your address please, ma'am?"

Ella rattled off her address without thinking about it, when a change in the light of the front window caught her attention. He was there. The man with the voice, standing at the window, staring at her. Fear hit her so strongly, she stuttered, then stumbled, and almost dropped her phone.

"Ma'am, are you there?"

Ella couldn't answer.

CHAPTER 13

*T*revor's phone buzzed in his pocket, waking him. The feel of the day told him it was morning before he ever saw the time. He'd slept all night. He pushed himself into a sitting position, knees up, and pulled out his phone. The number had no name associated with it, but when he saw the text he knew immediately who it was. Kalista.

He's here. 1200 block Chestnut Ave.

Trevor was on his feet and running in a breath. He made it to the parking lot in record time, unable to worry about backup, his brothers, or anything else. Khain would be his.

He popped the blue bubble onto the top of his truck and flipped on the siren, then floored it, maneuvering around stopped traffic and running red lights. In only a few minutes, he turned the corner onto Chestnut Avenue, his tires screaming in protest.

Up ahead, he saw two parked police vehicles, and a calm officer on the sidewalk questioning a civilian woman while another officer walked sedately through a yard a few houses down. Trevor skidded to a stop, unsure if he was at the right place. He rolled down his window and sniffed the air.

Khain had been there, but he was gone.

"Damn it!" Trevor yelled, punching the dashboard in front of him. Would he never meet Khain face to face?

He swerved to the curb and parked his truck, jumping out and heading across the street. A delicious smell hit him and his steps faltered for a second as he identified it. Cinnamon and sugar, it reminded him of when he was young, very young, while his mother was alive. Trevor pushed the thought away angrily. No time.

"Report!" he barked at the officer on the sidewalk who was talking to a tall human female whom Trevor could only see the back of. He turned away and strode to the other officer while the first left the woman and ran to catch up with him. The three met under a maple tree that had lost most of its leaves. Only twenty or so held on resolutely in the cool, crisp wind.

Trevor didn't wait for anyone to start. "Was it him?" he asked the two officers, his voice low. He knew damn well it had been, but he needed to know what the first two on the scene thought.

"Definitely, Lieutenant," one of them said while the other nodded. "He was gone when we got here, but we smelled him as soon as we turned on the street. A *felen* was here too, but he left already."

"Where?"

The officer pointed to the house they were standing in

front of. "We think he may have crossed over inside that house and disappeared from there too."

"Who's been in the house?"

The second officer held up his hands. "We only went inside for a second, to make sure he was gone."

"Good, don't let anyone else in. My team will be here shortly." Trevor pulled out his phone and sent an alert to Mac, Harlan, Becket, and Crew, noticing when he was almost done that the cinnamon and sugar smell had gotten stronger.

He looked up. The woman with the black hair took two more steps towards them and stopped, just outside of their circle, her arms crossed over her chest. She was dressed only in a sweater and jeans and Trevor knew she must be cold, but that wasn't what stopped his breath. She was gorgeous. Her skin, as cool and pale as cream, contrasted with her long black hair in a way that made his eye want to hug every curve of her cheek and brow. The delicious sweet scent came with her and hovered around her, like she'd spent all morning baking cinnamon rolls in a small, hot kitchen. She raised a dark eyebrow at the officer who'd been questioning her.

"Ah, is it safe? Can I go inside?"

At the sound of her voice, Trevor felt some great surge of emotion, some unnamed desire inside him. One word popped into his head like a neon sign he couldn't ignore. *Mine.*

Trevor tightened down his inner will, surprised to feel his fangs lengthening in his mouth slightly, like something was spurring him to shift. *Shiften* couldn't shift in front of humans unless Khain was nearby. He lifted his head and turned slightly, scenting the air. Khain was not around. He shook his head and looked at the clipboard in the officer's hands. At the top was the woman's name. *Gabriela Carmi.* "Miss Carmi, or is it Mrs. Carmi?" he asked, his voice and his chest tight.

She waved her hands elegantly, like doves set loose at a wedding. "Ella. It's just Ella."

Trevor nodded, his stomach twisting into coils as he smelled her rich scent and ate up the sight of her. "Ella, this man who was in your house. Did you see him?"

Ella shook her head, watching him carefully, her head tilted back slightly so she could look him in the eye, exposing the creamy length of her neck. "No. Just heard him."

Trevor licked his lips, trying not to imagine what her skin would feel like if he ran his fingers over it. Or what it would taste like to his tongue. "Did he say anything?"

Ella frowned and Trevor thought he'd never seen anything quite so beautiful. "No," she said after a moment's hesitation, her breath frosting as she spoke.

Trevor sniffed the air, but he could smell no deception, although she looked like she wasn't being entirely truthful. But why would she lie? He wished for Troy. Troy could sniff out any lie, any liar, not that he would ever call her that.

He noticed her pulse beating in her neck and he watched it, fascinated by the bluish tinge he saw at the delicate cut of her collarbone. She was cold. He should offer her a coat. His truck to warm up in. Or to drive. Maybe to have as her own. Or he could get her a new furnace for her house. Or give her his house to live in as long as she wanted. Or how about a ring, a big one, just in case she liked that kind of thing. A woman like her really shouldn't go without—.

"Ah, Lieutenant?" One of the officers said and Trevor pulled himself back to reality. Both of the officers were staring at him warily and Ella Carmi looked almost scared of him.

How long had he been staring at her?

***

Ella held her breath as the big cop with the gorgeous face, the slight New York accent, and the cleft in his chin stared at her. She was a sucker for a cleft chin, always had been, not that she'd ever had much experience with men other than looking at them. Playing constant nursemaid didn't leave much time for that kind of thing. Not that she was a virgin, oh no. She had let one man perform the hymen maneuver on her during her failed attempt at college. It hadn't been anything to write home about. Her other boyfriend hadn't even tried. But when Lieutenant Luscious looked at her, she felt a loosening in her hips and a tingle at her core that made her unable to think about anything but beds, soft lighting, and tongues in naughty places.

Then she remembered the guy who seemed to be hunting her down.

Ella bit her lower lip, hard, trying to draw herself back to reality. The big cop was looking at her again and their eyes met, making reality skitter away. She put out a hand, feeling light-headed, but there was nothing to hold on to. She stepped back with one foot and tried to ground herself, keep her balance. He was just so big. So handsome. He made her feel so—

He was speaking again, slowly at first, then with more speed and confidence. She tried to focus on his words and not the crazy way she was feeling. "Ella, you can't go back in your house until the crime scene team does a thorough sweep of it. I have somewhere you can go until then. In fact, I think it's best if you stay away from your home for a while, just until we get this straightened out. We may know who this man was, and he's dangerous."

Ella nodded. That sounded good. She didn't want to be alone anyway. But more than that, she didn't want this handsome cop to see her zone out, and that's what she felt like she was about to do. Just stop speaking, stare off into space, like some sort of a coma patient who walked and talked every once in a while. It had happened eight times in the last two years, five of those times just in the last three months, and it scared the crap out of her more each time. If she did it in front of the big cop, she thought she might die.

"I'll have Officer Adin take you there in just a few moments, but I have to ask you a couple more questions before you go."

Ella nodded, hoping she looked ok, feeling like a balloon with a delicate spider web for a string, one puff of air and she'd be gone.

The big cop motioned her to walk on the sidewalk with him, then gave the other two officers some sort of instructions. Ella put one foot in front of the other, until she was pretty sure she was walking ok.

"I have a few strange questions for you, but please answer them honestly. They might shed some light on who this guy was."

"Ok."

"Were you downtown at all yesterday? Anywhere near 15th Street?"

Ella stiffened, unable to help herself, and a sudden fear shot through her. "No," dropped out of her mouth, completely unbidden and before she could correct the lie, the cop asked another question.

"Are you married?"

"No."

"How old are you?"

She could answer that one. "Twenty-five."

He turned glittering blue eyes on her and she almost shrank at their intensity. "And your parents?"

"Ah, what? I mean, what do you want to know?"

"Are they here, in Serenity?"

"No. My mother and father are both dead."

The cop pressed his lips together, and she expected words of condolences. Instead, he said, "Tell me about your father."

Ella knew the question was strange, knew it made no sense at all, but she wanted to please the man. Wanted to keep talking to him, because it seemed to make her feel better, seemed to ground her in reality. So far, she hadn't zoned out. Hadn't lost it. She was still there, talking coherently. "His name was Howard. He sold insurance for Country Home. He was a sweet man, always laughing, but he never had a ton of money. That didn't matter, though. He was still the best dad that ever existed. He came to every play I was ever in and always had time to talk to me. Everyone told us how much we looked alike." She put a finger to her nose. "I've got his nose, his eyes, and his smile."

She smiled as if to prove it, feeling suddenly sick to her stomach. Howard had been her imaginary father, the one she'd retreated to her room and made up every time Shay hit her or their mother had told her to *quit being strange, why can't you just be normal every once in a while.* Why was she lying? Why was she spilling out this story, this absolute *fabrication*? Her mother would never, ever discuss her father, and when Ella tried, her mom would go still and silent and not speak to her for weeks. Shay loved that, and used to whisper about it when she really wanted to hurt Ella.

You're so fucked up your own father didn't even want you!

The cop turned slightly towards her, his eyebrows furrowed and his nostrils flaring slightly. She could tell he was disappointed, but she couldn't understand why. Could he tell she was lying? Oh God. She opened her mouth and tried to tell him it had all been a mistake, but the words wouldn't come. Her mind drifted instead, as it tried to cope with everything that had happened that day, with what was still happening.

The cop stopped walking and she realized they were next to one of the patrol cars. He opened the back door. "Just sit in here, Miss Carmi. Officer Adin will take you somewhere safe in just a moment."

Ella climbed inside, unable to meet the big cop's eyes, her mind unable to reason any of it out. She just needed a moment to think. A moment to breathe. A moment to recover.

He slammed the patrol car door behind her and walked quickly away, giving her the moment she no longer wanted.

CHAPTER 14

*T*revor drove back to the station slowly, thinking hard, confused as to his reaction to the woman, Ella. He'd never in his life reacted to a woman like that. Like most of his kind, he found human women attractive on a sexual level, but he had never had that chemical and emotional attraction to one that made him think about… more. He knew it happened all the time, more so now that there were no female shifters, but it had never happened to him.

Idly, he wondered if she could be a one true mate, even as he knew she wasn't. Her name was not *like flora*, and she knew who her father was. The only thing she had going for her was her age. Trevor wanted to kick himself for his attraction to her.

He shifted into low gear and let his truck coast to a halt at a stoplight, glad for the extra time to think before he arrived at the station. Maybe she was a half-breed. He'd heard of *wolven* being attracted to half-breeds almost like full *shiften*. Rarely could the half-breeds shift, but he'd heard stories that their children with *shiften* frequently could. Too bad there were no sort of databases of half-breeds that he could look up to figure out if she was. Wade would have been able to tell, maybe even Crew. But Trevor did not have their touch, and as sensitive as his nose was, he'd never been able to sniff them out either. He wondered if Troy would have known. Troy and Trent both seemed to have abilities and insights that Trevor did not, possibly because they had never shifted into human form. It kept them wilder.

The light changed and Trevor drove on, his mind spinning. He had a few things he wanted to do before his team came back to him with the results of their investigation. When he got to the station, he parked quickly and ran inside.

As he walked in the door, Trent hailed him mentally. *We heard Khain crossed over again. What's going on?*

Not sure yet, he sent back. *He was gone when I got there. The human involved was unharmed.*

Poodle-fucker is up to something.

Trevor laughed in spite of himself. *Agreed. Maybe you and Troy should find a handler. Patrol the two areas he's shown up at the last two days.*

On it.

Trevor hurried to his office, glad not to meet anyone on the way. He hurried to his black office chair and pulled his laptop close, opening a browser. *Meaning of Gabriela,* he typed in.

God's able-bodied one.

Huh. He accessed the police department's criminal database and looked up the last name Carmi. A Frederico Carmi had been arrested for terroristic threatening in 1972, and that was all he found. Not helpful.

His phone rang and he snatched it up. "Burbank," he snarled, harsher than he wanted, but when he heard Mac's voice, he wasn't sorry.

"Nothing. He left no trace. Didn't force the door. Just crossed over inside the front door, walked around a bit, then crossed back over from in front of the window. The *felen* said he was on our side for exactly ninety-six seconds. They said he's still tracking differently, and it's harder to get him but not impossible," Mac said, his voice surprisingly free of hostility for once.

"Interesting," Trevor said, wishing they had a way to track him when he left their world and went into his own. A way to reach him there. A way to go on the offensive and not always be on the defensive. "I'm sick to fuck of being on the clean-up crew," he said into the phone. "Get with Harlan, maybe some of the sub-rosa team. Tell them we need a new strategy. Entertain any suggestions, no matter how crazy. Something big is about to happen and we can't sit around and wait for it."

"Good plan," Mac growled and hung up.

Trevor stared at the phone before hanging it up. That couldn't have been approval he heard from Macalister Niles.

His mind went back to Ella Carmi. He snatched up his phone again and dialed Wade.

"Chief Lombard."

"Wade, can prophecies ever be wrong?"

"Trevor," Wade growled. "Is this about this morning's visit by our favorite asshole?"

Trevor ground his teeth. "Yeah."

Wade sighed. "You tell me about it when you get a spare moment. As for your question, no, I don't believe a prophecy has ever been proven wrong, but yes, theoretically, they could be. When we go under, language is different. We aren't reciting something someone has told us in a conversation. We are interpreting messages that could be coming in any form."

"Like what kind of form?"

"They could be images. Scents. Sounds. Intentions. Ideas. Thoughts. Almost never words."

Trevor grunted. "That sounds to me like you could very easily get them wrong."

"Yet I don't believe I ever have."

Trevor thought about that, hard. "And my dad?"

"Your dad was a *Citlali* with great power and a greater gift. I would bet my life that the One True Mate prophecy is 100% correct."

Trevor caught his lower lip between his canines and worried it a bit. "Khain entered a woman's house today. She got away. She's twenty-five but she knows her father and her name is Gabriela, which isn't any sort of flora."

The line was silent for a moment. Trevor was just about to ask if Wade had heard him when he spoke. "Was she a warrior?"

"A warrior? No, I mean, she was a woman. Soft. Pretty."

"Don't be fooled by softness, son. It tells no tales."

Trevor huffed air out of his nose. "Thanks, Wade." Was being cryptic in the job description for *Citlali*? Or did they work at it?

Trevor hung up, still thinking of Ella Carmi. Had he made a mistake by sending her to the safe house with Adin and his partner? If Khain had been after her specifically, he could try again. Track her somehow. Two patrol officers were no real match against Khain. Two were better than one, who

Khain could easily best, but at least four strong shifters were needed to drive Khain away, and more were better.

Maybe when Mac reported in again, he should send him over there, him and Harlan. They were the strongest—

Trevor felt his fangs elongate and a growl come out of his throat at the thought of Mac being anywhere near Ella Carmi. He watched as the claws on his right hand grew long and razor-sharp.

Trevor reeled himself in and stood, grabbing a coat from the back of his door.

Trent, Troy, I need you.

He would check in with his team, then go watch her himself. At least for a few hours.

CHAPTER 15

*M*any hours later than he wanted to, Trevor and his brothers pulled into the driveway of the police-controlled house where Ella was safely ensconced. Mac had followed his instructions without hesitation for once and by the time Trevor had found him, he was in the tunnels, in an intense meeting with Canyon, Timber, Jaggar, and Sebastian, demanding a new strategy, an offensive strategy. Trevor backed Mac up, emphasizing to his team that the game was now changed. They needed a way to hunt and track Khain. He was done with damage control. The foursome hadn't had any ideas but that didn't matter. Getting them thinking was what was important. They would come up with something.

He'd finally made it out and drove straight to the safe house. A perfect blend of ecstasy and anxiety filtered through him at the thought of seeing her again. His boot-clad feet crunched on the stones of the driveway as he walked towards the front door, his eyes on the soft light coming from inside, his brothers falling into line behind him. He could see his breath in the cool night air.

He knocked and waited. Adin opened the door in a few seconds. "Lieutenant, hi. We got the extra officers you sent over."

"Good. You and your partner can go until second watch tomorrow. The K9s and I will assist with the night shift."

Adin raised his eyebrows but didn't say anything. He stepped back so Trevor and the wolves could enter, then went to gather his stuff and his partner. "She's in a bedroom in the back," Adin said from across the room. "The last on the left."

Trevor stared down the hallway, his stomach doing flips. He nodded at the two officers in uniform sitting on the couch watching Bait Car with the sound down low. He approved of them being out there, and Ella not being out there, even if he didn't know why.

He could feel his brothers behind him as his feet took him towards the hallway. Both were open, but wary, and both had noticed a change in him, although neither one had asked him what it was about yet. Could they know? No. Neither one of them had given him any shit yet, and if they knew how he was feeling for a human woman, they'd be raking him over the coals. Troy especially.

The hallway loomed large as he travelled through it, the warm, rich scent of cinnamon and sugar catching him by surprise. Oh yeah, she smelled like a fucking bakery. He'd almost forgotten.

You smell that? he sent to his brothers.

Smell what?

Nothing.

Trevor licked his lips and thought about stopping, turning around, staying away. His body had other ideas. He stopped in front of the slightly-ajar door and knocked on the door frame.

"Miss Carmi?"

"Ah, come in." She sounded nervous. He hated that. What could he do to make her feel better?

He pushed the door open. The bedroom was small with a single bed in the middle of the room and the wall lined with chairs. She sat in one of them, by the slightly-cracked window, looking out. He winced at the security breach. How had she gotten it open? All the windows should be sealed from the inside *and* outside.

She looked at him, eyes wide. A hot liquid filled his chest, making him feel much too heavy all of a sudden. "Miss Carmi," he started, but then he felt his brothers push past him. Both of them swarmed quickly into the room, heading straight for Ella. He tried to call them back, they were big and he didn't want to scare her, but her face broke into an immediate smile when she saw them and he almost sagged with relief.

"Oh cutie, you are so beautiful," she cried, grabbing Troy by the face and petting his head and neck, leaning forward and kissing him on the nose. Trevor thought he might die with envy. Trent reached her then and she let go of Troy to smother Trent's furry face with kisses and tell him what a gorgeous doggy he was, and how big he was, yes, and what a very good boy he was. Her fingers traced his *renqua*, then went back up to his neck.

Trevor watched in surprise. His brothers generally did not like humans, although sometimes they made exceptions for human women, especially *pretty* human women, but he didn't sense any objections from either of them at being called a doggy.

Ella continued to pet his brothers and coo over them relentlessly, paying him absolutely no attention at all. He almost didn't mind. It gave him a chance to gaze at her. Her red lips and pale skin, her powder-blue eyes, her full cheeks and breasts, and the way her hands moved.

Hey, mutts. Have some pride, would you?

Troy shot him an evil look. *Shut up you jealous fucker. You just wish it was you.*

Trevor smirked and sat in one of the chairs by the door, as far away from Ella as he could get. He hadn't expected this, but he couldn't say he was disappointed.

Ella finally looked up at him. "Are they police dogs?"

Trevor nodded. "Our best, except for the bigger one there, he's on probation. Can't stop him from drooling all over the back seat of the car." Trevor smiled as Troy bared just one fang at him.

"They're so big."

Trevor didn't respond. He found it best not to offer explanations.

Both wolves pressed against Ella's legs and she continued to pet them, but when he met her eyes again, he could tell her demeanor had changed.

"I'm glad you came. No one will tell me what's happening. I agreed to come here because I was scared, but now that I've had time to think about it, I want some answers, and I don't want to be treated like a child anymore."

Trevor only stared. The standard line when dealing with a Khain sighting was supposed to be a lone madman with explosives, but he couldn't force out the words. He didn't want to lie to her.

Her eyes narrowed. "So you aren't going to tell me what's going on either?"

His brothers both turned and sat on either side of Ella, facing him, like they were on her side. He looked to them for help, but got none.

She stood, stepping carefully around the wolves. "Lieutenant, spill it, I can take whatever it is."

She stared him down and he could feel the force of her will, the force of her anger, and he could not resist it. He held the arms of the chair as if they might keep him from floating off into space. "You-you wouldn't believe me if I told you the truth," he said weakly.

She stared at him for a long moment, then sagged visibly. She made her way back to her chair and curled one arm around each wolf, pressing her face first against one and then against the other.

"Yeah, you might be right," she said sadly, and his heart broke.

***

Ella sat quietly in the chair, holding onto the beautiful dogs for a long time. Why couldn't anything be simple? Her whole life up until that point seemed like one long mess after another.

From the corner of her eye she watched the big cop. Officer Adin had told her that his name was Lieutenant Burbank. He dwarfed the chair he was in, staring at his boots with a gruff look on his face. She still thought he was the most handsome man she had ever seen. His hair was light, but not quite blond, and he had a five o'clock shadow that was also light, but did not hide his gorgeous cleft chin. He looked tired. Worried. Burdened.

But he made her feel safe. The instant he had entered the room, she'd known he would be able to protect her from the man who had come after her twice now. *Three times.* No. She didn't want to face that yet. Could he really be the same person from fifteen years ago? She ran her fingers through the fur of the dogs as she turned her mind back to the man in the room with her. The dogs made her feel safe too. They were massive, and obviously bred for police work; fighting, chasing down criminals. She hoped they would stay the night. She would sleep much better knowing the three of them were in the house.

Ella eyed the small bed, wondering if she was really going to sleep there. She wanted to go home, but then again she didn't want to be alone. Not now. Maybe not ever again?

Her attention found the Lieutenant again and she watched him. His face was screwed up like he was trying to make a decision or work something out in his head. She didn't want to burden him anymore. She didn't know how, but she could tell he had her best interest at heart. He just wanted her safe. If he wanted her to stay, maybe she would stay. Just for the night. She'd figure something more out in the morning. Besides, she didn't want to give him a hard time.

Not after she had lied to him.

Ella winced, wanting badly to come clean, but not knowing where to start. She hunched in her chair and turned her attention back to the dogs, running her hands through their fur, kneading their strong neck and back muscles, letting the feel and the demeanor of them soothe her.

Dogs were the best people, she knew that. Life would be a lot easier if she only had to deal with animals for the rest of her life.

CHAPTER 16

*E*lla woke up with a start, blinking against the early morning light. She'd slept in the chair with her feet up on another chair and it had been uncomfortable, but she felt rested. Someone had draped a blanket over her during the night. The big cop, it had to be.

She dropped her feet to the floor, smiling when she saw the two huge black dogs there, both awake, both with their heads on their paws, watching her protectively. She was halfway in love with them already.

"Hi," she whispered and the one with the white figure 8 on his left shoulder shook his head and barked out something that almost sounded like hello. She smiled. "Neat trick, boy. Who taught you that?" She ran her finger across the strange marking on his shoulder, wondering if it was a brand of some sort. She'd never seen an all-black dog with such a strange marking on only one spot of its body. The other dog had one, too, in the exact same spot. His looked like a bomb dropping from the sky. She saw only one other white spot on the very tip of the tail of the dog she was petting and none on the other dog.

The two dogs stared at her with quiet intelligence, then glanced at each other. Two strange voices filled her head.

… Bet she is …

… don't say … Trev… needs to …

Ella shook her head and banged her palm against her forehead. No new voices allowed, damn it! Both dogs looked at her and she swore she saw alarm on their faces. She bit her lower lip and petted them each with one hand, scratching under their chins. "Sorry. Just ignore me. I'm crazy sometimes. But your—" She frowned. "Boss? Master? Lieutenant? He doesn't need to know, ok? So don't rat me out."

The bigger one with the white bomb on his shoulder opened his mouth and his tongue lolled out. He looked at the other dog and Ella swore they were smiling.

Master … like overgrown circus …

Ella shot to her feet, pressing her hands to her temples. NO! She stepped over the dogs and paced around the bed, trying to deny she was hearing more voices. Both dogs scrambled to their feet also, watching her closely. "It's ok, puppies. Don't worry about me. I'm … I'm. I just have to pee." She ripped the door open and ran across the hall, shutting that door and doing her thing, then she stared in the mirror at her rumpled hair and sallow face. Sleeping in a chair sucked.

She slapped water on her face and tried to calm her hair with her hands, then brushed her teeth with her finger. She had to go home. Like now. She needed clothes, she needed to feed the cats, she needed to retreat back into her drama and keep her craziness away from people who had jobs to do.

People like Lieutenant Burbank. She sighed and wondered if he had a girlfriend. Probably. Or maybe a wife and five or six kids. She hadn't thought to look for a ring because she was a complete idiot about most things, men especially.

Ella exited the bathroom and found the smaller black dog with the figure 8 on its shoulder and the tuft of white on the end of its tail sitting outside the door waiting for her. She touched its head and smiled at it. What a good dog. Maybe she should go to the pound, get herself a dog. Someone to be there, to protect her. But what would the cats think?

She padded down the hallway in her bare feet, listening to one of the police officers talk. She recognized the voice as one of the officers from yesterday. Not the big lieutenant. Officer Adin, the one who had been so nice to her.

"Troy, don't bullshit a bullshitter. There's no way the Bears are going all the way this year."

Ella heard the big dog whine and it sounded like a laugh to her. She smiled at how vocal the dogs were. She loved it. Were they trained to be like that or was it natural? She knew huskies talked a lot but the two dogs didn't look like huskies. They were too big, too thick and had the wrong color eyes.

The hallway ended and she stepped hesitantly out into the living area, the slightly smaller of the dogs at her heels. Officer Adin was at the stove, in uniform, frying something that smelled like bacon, and the bigger dog sat on his haunches next to him. The dog's eyes met hers as she entered the room. Ella's stomach rumbled in hunger but she ignored it as she looked to her right. The second officer she had assumed Adin was talking to was not in sight.

Officer Adin's back was to Ella. He shook his head at the frying pan and kept talking. "See, we ain't got the dream team—" The bigger dog barked once, sharply, causing Officer

Adin to whirl around, spatula held high. "Oh, hi. Did we wake you?"

Ella shook her head. "Um. Sorry. Where is Lieutenant Burbank, please?"

"He had to go to his office."

"I need to talk to him."

The officer dropped the spatula on the counter. "What do you need, sweetheart? I can help you."

Ella pursed her lips. "I need to go home."

Officer Adin shook his head. "No can do. The boss says you gotta stay here for now, until we know what happened yesterday."

"Sorry but, am I under arrest?"

Officer Adin looked at her strangely. "No."

"Ok then, I'll get my shoes and go. Thank you for your help."

"Wait! No, ok, let me get Lieutenant Burbank on the phone. You talk to him. He'll kill me if you just walk out of here."

Ella's eyes narrowed and she crossed her arms over her chest, watching Adin. Within a few minutes he handed her the phone.

"Hello?"

"Mrs. Carmi," the smooth voice with the slight New York accent she recognized as the big cop said. "I really need you to stay there. That's why I left the-ah-the dogs with you. They are going to help Officer Adin keep you safe."

"Safe from what exactly, Lieutenant?"

He didn't speak for a moment. "I thought we covered this last night."

She sighed. "Did we? I thought we didn't say much of anything and I let you get away with it because I was scared.

But in the early morning light, last night's fears seem less grounded. I don't even know who I'm hiding out from, or why he would want anything to do with me."

His voice lowered dangerously. "You aren't safe from that-that criminal just because the sun is shining. Don't fool yourself."

Ella stared at the phone and a sick dread filled her. She wondered if she told the Lieutenant about the man with the barbaric voice, if he would know who she was talking about. She pressed on anyway. Unless someone was going to tell her something, she wasn't going to just sit around and let them do their thing while she sat in a room and stared out the window. "Still, I have a life, Lieutenant. I have things I must tend to. If you're so worried about me, maybe you could place a squad car outside my house." She tried to hold the apology in but she couldn't. "Sorry, that's just how I feel." Argh. She did that way too much.

The silence on the other end of the line filled her with hope and trepidation. She hadn't expected him to consider it. What if she had one of her episodes? She didn't need a police officer witnessing it.

"You really shouldn't be alone," the Lieutenant said and she heard something in his voice. Something that scared her. Could she really afford to turn him down? He spoke again. "Look, I've got some things I need to do today away from the station. Errands. You have some too, yes? Maybe we could help each other out. You stay with me. And then tonight I'll bring you back to the safe house and you'll sleep there again. Just until we figure out what's going on."

Ella's heart pounded at the thought of seeing the big cop again. The big *handsome* cop. At the thought of spending the day with him. She took a moment to make sure there was no eagerness in her voice. "When will you figure out what's going on?"

"My team is working on it now. The best males on the force. As soon as I know something, you'll know something."

Ella doubted that, but he knew what to say, that was for sure. "When will you be here?"

"I'm leaving now."

***

Ella sat on the couch next to the window, watching the driveway, trying not to admit to herself how excited she was, completely refusing to think about why the police lieutenant was really coming to get her.

When his big red truck pulled in to the driveway, she blushed as their eyes met through the window. She stood and ran to the bathroom before she peed her pants with her completely inappropriate excitement. She was so lame.

When she worked up the courage to leave the bathroom, both dogs were sitting at the door looking up at her. "Good boys," she whispered. She squatted down to pet them, burying her face in the fur of first one, then the other. "Help me out, ok. I really like your Lieutenant. I know he's probably married or taken or not impressed by twenty-five-year-old women who've never held down a job or learned to drive or even fit in at school or her own family, and I can accept that, but at least keep me from embarrassing myself." One of the dogs licked her face and whined while the other pressed his head against her chest. "Thanks, boys. You're such good doggies."

She stood and the dogs pressed against her, their backs reaching almost to her waist. God, she loved a big dog and these were the biggest she'd ever seen up close. She drew strength from them and made her way out into the living area.

He was there, leaning against the door frame, wearing similar, but not the same, clothes from the day before. Dark blue khakis, black boots, a t-shirt that stretched invitingly over his muscles, along with his badge and gun at his waist. He looked positively yummy and she felt faint for a moment. She bit her tongue, hard, tasting iron in her mouth. What in the hell was wrong with her?

"Hi," he said, pushing off from the wall and smiling at her. The other officer seemed to have left.

Oh God, the smile made him look even more handsome. She felt for the dogs. They were there, by her side, their soft fur providing a sort of touchstone for her.

"Hi," she smiled back. He looked at the ground and she looked out the window, then snuck a peek at his left hand. No ring. No tan line. But the hand itself was big, strong-looking, sexy as shit if you were into guy's hands, which she most certainly *was*. If he held her hand, his big hand would dwarf hers. She licked her lips and wished fiercely that it would happen, even as she knew it never would. "Your dogs!" she said, trying to fill the silence with something, anything other than her awkwardness.

"Hm?"

"Thank you for leaving them with me. They made me feel safe. They are *so* well-trained."

A grin crossed his face and he looked at the dogs. "Aren't they? We had to work with them for months. Years, really. And yet they still sometimes don't get the harder commands. But still, they are just dogs."

Ella cocked her head, feeling like she was missing something.

"Trent, Troy, come!" Lieutenant Burbank called, and he seemed to almost be laughing.

The bigger dog growled and rushed forward and bit the lieutenant on the shin, right through his pants.

"Ow! What the f—"

The dog trotted back to Ella and sat down next to her.

"Oh my goodness. Did he bite you? Are you hurt?"

The lieutenant grimaced and narrowed his eyes at the dogs. "No, it's nothing."

"Is that a hole in your pants? Did he really bite you?" She backed away from the dogs, nervous at the turn of events.

"Don't worry. Please. It's a joke. Their—ah—their handler likes to play jokes on me like that sometimes. He really actually can be a dick," he said, glaring at the big dog whose mouth was open and his tongue out, looking as amused as a dog could look. The other dog was staring at the floor and as Ella watched he shook his head, left, right, then back again, like a disgusted human would. She blinked and backed up until she ran into the wall.

A rush of words crossed her brain.

Hampster-humper... don't ... that again ...

Cat-fucker ... deserved ...

Kibbles-n-bits ...

Enough!

Ella pressed her hands to her forehead and whimpered. The man and the two dogs both looked at her, concern on all their faces. This was it. She was cracking up once and for all. The big cop was going to have a front row seat. She felt her cheeks heat and her muscles tighten with the strain of trying to hold it all back.

She slid down the wall and landed on the floor with a thump.

CHAPTER 17

Trevor ran to the woman but by the time he reached her she was already holding out her hands. "No, I'm fine. I'm sorry. Just give me a second to sit here. It's been a rough few days."

He veered off and went to the fridge instead, opening it and finding a sparkling water inside. He took it to her and knelt next to her. "Here, drink this, it will help."

Trent and Troy had climbed into the woman's lap as best they could and she seemed to be trying to cradle both of them. At least she didn't look scared of them anymore.

She took the drink, then cocked her head at him and she did look better. The color was back in her cheeks. She took a long drink then gazed at him. "Did you call the dogs Trent and Troy?"

"Uh, yeah."

"What strange names for dogs."

"Yes well, police dogs and all that. Who knows who names them and why."

She nodded and took another drink. "Which is which?"

"The bigger one is Troy. He's older by a few seconds. This one is Trent."

She touched each *wolfen* in turn and repeated the names, looking them in their eyes. Marking them. Trevor loved the care she took with them.

She ran her fingers over Troy's *renqua*. "What is this? Do you brand them somehow?"

"No, uh, that's just a birthmark. We ah-get our Czechoslovakian Wolf Dogs from the same breeder and most of them have some sort of mark like that. Genetics or something."

"Fascinating. I've never heard of a Czechoslovakian Wolf Dog."

"Yeah, well, they exist," Trevor said, then mentally flipped Troy the bird when he chuffed and bobbed his head at the lame statement.

"You relax for a second. We have time," he said, standing and walking to the couch. He had a thousand things to do that day and he could only get two or three done with her in tow, but it was worth it to keep her safe. His heart had dropped into his stomach earlier when she'd called and said she wanted to leave.

Behind him, he heard the *wolven's* claws on the hardwood floor and he turned. She was standing up. "No, I'm ready." She sounded surprised and happy.

"You sure?"

She nodded her head and smiled at him and he thought his heart might burst at the loveliness of it. Like the sun breaking through the clouds after a week's rain. Or a boat hailing you after you'd spent a week adrift at sea. Or—

Hey Lover-boy, you're drooling, Troy told him.

He snapped himself out of it. "Let's go then." He noticed her frowning and holding her head again. He frowned himself and watched her, but she shook it off and walked past him, straight out the door toward his truck.

She climbed in the passenger seat. He let the dogs in back and got behind the wheel. "Where to?"

"My house, please. I need new clothes and to feed my cats. Well, my aunt's cats."

Trevor grimaced internally. She was a cat-lover. Oh well, she couldn't be completely perfect. Cats were ok, he guessed. Especially housecats. They were tiny. Not sexy at all.

The drive to her house took twenty minutes and they didn't speak once. In Trevor's mind he was watching her sleep, which he had done for much of the night, wishing she were someone else. He'd never in his life felt so attracted to anyone, and it killed him that she was a human. Hell, maybe Mac and some of the other guys were right. Maybe the One True Mates were only a myth. Maybe a better strategy would be to encourage all the shifters to look for human mates. The Light knew human women were plentiful and normally eager to mate with *shiften*. Half-breeds were better than no young at all, and sometimes the offspring were strong. Sebastian was a half-breed, and he was hard-as-claws.

As Trevor pulled in front of her house, he was struck by the thought that he was missing something. Khain had been in this woman's *house*. That had to mean something, especially combined with what the demon had done and said the day before. If Ella Carmi wasn't a One True Mate maybe …

"Do you have a sister?" he asked, knowing it was stupid even before it left his mouth.

"Sister? Uh, yeah. But she doesn't live here."

"How old is she?"

"Twenty-eight."

"Right." Trevor shook his head and turned the truck off. "Are you going to be here long?"

"No. I only need to do a few things."

"Can I use your bathroom?" He could feel blood from Troy's bite running down his leg into his boot and he wanted to take care of it. He turned to the dogs in the back. "Patrol the yard."

Watch for Khain.

Got it.

Ella pressed her hand to her temple then looked at him, the hand still there, as if she didn't even know she was doing it. "Of course. I'll show you where it is."

They all got out and Ella led him up the walk, her eyes on her keys. Trevor looked at the side of the house, at the splash of white paint there, and wondered about it. Before he could ask, she had the door open. "Down that hallway, second on your left," she said and headed the opposite way.

Trevor sniffed the air. Khain wasn't there and any smell of him had faded. The house smelled empty and safe, except for the warm, slight ammonia smell of two cats. He found the bathroom and stepped inside, locking the door, then pulling up his pant leg to look at the bite. It was the size of a quarter and seeping blood. That fucker, Troy. Trevor would get him back.

He dropped his pant leg and stood up straight, unbuckling his holster and placing it on the sink. He let go of the holds of his humanity, urging his body to change. It was painful, but as always there was strength and promise in the pain itself. He dropped to all fours as his clothes mostly fell off him, then just as quickly, he pulled his mind together and shifted back, gritting his teeth against the ache of transformation. He looked down and saw his unbroken skin where the bite had been a moment before. He grabbed some toilet paper, wet it, and cleaned all the blood off of his shin, then pulled his clothes back on, buckled his holster, and left the bathroom.

***

Ella stopped in front of her dresser and lifted her head straight up as if scenting or sensing the air. Something delicious was happening in her house. Something she wanted to be a part of, to know. She turned in a circle and found herself walking towards the door of her bedroom, then down the stairs, drawn towards something unknown. A vast contentment filled her. This was good, right. She was finally doing what she was supposed to be doing with her life. She had found her mate and he would provide her with purpose, with protection, with support and love, with everything that was good and comforting in life. She drifted down the stairs and toward the other end of the house, suddenly startled out of her reverie and thoughts by the sound of a door opening. Lieutenant Burbank appeared at the beginning of the hallway.

"Ah, found it, thanks." He hooked a thumb over his shoulder, back towards the bathroom.

"Oh! Right. Good. I'll just be a few more minutes." Ella turned and hurried back up the stairs to her room, embarrassment flashing through her body. She was a complete nutcase, she knew that now. She turned her mind to the task at hand. Change her clothes. Run a brush through her hair. Clean her teeth. Maybe a washcloth shower.

A few minutes later, she had accomplished all of the

above without incident. She hurried back downstairs, surprised to find the big cop standing right where she had left him, a strange look on his face, and Chelsea in his arms. The short-haired cat snuggled into its perch and lifted a paw lovingly to the lieutenant's face.

"Cats, ah, cats don't usually like me," the man admitted and Ella almost giggled at the look on his face. He glanced toward the window as if afraid someone might see him.

"She certainly likes you."

"Yes," he said and put her down, trying to brush himself off, but Chelsea jumped straight back into his arms.

"Sorry," Ella said. "Just put her down again. I'll open a can of food to distract her."

He did and Ella was right, the food did distract the cat. Ella stuck her head out the back door and called for Smokey, who did not come.

She closed the door and turned back to see the big cop staring out the front window, his body tense. "Trent needs me," he said and made it to the front door in three steps. Ella rushed to the window to see what was going on. Both dogs were pointed away from her, staring at something on the front lawn. Something small that she couldn't see. Weird. She watched the big cop rush down the front steps and join the dogs, his posture saying whatever they were looking at was dangerous. A rabid animal maybe? Or a snake? But there weren't any venomous ones in the area. The cop bent and when he stood, he was holding Smokey by the scruff of his neck. Ella gasped and rushed outside.

"That's my cat," she said, gathering Smokey in her arms and turning away from the dogs. "He's harmless. Did he just walk up to you?"

She swore the two dogs were frowning at her but she

didn't understand what was going on. Smokey was a friendly cat with people, but he didn't like dogs or other cats. He only tolerated Chelsea because she had been there first.

"What's on his shoulder?" Lieutenant Burbank asked, his voice gruff.

"That's nothing. He's missing a patch of fur. He's been missing it since the first day he showed up here. The vet said there was nothing he could do about it. I don't even notice it anymore."

"Missing? He's not missing any fur."

Ella noticed the frown on the lieutenant's face and the strangeness in his voice. She looked down at Smokey who lay completely compliant in her arms, his eyes on the two dogs. On his left shoulder, in the spot where he'd never had fur before, he now had a white figure 8 threading through the black fur, exactly like one of the dogs had. Ella blew out a breath and ran her fingers over the spot. She thought hard, back to the day before. No, he'd had no white fur in this spot then. Only the tip of his tail. Her mind flipped over. The tip of his tail was the only other place that dog had a white spot also. "I don't understand. He had a missing patch of fur here before."

"Was it in that shape?"

Ella thought back. "Sorry. I don't remember. But I don't think so. I think it was just an oval."

A look passed between the big cop and the two dogs and Ella felt like screaming. There was something they weren't telling her.

The big cop stepped closer and his nostrils flared. "What do you mean, when he showed up here?"

Ella looked up at him. Maybe if she were more open, he would be too. "I only moved here with my mom two years ago. My aunt always had Chelsea and another cat too, but the day we moved in, the other cat disappeared and Smokey showed up. We tried to find the owner, put up signs in the neighborhood, but no one ever called, so we just kept him. He's a good cat." She shut her mouth with a snap, feeling like she was babbling, trying to justify something.

The big cop stared at the two dogs again and Ella felt her neck muscles tighten into cords, giving her an instant headache. "Look, Lieutenant, can you just tell me what's wrong?"

"Call me Trevor," he said in an offhanded way, rubbing his cheek with his hand. "Sorry, I guess we're all keyed up."

Ella relaxed slightly. Smokey jumped out of her arms and ran off into the bushes. They all stared after him, and then the two dogs began to walk around the house again, noses down, neither going after the cat. Ella looked at Trevor. "And you can call me Ella." she said, feeling shy but happy at the same time, putting Smokey out of her mind for now.

He smiled at her. "Right."

Ella felt herself get sucked into that smile and she resisted the pull. "So, ah, I'm mostly done here. What did you have to do today?" she asked too brightly.

He held his hand out toward the street. "The department is having a-an event and I need to pick up some snacks. That's easy, right? You up for a trip to Cost-Smart?"

"Anything," she breathed, then had to hold herself back from a forehead slap. She said the stupidest shit sometimes.

He didn't seem to notice. "You need to lock up?"

Ella ran back inside and grabbed her keys and a small wallet she could fit in her pocket.

If she didn't think too hard about what was really going on, she could almost imagine they were going on a date.

CHAPTER 18

*T*revor pulled up at the warehouse store and eyed it, wondering if he should bring Troy and Trent inside with him or not. It would draw attention to them, but if Khain showed up, he would need them. A ripple of anticipation went up his spine at the thought of Khain showing up. He was more than ready to finally face the monster.

He turned off the truck, then went to the back to rummage around in the storage compartment for Trent and Troy's police vests. They'd been quiet the entire way, all of them lost in their own thoughts about what the appearance of an *echo* meant. Especially a domestic cat echoing a *wolfen*. It didn't make sense.

He pulled open the back door and held out one of the vests for Trent who walked into it and let him buckle it, then did the same to Troy.

"You never talk to them," Ella said.

"What?"

"You never say a word to them, or pet them or anything. I don't know, I thought it was strange. Sorry." Her cheeks flamed and she looked forward quickly.

Trevor caught Troy's eye and smiled. He wouldn't dare pet one of them. Wrestle maybe, but no male would ever pet Trent or Troy and expect to keep his fingers. As for talking to them? Maybe he was acting weird. He didn't know how humans treated their pets. He sure as hell was not about to call them cute puppies in a baby voice.

"Maybe it is strange. I'm not in the K9 unit. I don't have a ton of experience with their work." It wasn't totally a lie. He winced, hating the thought of telling her any untruths.

"Why do you have them now?"

"Ah, well, because they are a team, and ah, they are the best at dealing with certain kinds of situations and, well, I might need them..." He took off towards the store, hoping swift movement would deflect any more questions.

He stopped to grab a cart and she caught up with him, his brothers alert and menacing at her heels. She looked at the cart he was pushing. "Why is it so big?"

Trevor looked down at himself, startled, then realized what she was talking about. "The cart? Because this is a warehouse store. Everything comes in super-size packages. You've never been here before?"

"No," she said, her eyes on the ceiling of the store, then crawling over the pallets and pallets of items just inside the door.

"You're in for a treat," he said, nodding at the woman just inside the door and holding up his membership card. People whispered and scattered out of their way, scared of Trent and

Troy. They were certainly handy to have around. Criminals took one look at them and just gave up.

They pushed their way through the aisles and he grabbed items they would need for the rut the next night. Pickett's funeral was during the day but it would be catered. The *zyanya* would be next, and then right to the rut. Trevor would not be going but he'd told Mac he would pick up some refreshments so none of them fell over in a dead faint during their hedonism. Trevor shook his head. A rut with humans, a *scheduled* rut with humans—what was the world coming to?

Wade approved so it wasn't Trevor's business to judge. He pushed the giant cart through the aisles and grabbed bottled water, hard cheeses, salami, sausages, bratwurst, and burgers. As an afterthought he threw in a few buns and chips for the females. Ella stayed quiet, following him and taking everything in.

He pushed all the items to one side of the cart and grabbed some things he needed at home. Bacon, six whole chickens, two gallons of mayonnaise—Ella laughed and he turned to her.

"Is that mayonnaise? Who needs two gallons of it?"

Trevor held it up. "You'd be surprised. Trent loves the stuff. He's weird." He ignored Trent's calculated huff and the delicate lifting of one side of his mouth so only one fang showed.

Her eyes narrowed and she looked at him sideways. "Do you mean the dog Trent?"

Too late, he realized his mistake. "Yeah, um, I don't work with them, but I've been, uh, boarding them lately."

"They don't stay at the station?"

Trevor pushed the cart quickly out of the aisle and headed towards the rear of the store. "Nah. They get lonely."

She ran to catch up but he set a pace he hoped would keep her from talking. Past the sodas, he picked up a squeaky toy from a pile and squeaked it, grinning at Troy. Troy wouldn't dare bite him in the store. He hoped.

Ella pointed to a bag of dog food. "Do you need any of this?"

Trevor laughed. "Hell no, they eat steak. The last time I brought some of that home as a joke Troy went in my closet and shit in all my shoes. Never again."

Ella stared at him, her eyes wide. Trevor wanted to punch himself in the side of the head. He was normally not that stupid. She was affecting him. Making him babble.

"I'm done," he announced, then pushed the cart towards the front of the store, hearing two voices laughing in his head.

After he'd paid and boxed his items, he stopped and looked at Ella. "Hungry?" he asked, nodding to the food court. "It's not fancy but the food is good and I'm paying."

"Oh no, you can't."

"I can," he said with a simple grin, hoping she would let him. "I want to."

She smiled back and his stomach dipped. "Ok then."

They stood in line and when they got to the front, Ella ordered a small soda and a slice of pizza.

Trevor didn't even have to look. "Fifteen foot-longs please, and a soda."

Hey, Troy barked inside his head. *I'm thirsty.*

You're gonna have to drink water. I'm not giving you soda in front of her. There's a bowl in the truck.

Troy didn't answer and Trevor knew that was bad. He would have to deal with the consequences later. He gathered up his fifteen hot dogs and went to the condiment area. He threw the buns away, slathered five with onions, five with ketchup, mayonnaise, and onions, and left five plain, not noticing Ella's confusion.

He led her to a table in the corner where they would draw the least attention, then set ten of the hot dogs on the floor. Troy finished his five before Trevor could lower his butt into the chair, but Trent ate more delicately, licking off the condiments first, then munching one wiener at a time.

Ella sat and took a bite of her pizza slice. "You really do feed them people food. It doesn't mess with their digestion?"

"Nah, that's why I threw away the buns. They would have."

Ella eyed his food. "You don't eat the buns either."

He swallowed a bite. It went down hard. "No. I don't," he finally said. "Low carb."

She nodded knowingly, then looked down at the two canines. "They look so much like wolves."

Trevor sucked a piece of meat down the wrong pipe and Ella watched him, concerned until he stopped coughing. "They do. How much do you know about wolves?"

She smiled and her voice took on a new excitement. "More than you, I'll bet. Wolves are amazing animals. Highly intelligent. More social than humans. So gorgeous and cunning." She leaned forward. "Did you know that the loss of wolves in this area is responsible for the current suffering of the ecosystem in the northern woods?"

Troy's ears perked up and he placed his head on the table. Ella fed him a pepperoni.

"Suffering?"

"Yes." Trevor watched her lips move and the animation of her gorgeous face as she explained. His mind started to slip, imagining kissing her, and he had to pull himself back to her words.

"You really like wolves," he mused, almost to himself when she was done speaking.

"I do. Always have. I still have my wolf teddy I got for Christmas when I was four. I had to carry him around all day with me to keep him safe from my sister. One time she gave me a black eye and cut my arm with a paperweight but I still didn't let go of Baron. I sleep with him every night." She stopped as if embarrassed, then looked out over the crowd of people eating and shopping.

What she said warmed him from the inside. He wanted to take her hand, but he didn't.

She faced him again and lifted her chin. "You know wolves have been reintroduced into the wild in Idaho, Montana, and Wyoming after years of dwindling packs?"

He nodded.

"I think that's a good thing, don't you?" Her voice held a dangerous fire that he was certain he didn't want to mess with, but he ached to hear more of. Maybe as she moved underneath him, naked, panting and clawing at him.

Trevor pushed the image out of his mind and looked down at his food. "I think it's a great thing."

She sat back, mollified, finishing the last of her slice, then looking wistfully at the food counter.

"Want another one?" he asked.

"Oh, I don't want to—"

He stood. "I'll get you another one. Be right back."

She smiled at him brightly, making him decide to buy her two more slices. Maybe four. And some ice cream. And another soda.

Anything she wanted.

***

Several hours later, after four phone calls, two more errands, and amazing conversation with Ella, Trevor pulled up in front of the building downtown. "I'll only be a minute. I need to ask someone a few questions about an incident that happened two days ago on 15th Street. You can come in if you like."

Ella gazed at the building, then shook her head, looking upset.

Trevor stopped for a beat. "You ok?"

She nodded quickly.

"Ok, I've got to take Troy in with me, but Trent will stay with you."

She nodded again.

Trevor slipped out of the truck and looked over the new building. A faded and twisted sign sat in the window, reading *You Need It*. Blake had told him Mrs. White, the shopkeeper of the place that Khain had blown up, was trying to reopen her shop there. He walked inside with Troy, still wearing his police vest, following at his heels.

The curtains were drawn and the lights were low, giving the place an eerie look. Did items sell better that way? Maybe, if they were creepy items. He blinked in the low light and walked toward the counter, where a man who looked like he should be home in bed was placing jewelry into a glass display case.

"Is Mrs. White here?"

"I'm not open yet. Go away."

"Sir, my name is Lieutenant Burbank, of the Serenity Police Department. I need to ask Mrs. White a few questions."

"She already told that other officer everything she knows. You know, the sniffy one." The man put his nose up in the air and sniffed hard, presumably imitating Blake. His eyes landed on Troy and he stepped back. "What in the hell is that?"

"Police dog, sir."

"Get him out of here! He'll, he'll pee on something!"

"I can assure you that he won't, sir," Trevor said, trying to keep the laughter out of his voice and the smile off his face. "Just tell me what I need to know and we'll leave quickly."

The shopkeeper hunkered over the counter and stared at him. "What?"

"Are you an employee here?"

The old man snorted. "I'm the owner. Part-owner. This is my wife's baby. She loves ugly old crap."

Trevor nodded. *Lucky for you*, he thought. "You are Mr. White, then? Your wife, where is she?"

"At the salon. She'll be in tomorrow."

"I see, thank you," Trevor said, making a mental note to come back the next day. He hadn't read Blake's report yet and he was trying to put it off until he got to interview Mrs. White himself. He liked to do his interviews fresh, without the opinions of other officers tainting what he saw.

As he turned to leave, a trinket caught his eye. A pendant on a gold chain of a snarling wolf with amber eyes. The little gold piece grabbed him by the throat and demanded something from him. What, he didn't know, but he had a guess. Just looking at it made him think of the beautiful woman waiting for him in his truck.

"Ah, Mr. White, is that piece for sale?"

"Everything is for sale, son, for the right price."

"Could I see it?"

The old man lifted the pendant out by its chain and placed it in Trevor's hands. Ella's laugh, Ella's smile, Ella's voice, the curve of her hip, even her mangy cats filled his mind. *I love wolves*, he heard her say and he was lost.

"I'll take it," he heard himself saying, like a lovesick idiot who was too stupid to know that he was chasing a *foxen's* errand.

The shopkeeper raised his eyebrows. "That's a new piece. Not priced yet. But I can assure you it's quite expensive."

Trevor pulled out his wallet and placed it on the counter, then dug through it with one hand. He pulled out a credit card and held it out. "That's fine. I want it."

Mr. White leaned back, pinning Trevor with his stare. Troy shifted and Trevor knew the *wolfen* was trying to figure out what exactly Trevor was doing. He couldn't explain it or justify it. He had to have that pendant.

Mr. White ignored the credit card, took the pendant and held it up. "The gold in this piece is worth almost two thousand alone by weight, and the gems in the eyes might be yellow tourmaline, we're not sure. I don't know that my wife is willing to sell until we know for sure."

Troy whined, telling Trevor the old man was lying about something. Mr. White flipped the pendant over, displaying the angel that was perfectly carved into the other side, which made Trevor want the thing even more. He held himself back, trying not to show his eagerness. But he wasn't walking out of there without the pendant.

Trevor took a deep breath as the man ran his fingers over Ella's pendant, explaining why the thing was going to cost so much money. *Whatever, dude. I don't care how much it costs.* Troy whined again, probably telling Trevor to relax.

Trevor did, focusing on the wall behind Mr. White's head until he stopped talking. "So how much?" he asked bluntly when that glad moment finally arrived.

"Ninety-Two hundred."

Trevor held out his credit card again and this time Mr. White took it.

Troy moaned in his head. *You are awful at haggling. He would have let it go for five thousand. You couldn't even check in with me?*

Trevor turned his back on Troy, unwilling and unable to explain himself. When the pendant was safely wrapped up and in his pocket, only then was he able to breathe easily.

He didn't know when or how he was going to give that pendant to Ella, but he knew it was meant for her, as sure as he knew his own name.

CHAPTER 19

*E*lla sat in the passenger seat of Trevor's truck, feeling like she was in a young adult novel. Trevor had been so much fun to talk to, such a gentleman, and so interesting that she almost felt like they'd been on a date, and not part of some weird, forced protection team. He fascinated her. No sign of a wife or girlfriend or kids yet. She watched him from the corner of her eye. He had to be almost thirty. How was it that he wasn't taken yet? Unless there was something wrong with him…

"We just have one more stop," Trevor said, turning on the windshield wipers. "Crud, I was hoping the rain would hold off until I got the stuff in the back of the truck to Mac."

"Who's Mac?" Ella asked.

Trevor growled loudly, the sound reverberating low and deep in his throat, his lip lifting like a snarling dog's would. Ella stared at him, her eyes like saucers, her heart beating hard in her chest. Had she heard what she thought she heard?

He leaned over the steering wheel and coughed hard, whacking himself in the chest with his fist. "Excuse me," he said, not looking at her.

Ella stared hard at the dashboard, the pounding of her own blood in her ears almost blocking out what she could only describe as snickering that she was hearing in her head.

Trevor opened his door. "I'll be right back. I have to cover the truck bed." He jumped out and ran to the back of the truck. Ella twisted in her seat and watched him as he pulled on a roll of leathery fabric just behind the cab, pulling it to the very back of the truck and snapping it in several places to cover all the groceries they'd bought.

Trent licked her hand and she petted him, smiling at him. Troy looked jealous so she twisted farther and petted him too. "Such good puppies," she whispered, as Trevor jumped back into the vehicle.

"Mac is no one," he said. "Just a coworker. I need to get this stuff to him and then I can take you back to the safe house."

"You aren't going to stay with me?" Ella said, almost pouting, before she could stop herself.

Trevor put the truck in gear and started driving. Ella felt her heart sink as he seemed to be thinking of how to tell her no.

But then he didn't. "I'll stay with you."

She smiled, her heart full. "Thank you."

"Anything you want," he said softly, his eyes on the road.

Ella let the words hang in the air. He was just being polite.

Within a few minutes, they pulled up into the police department parking lot and parked in an empty space. Trevor made a phone call and then scrambled out of the vehicle. "Wait here, I'll be right back."

Ella waited, twisting in her seat again to pet the dogs and surreptitiously watch Trevor's muscles flex as he carried the heavy items from his truck to an expensive-looking car three spots down. A man came out of the building and approached Trevor, dressed exactly like Trevor. He was tall and dark with a broad chest and a handsome but mean face. Ella didn't like him immediately and she felt surprised at her reaction. Normally she liked everyone, but then she realized why she didn't like him. He unlocked his car trunk, then stepped up to Trevor and his facial expression and gestures made it obvious he didn't like Trevor, or at least was mad at him. Ella bit down on her lip, upset by that. She watched the two men argue in the cold rain and wondered if none of the cops ever wore jackets. She hadn't seen Trevor wear one yet and Mac, if that's who he was, wasn't wearing one either.

Trevor glanced over at her and Mac's eyes followed the glance. He said something to Trevor and for the first time Trevor's response became heated. He placed his body in between Ella and Mac so she couldn't see his face anymore, but his body told plenty of the story. The two men were about to fight and it was going to be a bad one. Troy whined and Ella did the only thing she could think of. She opened the back door to let him out. Troy and Trent swarmed out, both of them running straight to Mac and jumping up, putting their big paws on his chest and their snarling snouts in his face. Ella gasped.

"Still using your mutts to do your dirty work," she heard Mac say, and then he turned and walked away, knocking the two dogs to the ground. They paced, their angry energy obvious in the set of their bodies.

Trevor loaded the water and food into Mac's trunk, then slammed it and headed back to the truck to a shocked Ella. "Done," he said. "Want to go out for dinner, or get something on the way?"

Like absolutely nothing had happened.

CHAPTER 20

*E*arly the next morning, Trevor opened one eye and watched Ella sleep in the chair across from him, the *wolven* at her feet. He hated that she was sleeping in the chair again, and if he had any guts at all he would put her in the bed, but he didn't. He felt like a full-fledged chicken at the moment. She was scrambling all his brain circuits, swiping all his nerve. One disappointed or pained look from her and he would crumble.

The only good thing about her being in the chair was it made him feel like he could stay in the room. Like they weren't actually sleeping so it wasn't completely inappropriate for him to be there. The door was open, the other officers stuck their heads in a couple of times through the night. His sleep was light enough that he had heard them coming and waved at them, pretending that he was just watching over a victim, keeping her safe. Everything totally on the up and up. He was not watching her sleep and wondering what her skin would feel like under his fingers. He certainly was *not* memorizing her features or imagining how her curves met under her clothes.

Trevor shifted in the chair and closed his eyes but a buzzing in his pocket brought him to full alertness. A text from Wade.

I want that safe house shut down today. Unless something more happens, you can't keep that girl there tonight.

Trevor couldn't believe what he was reading.

Khain was in her house. What if he comes back?

He won't, as long as she's with you. He smells wolven, he stays away. You can't keep her forever.

Trevor bared his teeth. Risky business, leaving her alone to see if Khain would come back. He sent another text.

What if she's a one true mate?

Is she?

Trevor thought for a long time. He wanted her to be. But that meant nothing.

I don't know. She could be.

So question her. Eliminate it or confirm it. Today. If she is one, I want her in my office asap.

There was an echo at her house. Housecat. It mirrored Trent.

Wade didn't send anything back for several moments and Trevor knew he had rattled him. *Echoes* meant serious business.

Any message?

Nothing yet.

It could be a coincidence. You know what you have to do. See you in two hours.

Ah, right. The funeral. Trevor let his eyes slip closed, his phone held loosely in his hand. He didn't want to leave…

One hour and a half later, Trevor came awake with a start. Trent was nudging him.

Funeral.

Trevor stood and rushed to the door. He'd overslept and he'd have to go looking like he did. He had a dark jacket in his truck.

"Are you leaving?" Ella's voice drifted out to him. He froze, then turned back to her. She was standing on the other side of the bed, her hands clenched.

"Yeah, there's a funeral today…"

"Oh no." Her sad face broke him. "Someone close to you?"

"Yeah, a cop I knew."

Her face lit up with alarm. "A cop died? What happened?"

"That incident on 15th that I told you about two days ago, there was an explosion. He got caught in it. He didn't have a chance, really."

Ella's face lost all its color. "Oh no," she moaned. She collapsed onto the ground and buried her face in her hands. Trevor could hear her sobbing. He rushed to her, but the wolves surrounded her, licking her and whining to get her attention, blocking him completely. She held on to them tightly, but would not lift her face.

"Ella, what, what is wrong?" he asked gently, crouching down next to her.

She shook her head and continued to cry. He watched as she pulled herself together forcibly, with a great effort of will. When she looked up at him, her face was streaked with tears and her eyes were red. "I, ah, Trevor, I have to tell you something. And if you have to take me to jail, I completely understand."

"Take you to jail?"

"Trevor, I lied to you. I was there. During the explosion. I was in that store. I-I can't tell you exactly what—" She buried her face in her hands again and began to cry softly.

Trevor just stared, unable to process what she had said. If she had been there, that meant she had seen Khain. Could that be why he had gone to her house the next day? Trevor knew he could mark humans. But why?

"How did you escape?"

She looked up at him again, actively sobbing, as the two *wolven* whined and rubbed their heads on her. She took their comfort gladly, wrapping her arms around each of them, then shook her head. "I have to tell you something else first, so maybe you'll understand. I-I'm crazy."

Trevor smiled until he saw the emotion on her face.

"It's true. If I'm not totally there yet I'm heading there. I hear voices. I black out sometimes, just lose my grip on what's going on and when I come back, it's minutes or one time, hours later." She scrambled to her feet, Trent and Troy jumping out of her way as if they knew it was coming. She eased past Trevor to the other side of the room, then paced. "I've started sleepwalking. Doing weird things in my sleep. I painted something on the side of my house."

She stopped and stared at Trevor, her face crumpling. "I think I hurt your friend. The cop who died."

Trevor shook his head. "That wasn't you."

"You don't know that! I did something. I—There was another man. He came in the place and he was scary and big and I saw his face change—that's part of the going crazy, I know, and when he came after me I did something."

"What?"

She threw her hands in the air and stared at the ceiling. "I don't know!" She dropped her hands and stared at him. "I think I caused the explosion."

"How could you possibly—?"

She shook her head and tears dripped off her face. "I don't know. Maybe I... made a bomb in my sleep or something."

Trevor stepped to her, not quite daring to touch her. He hovered his right hand over her shoulder but dropped it and tried to catch her eye instead. "Listen to me. That... man who was there? We know who he is. He's done this before. He's the one who killed the officer. I recognize his handiwork. Believe me, Ella, it was not you."

Ella sobbed again and dropped her face into her hands, although in relief or disbelief, he couldn't tell.

"The funeral starts in a few minutes. You should come with me."

Her tears dried up, leaving only sniffles, but she still wouldn't look at him. "But I lied to you. Don't you have to arrest me for obstruction of justice or something?"

"No. No way. I know you had a good reason. And you've told me now. I'll need to hear the whole story but I don't want you to be so upset. Would you like to be hypnotized?"

She looked at him then. "Really? You can do that?"

"Not me, but I have a co-worker who does it often. It will keep you calm. Help you remember everything."

Something dark passed over her face that he couldn't decipher but she pushed it away. "Yes," she said firmly. "I do want that."

Trevor stared at her, even as his phone started to go off. He was late, but what he wanted to know was the only thing more important than the funeral. He had to know if she knew. "Ella, I have to ask you. The man who broke into your house, was he the same man at the store, where the explosion happened?"

She nodded slowly, absolute terror in her eyes. Trevor nodded back.

He would have no problems getting her to come back to the safe house after the funeral.

***

Ella slid out of Trevor's truck at the cemetery, not surprised at the sea of blue she saw. It looked like the entire police force had turned out for the funeral, most of them in their dress uniforms. She hated that she was dressed in ordinary, everyday clothes, and not something befitting of a funeral, but they hadn't had time to get her different clothes. She pulled her jacket tighter around her, dismayed that the day was unseasonably warm for fall. The sun beat on her hair and her shoulders and she could already feel the heat of it, but she would deal with it.

Trevor and the dogs came around to her side of the truck. "We'll stay towards the back," he told her, motioning for her to walk towards the crowd.

She did, and they arrived on the edge of it just as a police officer was finishing his speech. "That's Deputy Chief Lombard," Trevor whispered. "My boss."

Ella looked him over. An older man with just-beginning-to-gray hair and a kind face. He looked wise and thoughtful.

"… Officer Pickett will be much missed, but his spirit and dedication will live on forever in his memorial. We have lost many brave males to this fight, but the fight is not lost, because of the braveness of those who have gone, and those still on this earth. If I could say one thing to Bardron Kato Pickett, it would be this. We remember you standing tall and true, brother. We watch you as you go into The Light and we envy you your peace. May your fight be forever over, and may your image forever walk with us, in friendship."

Ella felt tears threaten for this man she didn't know as the crowd moved and began to break apart. She clung hard to the hope that Trevor had given her, that she couldn't possibly be the one responsible for his death. She heard the sighing of the crowd and looked around, surprised that she didn't see any women. Well, one maybe, up at the very front, staring at the deputy chief, as the men around her stared at her with something like awe, like she was a celebrity. She turned to Trevor to ask him who she was, but Trevor's face held a sadness that made her forget everything but him. A small tear ran down one cheek to his chin.

Ella reached up and laid her hand on his shoulder, not realizing her life would change when she did so. The touch rocketed through her body, starting in her fingertips and almost shooting out her toes and the top of her head, like a wave of soft pressure rippling through her. A wave that brought clarity and calm emotion flowing after it.

Trevor Burbank was not just some cop doing his job, keeping her safe. He was the answer to everything that was wrong and off in her life. He was her other half, and now that they were together, she was ok. The slow crumbling of her mind would stop and reverse. He was for her, she was for him, and together, they would build something good, pure, and unbreakable.

She stared at him, unable to speak, or look away, even when his eyes met hers and she could see that he was feeling everything she was.

***

Contentment and joy swept through Trevor like a cold fire, burning away everything that had been there before. He turned his eyes to Ella. His *renqua* burned with her touch, even though her hand was on his other shoulder, but somehow he knew that she was causing it. The burn was soothing, and it brought a message. But did he dare hope the message was true?

He reached up and took her hand from his shoulder, lacing his fingers into hers, not caring that his whole world could see them if it just turned around. This was their moment. It belonged to no one but them and he wasn't going to miss it—

"Trevor, your eyes…"

"What?"

"They're yellow."

Trevor pulled his hand out of hers and grabbed his phone, turning on the camera and pointing it at himself.

But no, his eyes were the same color he saw every day when he looked in the mirror. He looked down at Trent and Troy and they both shook their head slightly. They hadn't seen it.

You smelled different, but only for a second, Troy sent. *Actually, you both did.*

Ella frowned and looked down at the dog and for a moment, Trevor had to wonder if she had caught any of that. But no, how could she? Only a few *wolven* could communicate telepathically with other *wolven* they were close to, and no humans could that they knew of, and she was not *wolven,* was she?

A thought hit him. What if she was a half-breed? That would explain his attraction to her.

He grabbed her hand again, but the sensations did not return.

CHAPTER 21

Harlan coming, Trent warned a split second before Harlan called out to him.

"Trev," Harlan's deep voice called from behind him. Trevor whirled around, dropping Ella's hand and positioning himself between Ella and Harlan.

"The *felen* have hit up dispatch. We've got a disturbance."

A week ago, Trevor would have been thrilled to hear such news, would have taken off like a rocket towards it, even though it didn't make sense. Now though, all he wanted to do was stay with Ella. "What do you mean, a disturbance?"

Harlan drew close, tall and big, like all of the KSRT, but not quite as tall as Trevor. He peeked over Trevor's shoulder at Ella. Trevor tolerated it, but barely. He eyed Harlan's jugular and lifted his lip, feeling his fangs try to grow.

Harlan spoke softly. "They think he's trying to cross over."

"Trying?" He turned to Ella and gave her an apologetic

look. "Will you excuse me for a second?" She nodded and looked around nervously. Trent and Troy drew close to her sides and she threaded her hands in their fur, relief strong on her face.

Trevor walked ten feet away with Harlan. "Since when does he *try* to cross over? Khain doesn't have any difficulty getting out of the *Pravus*."

Harlan spoke quickly. "The *felen*'s exact words were, 'there is a disturbance in the *Pravus*. Either he's having difficulty crossing over, or something big is happening over there. We request *wolven* backup just in case.'"

Trevor watched Ella, noticing the vulnerability of her pale skin, the beauty of her form. "Just in case of what?"

Harlan shook his head. "I'm not the expert. What the fuck is wrong with you? I thought you would have asked me one word, where? And then you would have been gone."

Trevor faced Harlan. "Yeah, sorry. Where is everyone else?"

"Mac, Beckett, and Crew are already on their way, riding together. You can ride with me."

Trevor shook his head. "I'll head out by myself. Got a meeting with Wade in two hours and other important things to do today. Where?"

Harlan gave him a funny look, then recited the directions and headed to his own vehicle. Trevor made his way back to Ella.

"You have to go, don't you?" she asked as soon as he reached her.

He almost called it all off. Let the rest of the team handle it. But in the end, he couldn't do it. He was the boss. He was the one that Wade thought would end Khain once and for all. He couldn't pick and choose his battles. He had to be there for all of them. He nodded slowly. "Listen to me, Ella. You have to go back to the safe house. I'll send Trent and Troy with you and there will be two other officers there too. You will be safe there, I promise you."

She nodded slowly and did not argue. "Sorry you have to send people to watch me."

He shook his head. "Don't ever be sorry. You're…" He wanted to say so much more than he could actually bring himself to. "You're worth it."

He took her hand, feeling a thrill go through him when she didn't resist or pull away from him. "Come on, we have to find Officer Adin. I'm not leaving you until I put you in his car myself." He pulled her towards the crowd, scanning it with his eyes and nose. Trent and Troy followed.

You two, don't you leave her side. She's top priority.

Roger.

Got it.

***

Three hours later, Trevor drove slowly back into Serenity, passing the statue of the red wolf at a near crawl. He stared into the wolf's eyes, keeping only the barest of his senses on the road. When he drove far enough that the connection was broken, he stepped hard on the gas. He was already late for Wade's meeting.

Report, he sent out to Trent.

All quiet. She's napping.

An image of Ella's pretty face relaxed, eyes closed, body curled up on the small bed in the safe house swam in front of Trevor's eyes. What he wouldn't give to be with her, even sitting close to her, watching her as she slept.

The disturbance had proven to be a waste of time. Mostly. All of the KSRT and six *felen*, most of the *Pumaii*, had gathered on Blue River Bluff just to the north of town. Trevor had to admit that he felt something as soon as he got there and walked out to the bluff. Something that made him itch to shift right there, shift and run, shift and howl, shift and bite whatever there was to bite.

All the *wolven* had held their form, but barely, only by walking constantly and holding on tightly with their minds. Two of the *felen* had shifted and loped off into the woods as monstrous mountain lions that made Trevor's fangs lengthen. In human form, *felen* were attractive in a strange way, but as big cats, he felt a strange repulsion towards them. Like he would just as soon rip them apart than share the same ground with them. When *felen* and *wolven* shifted near each other, if Khain weren't around, it was always a bad scene.

When the *disturbance*, the ruinous scream from another world, finally stopped, Trevor was the first to leave. Let his team stay there if they wanted. He had a meeting he had to be at, so he had climbed into his truck and driven off, feeling his need to shift and to run only grow with every mile he drove away from the woods. Good thing there was a *Zyanya* scheduled that night. It would be an official *wolven* goodbye to Pickett, but also a running with the moon that Trevor had never felt he needed so badly.

And after that? The rut. Ella's image rose in his mind and Trevor shook his head. He would turn away a thousand ruts for the chance to sit across from Ella in the dark for just one night. But if the others needed it…

Trevor was pulled out of his thoughts by the police station appearing on his right. Within three short minutes he was standing outside of Wade's office, tucking his shirt, checking the creases on his pants. He raised his hand to knock, but Wade's voice came through the door. "Come in, son."

Trevor opened the door and pushed inside. A male sitting in one of the black leather chairs opposite Wade stood and faced him. Trevor stared him down coldly, afraid he knew who it was.

He was big. As big as Trevor, which was rare. His dark hair was cropped close to his head and he had no beard or facial hair at all. Trevor could see black tattoos on the man's wrists, peeking out from under the cuffs of the full suit he wore, one he looked both comfortable and uncomfortable in.

But none of that was relevant. All Trevor cared about was the smell coming off of him. It was cold and hot at the same time which could not be.

"This better not be who I think it is," Trevor growled at Wade, his eyes on the interloper who should not be in the police station, much less inside Wade's office.

Wade inclined his head. "Lieutenant Trevor Burbank, meet Graeme Kynock, Special Constable of the Police Service of Scotland, on loan to the KSRT, with possible future reassignment."

The male held out a hand to Trevor but did not smile. "Good afternoon, sir. My name is actually pronounced grayem" His accent was not thick, but definitely there. He rolled the R in his name which made Trevor want to bite him.

Trevor ignored the hand and turned to Wade, his brow furrowed, his fists clenched. "He's not *wolfen*," he bit out, barely able to control himself.

Wade didn't give an inch. "He's *dragen*. They have been valued members of the Police Scotland for centuries, working alongside our *wolven* brothers and sisters there."

Trevor narrowed his eyes and turned to Graeme. "You have females?"

Graeme dropped his hand. "No," he said simply.

Trevor took a step forward. "I thought all the *dragen* were gone. Killed off."

Graeme lifted his chin. "I am the last."

Trevor turned to Wade again. "I would like to speak to you alone." He was so angry he almost shook with it, his muscles tensed and full.

Wade didn't give an inch. "Whatever you have to say to me can be said in front of Graeme. He should know what he is getting himself into."

"Fine. How do we know we can trust him? What is he even here for? How am I going to explain to—to anyone that we're letting a non-*wolfen* work with the KSRT?"

Trevor was distracted by a noise coming from Graeme and he shot his eyes back to the male, falling into a defensive position. Graeme's clothes seemed to melt and twist and then merge with his body as he grew to five times his size, quicker than Trevor could watch it. This was no shift. It was something else entirely. Before Trevor could even think about shifting, a red and yellow dragon with a hooked nose and leathery wings loomed in front of him, his scales brushing the high ceiling, two chairs flattened underneath him. The dragon opened its mouth and Trevor could feel its hot breath coating him. It turned its head to watch Trevor with one flat eye, then shot fire across the room at a chair. The top half of the chair disintegrated into ash as the bottom half continue to burn.

Trevor took a step backwards and let loose his own shift, but his was slower, harder and could never rival the smooth transformation that Graeme again pulled off in front of him, almost instantly pulling his dragon-self back into a human form.

"Trevor, no," Wade warned and Trevor stopped and reversed his not-too-far-gone shift, leaving his fangs long. The dragon he had just witnessed could snap him in half with one bite, but Trevor would not admit that, even to himself.

A fully dressed Graeme Kynock ignored Trevor's snarl and walked to the flaming chair. With firm presses of his hands, he put out every flame, pulling it and the resulting ash into him.

Trevor stared, refusing to show that he was impressed.

Wade sighed, eyeing his three ruined chairs. "Don't you think that could be useful against Khain? A demon who fights us with fire and explosions?"

Trevor growled deep in his throat, unable to give up gracefully. "Sure, if we ever see him! Khain has barely been around for centuries, and some new defensive is not going to help us. We need to go on the offensive, sniff him out. We need new plans, new—"

Wade held up a hand as Graeme unbuttoned his suit jacket and pulled over a new chair to sit in, his hands clean, his countenance undisturbed. "I appreciate that we took you by surprise, Trevor. I should have told you that Graeme was not *wolfen*. But I need you to let go of your stubbornness just long enough to hear me out."

Trevor interrupted. "How can you be sure he isn't a spy? You know as well as anyone that we've been burned in the past by *shiften* we weren't familiar with."

Wade sighed. "I trust him, Trevor. Bring Troy in here. Have him give you an assessment of Graeme."

"Troy is busy."

"Then do it later. I find it very interesting that you're telling me you want to take the offensive with Khain. That's exactly what Graeme will be able to help you do."

"How?"

Graeme lifted his chin and stared over Wade's head. "I see a green bluff in the northernmost woods of Illinois. Under it, alongside it, in its very essence, is where Khain can be found. This is his home. His hideaway. I can find it, and force my way in."

Trevor's mind worked overtime. Could such a thing really be possible? He shook his head. The dragon was having delusions of powers he couldn't possibly possess.

Graeme looked at him, nostrils flaring. "You doubt me."

"You're not as stupid as you look."

Graeme stood and the fierceness in his eyes caused Trevor to step back. His clothes melded into his skin again, which became scales, and in under two seconds, the red and yellow dragon was back, not quite as big. His scaly head lowered until it was less than a foot from Trevor's face. Trevor felt a wind form around him but he did not look away. The force of Graeme's will pulsed outwards from him. Trevor could feel something big coming. He straightened his spine and stared at Graeme. Whatever it was, he would meet it head on.

In the corner, just a few feet from the destroyed chair, a rippling in the air began. A tiny black spot appeared. Trevor wanted to look straight at it, but he didn't quite dare look away from the beast in front of him.

The wind pulled at him, whipping even his short hair around and items began to fly off of Wade's desk. Wade gathered his computer and one notebook to him, but did not order a halt to the demonstration.

Trevor could see cords standing out in relief on the dragon's neck as his body reacted to the strength of his will, to the effort it took to do whatever he was doing.

The black spot in Trevor's peripheral vision grew larger

and he had to look at it. The sight of it caused his gut to tighten and his balls to shrink. Few things scared him in his life, but that tiny black ball that he could only assume was an opening into the *Pravus* filled him with liquid dread.

He tensed, fell back, readying himself to shift, to fight, to die if necessary. He regretted not having more time with Ella, but he pushed her out of his mind. His animal snarled in his head, wanting to come out, needing to be the one in charge, but Trevor held back with all his will. He had to see this with all of his reason intact.

The black hole whirled and sucked and grew and Trevor was able to see into it. It was only a foot or so in diameter but through that tiny window he could see a land of yellow, cracked dirt stretching out in all directions. No plants. No anything, except fires leaping out of the cracks like geysers. As Trevor watched, a book from Wade's desk sailed past him into the hole and more books tried to follow.

The smell of Khain filled Wade's office.

With a raging growl, Trevor gave in, shifting, turning into the animal he would fight as. His clothes dropped to the floor and he pulled back on his haunches, ready to leap as soon as the opening was big enough.

No! a tortured voice commanded from inside his head. *You shall not enter!*

The hole snapped shut with a popping sound, cutting a stack of stapled papers that had been sucked in partially clean in half. Trevor stared, his wolf side unable to believe there was nothing to fight. He turned towards Graeme. He would do.

But Graeme had transformed back into the human and was laying on the floor of the office, unconscious.

CHAPTER 22

*T*revor paced outside the safe house, needing badly to shift and run, but he couldn't here in the middle of a suburban street. He wouldn't anyway. He needed dirt under his feet, the moon calling to him. He could feel her, the moon, growing fat and heavy, just waiting for the sun to finish its descent and then she would rise. She would show him the way.

So many thoughts filled his mind. When the *dragen* had finally come to he had explained that all of the *Pravus* smelled like Khain, and entering there would have done no good.

"To be a *shiften* alone in the *Pravus* means madness," was all he would say by way of explanation. Trevor didn't know how his messed-up ability was going to help them if no one could go over there, but he'd been too agitated to try to figure it out. He'd gone down in the tunnels to talk to some of his guys down there, tell them what he'd seen, and then he'd run the tunnels until sunset.

He didn't know what to do. Trent and Troy wanted to attend the *Zyanya*, and maybe they needed to, like Trevor himself did. He couldn't tell either of them no, not with the guilt he carried about them, but who would stay with Ella? Her safety was paramount.

Finally he decided. He made a few phone calls, then waited in the street, his face turned toward the east, feeling the call of the moon.

Wade pulled up in his black jeep and stopped in front of Trevor. "You've got some explaining to do."

"Sorry boss, I can't trust anyone else to do it. You don't need the *Zyanya* like the rest of us do."

Wade nodded thoughtfully. "But why are we still keeping her?"

"She's special," Trevor said simply.

Wade raised an eyebrow but didn't say anything. Instead, he parked his jeep and got out. "You coming in?"

Trevor shook his head. If he saw her, he might not leave, he knew that.

"Ok, I'll send your brothers out."

Trevor waited until they came, his agitation eating him alive. He had to follow the moon. Trent nipped him on the thigh.

"Ouch, hey!"

She was waiting for you. Trent's voice was a low, pleasing rumble in his head.

I'll see her when we get back.

You should bring her.

Are you moonstruck? None of us will be able to shift.

A look passed between Trent and Troy. Trevor leaped

forward and grabbed them by the collars, physically shaking them. "What? Tell me!"

Troy thinks she might be part wolfen.

Trevor held his breath and let go of his brothers, then stared into the sky. Did he dare hope it? *A half-breed?*

No. Maybe a quarter or less.

Trevor bit down hard on his tongue. A quarter *wolfen*. Not quite human, but never, ever would she shift. Even half-breeds only learned to shift something like a quarter of the time. But still…

He shifted back and forth on his feet, then took off down the sidewalk, walking hard, almost running. The sky was almost fully dark, and the moon would be up soon. But if Ella was even part shifter, did that change everything? Possibly. Even as it changed nothing. He wanted her so bad he could taste it. The only question was, was he willing to give up his One True Mate for her?

***

Ella slid the window open an inch, thinking. She knew Trevor wouldn't leave her there without the dogs unless she was safe, but she didn't want to stay. She wanted to be with Trevor. Chief Lombard had gracefully explained that Trevor had an event he had to attend and would be back in a few hours, and that he would stay with her until then. She had nodded and feigned tiredness, then stared at Trevor's truck in the driveway, wishing she could go with them.

Voices filled her head and her hands flew to her temples, trying to block them out.

She was … for you.

I'll see her when we get back.

Ella's head lifted and she stared hard out the window. That had been Trevor's voice she heard inside her head. He was sad. Conflicted. And yearning something she didn't understand.

You should … her.

Are you moonstruck? None of us will be able …

Troy thinks she … wolfen.

Ella rubbed at her cheek with her hand and stared hard out the window at the three forms she could barely see, standing almost on the street. She swore Trevor was having a conversation with the two dogs, and she was witnessing it, and *hearing* it. But how could that be? And what was that word? *Wolfen?*

She'd never heard it before.

If only she knew where they were going.

A moving image filled her mind, like a movie, of Trevor and the two dogs running, sprinting along a path in the woods. She could see them clearly because of the yellow moonlight leading their way. Trevor was naked and her breath caught in her throat as she watched his big body move with a sinewy grace that captivated her. Heat filled her so fully that she whimpered with it and her knees buckled. She saw him from the side and the back, but what she really wanted was to see him from the—

Ella made a decision without being fully aware she was making it. She slid open the window all the way, then climbed out of it, slipping easily to the ground, knowing she would be hard to see in her black leggings and dark shirt. The air was still warm, the heat trapped by a layer of clouds above them. The moon began to peek through to the east and she stopped for a moment, transfixed by it. She pulled her attention back to herself and ran for Trevor's truck, watching the man and two dogs in the street, who all had their back to her. One of the dogs lifted its nose and slowed, but didn't turn around.

Ella climbed over the tailgate of Trevor's truck and lifted the vinyl cover just enough that she could squeeze inside. It was warm and dry and clean in there, and she crawled forward, finding a piece of flattened cardboard to curl up on. She didn't know if she would be found and she didn't care.

Something big was going on and she ached in her soul to be a part of it. If Trevor found her, she would convince him to bring her, somehow.

What if he's going to be with another woman?

Ella pushed the thought out of her mind. It was too awful to contemplate.

The man and the dogs came to the truck silently, the only noise the crunching of their feet on the gravel. Ella listened hard, scared she would be discovered. Trevor's footsteps stopped a few feet from the truck and she got the sense he knew she was there somehow. She held her breath and didn't move.

Trevor exhaled sharply. "Ouch, fucker, quit biting me or I'll demote your ass."

But he moved forward and opened his door. Ella heard the two dogs jump in and someone slide the back window open, then the truck started up and they moved. Ella relaxed and didn't try to figure out where they were going. She was just happy to be along, but when they slowed to a crawl twenty-five minutes later she thought she had an idea where they might be. The length of the drive, combined with the train tracks they'd gone over, and the smell in the air told her there was a good chance they were near Big Claw woods.

The truck bumped slowly over ground too uneven to be a road. Ella braced herself with her feet and held on, trying to minimize her bouncing. She didn't need to be covered in bruises the next day.

After ten agonizing minutes, they stopped and the engine turned off. Ella heard the sound of other vehicles approaching and stopping, car doors slamming, men talking, laughing, joking with each other, their verbal barbs mean and spiteful. Trevor's door opened, then closed.

Ella held her breath, not daring to move a muscle. More cars came and stopped. More men got out and walked away, somewhere ahead of them. Ella felt an energy from that way. A building crescendo of something enticing, something powerful.

She crept to the very back of the truck bed, trying to be as quiet as possible, even though she didn't hear anyone around her anymore. A loud howl filled the air and she froze. A wolf? Dozens of more voices joined it, then maybe hundreds, until the sound was like a great sweeping wave that covered her.

Ella stared straight into the darkness, shaking, but not with fear. There were no wolves in these woods. Unless…

No longer able to be quiet or careful, she punched a hand upwards at the truck bed cover, unsnapping it in two places, then stuck her head out, trying to see where the already-fading noise was coming from. At least a hundred vehicles sat in a clearing. Above her, on a hill, there was movement in the trees, but she couldn't tell anything about it. Only that many, many things were moving, and fast.

The last form moved out of sight and the last howl drifted to a stop, and she was alone.

In the woods.

In the dark.

CHAPTER 23

*E*lla lay in the dark bed of the pickup truck staring up at a sliver of the night sky, trying to get her mental feet underneath her. Was this even happening? Could she be imagining it? If she wasn't, what exactly had she seen and heard, and what could it possibly mean? Thank goodness the night was warm, warmer than it had been in weeks.

She didn't know how long she lay there. Time seemed to float away from her somehow. In the dark, it meant nothing. Only when she heard male voices again, did she scramble to her knees and do her best to snap the vinyl cover closed again on the back of the truck. Even if Trevor found her, she didn't want any of the men he was with to see her.

But Trevor, he was a different story. He needed to find her. She wanted him to find her, to know she had seen. She wanted to *know* what the night had been all about.

She heard many footsteps thudding dully against the grass and dirt, and heard men's voices again, still joking, but the tone was much easier and more friendly now. These men seemed to like and respect each other, while the men who had walked up the hill all had seemed bitter and hostile.

Doors slammed, engines started, vehicles began to pull away. Ella listened for what seemed like a long time, never hearing Trevor's voice, until it sounded like all of the other vehicles in the clearing were gone.

"You heading to the rut?" a voice she didn't recognize said.

"Nah, you have fun." Trevor's voice. Ella smiled when she heard it. But what was a rut?

"Seriously?"

Trevor's voice was hard when he spoke again. "Seriously."

The other man didn't say a word for a few moments. "You holding out on me, dog? You got a girl?" he finally asked.

Trevor chuckled deeply and Ella licked her lips. Even he sounded more relaxed.

"Ask me again in a week."

"Lucky bitch," the other man snarled. Ella heard a car door open and close and a motor start up. Only after the other vehicle was gone did Trevor open his own door.

Within a minute, they were back on the road, Ella trying to decide how she would spring it on Trevor that she had tagged along and spied. Would he be mad?

The thought scared her and excited her at the same time. *You really are ready for the loony bin, Ella Carmi. Why do you want to see him mad?*

The truck bounced over the uneven terrain for a few moments, until Ella heard Trevor's phone buzz. The truck stopped.

"Oh no," Trevor breathed and Ella heard panic in his voice. She heard the faint sound of numbers dialing, then Trevor spoke. "What do you mean she's gone? For how long? Where, how?"

Trevor was silent for several minutes and when he spoke again, his words shook. "Find her. Good-bye."

She's ... truck.

"She's where?" Trevor barked out loud.

Ella's eyes went wide and she couldn't help herself. She pushed her head up against the vinyl, just high enough that she could see into the cab where Trevor and the dogs were.

Troy stared back at her, a large doggy grin on his face.

CHAPTER 24

*E*lla scrambled on her hands and knees to the back of the truck, snapping the vinyl cover off in two spots and jumping over the side, then re-snapping it just for something to do as Trevor came out the driver's side door, his expression shut down with anger.

"What do you think you are doing?"

Ella faced him, her heart beating too hard. "Me? What about you?"

His eyes narrowed and he cocked his head to the side. "What did you see?"

"Nothing, I didn't see anything. But I heard something." She stepped forward, surprised at her own boldness, but wanting so much from him she couldn't help it. She poked a finger into his chest and left it there. "You, Trevor Burbank, have a secret. Many secrets. I want to know what they are."

LISA LADEW

When her finger touched him, something changed again, like it had before, but also differently. It wasn't some insane, sure knowing in her being that he was hers and she, his. Instead, it was something that came from him. Something rich and heady, almost like a smell, or maybe a knowing. Her body responded to it like it was a chemical created just for her, heat flushing up and down her spine, causing hyper-awareness at her mouth and skin and core.

Trevor reached up and took her hand and the sliding of his skin on hers made her weak. The moon slipped behind a cloud, leaving her almost completely blind, even as she felt he could see her better than ever. Behind the woods, thunder rumbled in the distance, reminding her of a summer storm come to play in the heat.

Ella swallowed hard, staring at the dark face that loomed above her. She opened herself to him, wanting him to kiss her. Wanting his lips on hers so badly she knew she would beg if he told her to. The thought caused no shame. She was lost to him and she knew it. What she didn't know was why.

Noise pulled her attention to the truck. Two dark shapes leaped out the window and ran away from them, towards the woods.

Her voice only broke slightly when she spoke. "Your dogs. Are they scared of the thunder?"

Trevor stared at her hard and she could feel him making a decision. She felt herself get pulled into the mystery that was him just a bit more.

"No. They are giving us privacy."

Ella licked her lips, feeling suddenly dry as the desert and wet as the oasis. "What do we need privacy for?"

***

Trevor could smell her arousal. She wanted him. Her body was opening to him like a flower in full bloom and the scent of it surrounded him, making him crazy. He sniffed deeply. Vanilla. He couldn't take it. The part of him that was all wolf even in his human form whined and snarled to be let free, to take over. He resisted as well as he could.

He reached out his right hand and brushed her cheek, smelling her sweet scent flare as he did so. She was killing him, and she wasn't even trying, probably wasn't even aware of his agonies. His cock had grown thick and long in his pants and it beat in time with his heart. A lock of her hair brushed against the back of his hand. He pushed it behind her ear, then slowly wound his fingers into the mass of black silk. He exhaled hard at the sensation. He'd been wanting to touch her hair forever. Since the first time he saw her.

He tugged experimentally on it, watching her face closely, able to see her easily in the dark, as more thunder rumbled from far away and the smell of rain pushed towards them.

Her eyes closed and her lips parted slightly, as her sweet arousal scent broke out stronger. So he pulled harder, twisting her face to the sky.

"Ahhh," she exhaled, and even her breath smelled like sugar to him. He was completely lost to her and could not have stopped himself from touching her even if ordered to by Rhen herself.

He lowered his face to hers and took her lips hard and decisively, forcing another whimper from her as she kissed him back. Her hands snuck around his waist and pulled on his shirt, pulling it up and out of his pants so she could touch the bare skin at his waist.

"Ella," he breathed between kisses, his other hand moving

to the front of her body, eliciting a gasp from her as he cupped her breast. "I want you."

"So take me," she said, her eyes closed, her body pressed against his.

Trevor moved fast, turning her, dropping the tailgate of his truck with one hand, then lifting her and sitting her on it. He stripped off his belt and holster as he kissed her, and placed them under the cover of the truck bed just as the first rain drop hit his shoulder in the absolute dark.

"Oh God," she breathed, as he leaned into her and both his hands found her breasts, teasing her nipples into tight peaks he was suddenly obsessed with. He had to see them. Had to taste them. Had to own them.

He pulled back and lifted her shirt, placing it to the side. Her pale skin shone in the absence of light and her simple white bra attracted him like a missile to a target. He felt the pull of her stare and he looked up at her for just a moment. "You are so beautiful," he said, then reached around and popped the clasp on her bra, pulling back to watch like he was unwrapping a gift. In a way, he was. He licked his lips as she came fully into view. He stored her bra with his holster then leaned in and took first one breast, then the other into his mouth. Primal was the only word that could describe the absolute desire that spread through him at the taste of her skin. He suckled hard, forcing a moan from her.

The rain fell harder, soaking his clothes and short hair, even as she pulled at his shirt, trying to lift it over his head. He whipped it off and went back to his prize, his gift, her body. She moaned and leaned back against the vinyl truck bed cover, arching her body up to him, running her hands over him.

She pulled at him, trying to get him up on top of her.

"Under the cover," he told her. It would be a tight fit, but they would be dry.

"No, on top, if it will hold us. In the rain," she said, her voice thick with lust, and he got the feeling she was emboldened by the fact that she couldn't see him. He could see her though, and he intended to watch everything, every provocative movement as it unfolded. Already, he was imagining slamming into her from behind, and he just knew she was tight and wet for him.

He hopped onto the tailgate, lifting her easily onto the vinyl cover, already slick with rain water. She laid back, fumbling with her jeans, pushing them down and kicking them and her shoes off. Her legs were as pale as the rest of her and he thought he'd never seen anything so gorgeous. He ran his hand up one thigh until he reached the V of fabric covering her most sensitive spot. He held himself back as he danced around it with his fingers, then lowered himself onto the truck bed cover next to her, testing to see if it would hold. It did, bowing in the middle, but not unsnapping. She curled into him, throwing a leg over his hips, catching his mouth with her own as he ran his hands up and down her almost naked body.

"Fuck woman, how are you so perfect?" he breathed, tracing the curve of her hip and the softness of her belly, heat pouring off of her even in the cool night air and the small pool of water that was growing around them.

She moaned again and pawed at him. He wriggled out of his boots and jeans, not caring where they ended up. When her small hand touched his cock he snarled his approval, not able to help the animalistic sound.

"Oh God," she murmured.

"What, angel, what's wrong?"

"You're so big."

"What did you expect?" he growled into her ear, nipping her, pulling her head back by her hair, kissing his way down her neck, heading for her breasts, and then who knew what else.

"Wait," she said. "I have to see it." She knelt and pushed him down into the rain as the drops continued to fall on his chest and face and belly. On her knees, over him, she stared down at him, something like wonder on her face. She palmed him, then he saw her lick her lips and lower her head. He steeled himself. It had been too long for him and her touch was so heavenly he couldn't hold himself back, but as good as her mouth was, his animal wanted control, wanted the mating.

He groaned as her warm, wet mouth touched him, licking, sucking, swirling, never coming up for air, until he couldn't handle it. He pulled her up to him. "Ella, I have to have you, please, say it again."

She knew exactly what he wanted. "So take me."

He stripped off her panties in a flash and flipped her onto her stomach, where she arched up onto hands and knees. Fuck, her scent, like the sweetest food at the best bakery in the world. He pulled her onto his face and latched onto her clit and sucked hard, knowing it was probably too much, but unable to stop himself. If she said one word, he would be able to stop, but she didn't. She arched higher and tightened her legs around his head, then screamed out her orgasm into the night, spilling the taste of sugar cookies onto his tongue. He knew she couldn't taste like that in reality, he'd never heard such a thing, but to him, she did. The sound and taste of her orgasm drove him mad with desire.

When she pulled away, he raised and backed her onto him, fitting the head of his cock inside her warm, wet core, groaning at the sensation. Slowly, slowly he pulled her back and pushed into her, noting her tension and relaxation and soft noises of approval or alarm. When he was finally fully inside her, she relaxed and he began a steady rhythm that he knew would take him where he was heading, and her too, if he could get her there again.

"Trevor," she moaned, her hands slipping slightly in the water. She dropped to her elbows, creating a splash, and he watched as the raindrops rolled over her back towards her head, catching in her hair, wetting it. He curled his fingers around her hips, thinking her body merging with his was the most beautiful sight he had ever seen in his life. Heat poured off of their bodies, more than making up for the slight chill of the rainwater.

His thrusts sped up, her body and noises demanding more from him, more delicious friction, more hard pounding, which he gladly gave. She arched higher, the angle change driving him over an edge but he held himself back as best he could, seeking her pleasure before his, curling an arm around her to reach her clit, pressing and releasing, rubbing and sliding until she tensed again and cried out. He felt her clench around his cock and he went with it, finally letting go, spilling inside of her with clenched teeth and a strangled cry of pleasure.

She dropped onto the slippery surface beneath them and he followed, disengaging himself, realizing only then that they were in a puddle of cold rain water, and that he had just slept with a victim, someone he was supposed to be protecting.

The rain came harder, making him squint against it, and the night lit up as lighting struck somewhere north of them.

In the flare, Trevor saw Ella staring at him with frightened eyes.

CHAPTER 25

*F*emale groans of lust and satisfaction filled the air, tempered by masculine grunts of exertion and fulfillment. Mac prowled through the open warehouse filled with couches and mattresses, eying the bodies locked together over every spare soft inch in the low lighting.

It was a true rut, except that all the women there were humans.

Mac's gut ached to be a part of a rut with female shifters, dangerous creatures who would tear your guts out if you treated them wrong, but who would temper that risk with passion that made these women look as if they were asleep.

His head swiveled as the passionate cries of one woman reached his ears. Maybe that one wasn't asleep. The scent of her release filled the large room and his nostrils flared to better catch the scent. Gardenia mixed with something indefinable that made him lick his lips.

If she weren't already gathering a crowd of admirers, maybe he would have tried his hand with her, or his cock as it were, but no, her dance card was full.

His feet led him towards the center of the room, and as he walked he touched the women he passed, testing their scents first, to be sure they welcomed it. He ran a finger over the shoulder of a naked brunette being fucked doggy style by Harlan over the back of a couch. Mac could smell the sadness coming off of Harlan in waves, even as he rode the woman mercilessly.

Harlan was fifty-three, older than the rest of the KSRT, and had been around long enough to have seen an all-shifter rut. Harlan's mate had been killed by Khain, the day after their mating ceremony. Even though Harlan's biology demanded this release, Mac knew his heart wasn't in it. He missed his Eventine, who had been gone for twenty-eight years.

"May her spirit be forever cradled in The Light," Mac whispered softly, even as his hands found the woman's hair. She moaned and locked eyes with him, challenging him, inviting him. He smiled down at her and immediately her hands released their death grip on the back of the couch and sought his belt buckle. Moments later, she had his cock in her hand, gasping at the weight and breadth of it.

"Are all of you here huge?" she whispered.

Mac chuckled. Probably. The wet pink of her tongue met her upper lip and he needed no more invitation. His right hand tangled in her hair as his left hand drew lazy circles over her shoulder blade. Softly, slowly, he pushed the head of his cock between her lips, feeling each tiny tooth scrape as the pressure of the male ramming into her from behind forced her head towards his belly. She grabbed him before she could gag on him and began to work him hard. He had women daily, but to an unmated *wolfen*, nothing was better than rut sex. Sex shared with pack mates, their smells mixing, their fluids joining, the women being taken to heights of pleasure they'd never before let themselves fantasize about, but would forevermore dream of.

Mac intended to fuck, suck, and lick every woman in the place until she'd come at least three times, if the night was long enough.

But he would start with this one, then see where he ended up. He had been right, requesting a rut. Even if it wasn't the same without *shiften*, it was still a necessary part of their biology, and anything that necessary had to be right. Hell, maybe they'd end up with a few half-breeds out of it, which wouldn't save the *wolven*, but it was better than nothing.

Mac thrust his hips forward, feeling the head of his cock hit the woman's throat, watching her swallow to try to get more of it down. "Good girl," he crooned. "Swallow that cock. Take it all and you might get a bit of a reward." She locked eyes with him and he could tell she was quite enjoying herself. Good.

Because that was what a rut was all about.

Pleasure.

CHAPTER 26

*E*lla scrambled into the cab of Trevor's truck, spurred on by the lightning that arced to earth closer each time. She had her clothes in a ball, clutched to her chest. Everything was wet but her bra which she put on.

Trevor handed her a towel, but didn't look at her, then he climbed into the driver's seat, pulling his shirt on. He already had his pants and boots back on, although how he'd done it so quickly, she couldn't fathom. He was wet too, through to the skin.

He watched the woods and she wondered how the dogs would know to come back. For that matter, how had they known to leave? Had he trained them for such a thing?

Ella pulled on her wet clothes, dismayed at how awkward things felt between her and Trevor. She'd had sex with him. In the open. In the woods. During a rainstorm. He hadn't even worn a condom and he'd come inside her. Ella groaned inside her head. How could she be so stupid? And now he couldn't even look at her, which was ten times worse.

Two words flashed through her head.

Come back.

She whipped her head toward him and stared at him hard. It had been his voice in her head. Had he fucked her just to take her mind off of his secrets?

He avoided her stare completely, watching the woods still. He shifted in his seat and she felt embarrassment come off him in waves. The dogs were coming down the hill, picking their way over rocks and fallen logs. Why would Trevor be embarrassed? They were just dogs. She wouldn't have cared if they had watched … she didn't think.

Trevor leaped out of the truck and pulled towels from under the seat, lining the back with them, but the dogs looked drier than she and Trevor were. They jumped up into the truck. Ella watched Trevor's face and thought she saw his embarrassment spike. She looked curiously at the dogs, but they both jumped in to the seat and curled up, nose to tail, as if nothing had happened. Again, Trevor never said a word to them, or petted either of them. The three of them had the strangest relationship she had ever seen. But maybe that's how you were supposed to be with police dogs.

Trevor climbed in and started the truck, then drove off, taking them all back to Serenity. She thought about another night in the safe house and she couldn't do it. She wanted to go home. Sleep in her own bed. And she wanted Trevor with her. But only if he wanted to be there. This awkward silence was killing her but she couldn't think of anything to say. She finished pulling on her clothes.

Twenty minutes later, they pulled up in front of the safe

house. Ella stared at it, not wanting to get out. There were no cars in the driveway.

"Damn, I forgot to tell them I found you," Trevor said.

"Yeah, I was hard to find, wasn't I? All the way in the back of your truck." Inwardly she rolled her eyes at her childishness, but he started it.

Trevor finally looked at her and she stared him down, even as she heard a chuff that sounded an awful lot like a laugh from the back seat.

Trevor looked away and pulled out his phone, then sent a text message. He turned off his truck and opened his door. "Let's go."

Ella crossed her arms over her chest. "I don't want to. I'm sick of staying here. This is night number three now and I don't know if there's really any need anymore."

Both dogs sat up in the back seat and poked their muzzles over the front, as if interested in the conversation. Trevor looked at her again for a long time. "Well, I can't take you to my house."

Ella leaned forward, her bad mood broken. He wasn't getting mad back at her, he didn't want her to be alone, and he wasn't going to try to force her to go back inside. "Why not? It would be better than being here."

Trevor looked behind him and she swore he was looking to one of the dogs for help. He faced her again. "It wouldn't be right."

She scoffed, about to ask him if fucking her in the back of his truck was right, but something in his expression stopped her. A thought hit her. "Why, do you have a woman there? A wife?"

His eyes went wide with alarm and his body tensed. "No!" he said, holding up his hands. "No, I swear. I'm single. No females. I-I've always been single."

Ella looked at him aslant. "What do you mean you've always been single?"

"I've never had a serious girlfriend."

"Never? How old are you?"

"Thirty."

Five years older than her, which was about what she had thought. She pursed her lips. "What's wrong with you?"

Troy shook his head like his ears itched and made that chuffing sound again that could have been a laugh or a sneeze. Trent leaned over and bit him on the shoulder. Troy snarled at him, but pulled back and quit making noises. Ella didn't even pay them any attention. She was used to their strangeness by now.

Trevor threw Troy a dirty look, then faced Ella again. "I don't know what's wrong with me. I never met the right female, I guess."

Ella curled her toes in her wet shoes and bit her lip. How she wanted to ask if she was the right woman, or if what they'd just done had been nothing but a one night stand. She didn't quite dare though. She didn't think she could handle the answer she didn't want to hear. "How about my place? I have a guest bedroom."

Trevor shook his head. "Please," she said, reaching out to touch his arm. "I need to sleep in my own bed. I gotta take a shower. I need to feed my cats and just be at home. It's safe, I know it is. We don't need to be here."

Trevor looked down at her fingers and sighed. "Ok. Your place. As long as it sm—seems safe." He bent over his phone to send another text message.

Ella smiled. Usually she was no good at all at convincing anyone to do anything, but Trevor responded to her differently than most people, especially now that their awkwardness seemed gone.

The drive to her place only took ten minutes that late at night. Ella had never been so happy to see her aunt's house. They parked in the driveway and all got out, the dogs and the man following her up the stairs of the front porch, waiting expectantly as she unlocked the door. Trevor took her hand as she pushed the door open, pulling her back and telling her to wait there, in the doorway with the dogs. He moved through the dark front room and the hallway easily, with no fear or hesitation, his head held high. Ella watched his powerful form as it disappeared out of sight, realizing that she wanted him again.

***

Trevor moved through the rooms upstairs and down, smelling every inch of the house. Khain had not been there again. He wasn't sure if he was being smart or stupid, bringing her here, but he did know he could get in trouble with his boss. This was definitely against the rules.

But an awful lot of rules had been lifted or downright ignored lately. He would take his chances.

He tromped back down the stairs and smiled at Ella. "Clear. Come inside."

"Oh thank goodness," she said, moving into the kitchen and calling out for her cats. She opened some cans of food, and cleaned out their water bowl and their perpetual feeder. "Do you want to take a shower?" she asked Trevor as the dogs both took a seat in her dining area. "I could dry your clothes in the dryer, and Trent and Troy are welcome on the couch if they want to—"

Before she could even stop talking, both dogs ran for the couch, each jumping on opposite ends. They took up most of it easily and Ella smiled ruefully as if realizing there was no room for either her or Trevor now. "Wow, did you train them to do that?"

Trevor stared after them and shook his head. "I would love a shower."

"Ok, you know where the bathroom is. Towels are in the closet. Leave your clothes outside the door. When we are all dry, I'll make some food. Tacos, maybe?"

Trevor smiled at her. "Tacos would be great." Maybe this had been a good idea, coming to her house. "Um. How much meat do you have?" He stumbled over his words. "Because Trent and Troy eat a lot, but if you don't have enough we could go to the store."

"They eat tacos?"

Trevor pressed his lips together. "They love 'em. Just no shells. And Trent likes mayo on his."

Ella laughed and Trevor thought he'd never heard a more beautiful sound. At least the wolves were good for something.

CHAPTER 27

Trevor watched Ella finish off her last taco, thrilled that things had been going so well between them. The only sketchy moment had been when he'd put Trent and Troy's food on the coffee table instead of on the floor. Oh, and again when he'd turned on the TV for them, saying they wanted to watch The Amazing Sea Wolves of Chernobyl. She'd raised an eyebrow but laughed it off, while he kicked himself for being so stupid. She made him feel comfortable.

They'd been talking for over an hour about unimportant things. Her family, his job. Trevor had been careful, not wanting to lie to her, but skirting around the truth also. He almost wished she'd call him on it. He would spill everything, given the tiniest provocation, even though he could lose his job, his status, everything, for telling a human those kinds of things. He'd already mated her once so it was not a stretch. He almost didn't care, but if she thought he was crazy? Threw him out of her house? He would care about that. People that turned into animals was a hard thing for most humans to swallow.

"So you're a workaholic, then," she said, smiling at him over the almost-empty table, the lights down low, the only other sound from the low volume on the TV.

Trevor took a long swallow of his beer before answering. She said she didn't drink, but the beer was still in the fridge from before her aunt died. "I guess I am. My work is important, but I like to think that if there were something equally important in my life, I would give it the time and energy it deserved."

She cocked her head at him. "Like a relationship?"

Trevor swallowed hard. "Yeah. Exactly."

She nodded and played with her can of sparkling water, her eyes shaded. Trevor took a cautious sniff of the air, trying to scent her emotion, but he couldn't tell what it was. He'd never been any good at that. Troy was the master at it.

Hopeful, Troy sent from the couch, not looking at him.

Ella frowned and looked that way, making Trevor watch her closer. This was not the first time he'd gotten the feeling she caught his conversations with his brothers.

Now she's confused, now suspicious.

Trevor caught Troy looking at them over the back of the couch from the corner of his eye. He was still watching Ella. Her eyebrows furrowed and she pointed at Troy.

"Did you…?"

Troy ducked behind the couch quickly.

Trevor tried to hide his alarm by taking a swallow of his beer.

Ella shook her head. "Never mind."

Trevor spoke quickly. "How about you, do you work?"

Ella took a deep breath through her nose and let it out, like she was about to say something she didn't like. "I don't. I need to though. Although the only thing I'm probably qualified for is some sort of nursing, and I need to go to school for that. I've been taking care of my mom or my aunt since I was fifteen. They were sick."

"That must have been hard."

Ella nodded. "It was hard. And now they're both gone. So I have to get over it and figure out what to do with my life from here on out."

"Did you go to college?"

Ella's eyes unfocused. "I did. For a very short time. My mother took a turn for the worse after a few months so I came back home. She begged me to."

Trevor was about to ask her if she had any other family when a small noise sounded towards the door. He looked up to see the black and gold cat that had taken such a liking to him before, coming in the kitty door.

He watched it closely to see what it would think of the wolves in its domain. It came straight for him, jumping in his lap, ignoring everyone else. He held out his hands and tried to keep the look of distaste off his face.

"Wow, she really loves you," Ella said, and her voice was warm. Trevor smelled desire flare from her. That he could distinguish.

He forced his hands toward the cat. If Ella liked the cat and liked that the cat liked him, maybe she would like it if he managed to like the cat, too. Somehow. He rested his hands on the cat's back. Not too bad. Soft. It smelled ok, like grass and wind and dry corners. A strange vibration emanated from the cat and he pulled his hands back, barely keeping himself from pushing if off his lap to the floor.

"Aw, she's purring."

Trevor held himself back from any sudden movements. Cautiously, he placed first one hand, then the other back on the warm collection of fur and muscles on his lap. It felt good, the purring. Soothing, like something a mother would do to calm a child. "What's her name?"

"That's Chelsea. She was my aunt's cat, and now I guess she's mine."

Trevor ran a hand down the cat's spine, almost liking the way the fur felt under his fingers. Chelsea rubbed her face against his leg. They hadn't seen the *echo* yet and he wondered why.

Ella got up to clear the dishes.

Trevor half stood, wondering what the etiquette was when a cat was on your lap. Could you just push it off? "Let me help."

"I got it. You relax. You work too hard as it is."

Trevor sank back into the chair and ignored Troy's snorting from the couch. He had lots of practice ignoring Troy. Instead he watched Ella move, the sway of her hips as she walked, the way her hair shone in the dim light. He felt an erection swell in his pants and suddenly the cat had to go. He picked it up and placed it on the floor with one last pat to its head and tried to shoo it away.

Ella came back, around the table to where he was, putting one hand on his shoulder. "We never talked about where you were going to sleep tonight," she said softly.

Trevor felt his cock go rock-hard with those few words. He reached up and covered her hand with his, which made her arousal scent intensify, and just like that he was lost again. He wanted her so much it hurt.

"I'll sleep wherever you tell me to sleep," he rasped, his entire body suddenly thick and ungraceful.

"Good," she said, and pulled him out of the chair. She looked back at him. "Should I leave the TV on?"

He nodded, then allowed himself to be pulled up the stairs.

***

Trevor couldn't wait until they made it into whatever bedroom she was taking him to. By 3/4s of the way up the stairs he leaned forward and bit her on the ass, holding her hips in his hands. It had looked too enticing.

She shrieked and laughed and tried to pull him up farther, but he grabbed her and spun her around, ready to take her right there on the top step, against the wall. He sunk against her, plying her mouth with his, pressing his erection against her as she moaned and writhed under him. He wanted to do this right, wanted to make her orgasm at least five times before he came himself, but the need to be inside her was too great. Maybe he would be able to temper himself once that happened.

He picked her up, holding her thighs as she wrapped her arms around his neck.

"You're so strong," she murmured against his lips.

Now he felt like taking her right there in the hallway, holding her up the entire time, lowering her onto his cock like he was curling a weight. If only she would say more things like that. An insane urge to throw his head back and howl hit him, and he distracted it by continuing to the bedroom, setting her down gently, and stripping off her clothes.

She stood naked before him, looking at him shyly, letting him look at her.

"You're beautiful," he told her, not quite daring to touch her just yet. "The most beautiful woman I've ever seen."

She looked down and color flushed from her cheeks to her breasts, turning her coloring from snow white to pink blush and making her nipples draw into tight, hard points that made him weak. "I couldn't possibly be." Her hands covered her belly.

He drew her to him, unable to believe what she had just said. "How can I convince you?"

She considered. "Take me. Take me like you took me in the rain. Like you would die if you couldn't have me for one more second."

Trevor groaned deep in his throat, feeling emotion sweep through him. She knew him intimately.

He pulled off his shirt, kicked off his boots and dropped his pants, and when she licked her lips at the sight of his cock he almost came right there, almost sprayed the ceiling with the proof of his attraction. But no, he could not waste that.

He turned her and pressed her over the bed, then was up and inside her in one movement. She cried out hard but pushed back against him even though she almost sounded like she was in pain. "Are you ok?" he asked as her face pressed into the pillows.

"God yes," she gasped out, turning her head so he could see her profile. Only then did he notice the wolf teddy positioned on the pillow next to her head. He froze, fully inside her, his balls pressed against her body.

It was black, with silver and gray markings on its chest and legs that matched the markings of his own wolf exactly.

Ella wriggled against him and he began a stuttering rhythm, staring into the yellow eyes of the wolf teddy as he did so. Another *echo*.

He fell forward and knocked the wolf to the floor with a sweep of his hand. He would think about it later. For now, he wanted to concentrate on Ella. He propped himself up on his hands and watched the muscles in her back move as she pressed against him, her little sex noises the sweetest music in the world to his ears.

His eyes fell upon her left shoulder, exactly at the spot where a *renqua* would be if she were a *wolfen*, and he felt his fangs lengthen until they scraped against his lower lip. Thick desire to mark her, claim her, swept through him and he didn't know if he could fight it. He battled against the desire even as his elbows bent and his mouth opened. She wasn't his to claim, she hadn't given him permission.

A female *wolfen* would tear a male's throat out for claiming without her permission, and he had no doubt that an ordinary woman had the capacity to do something similar. His desire and his will warred with one another, even as he thrust into her, slamming his stomach against her ass and his cock deep inside her.

He dropped one more inch, knowing he couldn't, he shouldn't, when she tossed her head and raised up suddenly, the back of her skull colliding with his nose with a loud and disgusting crunching sound.

Trevor groaned and pulled out of her, grabbing for his nose as she held onto the back of her head and rolled over. Blood spurted between his fingers and pain blinded him.

"Oh my God, you're bleeding. I'm sorry, I'm so sorry," she said, still holding onto the back of her head.

"You didn't mead it," he told her, his voice thick with congestion, blood dripping down the back of his throat. His cock waved in front of him like a flag, refusing to soften even in the face of his pain.

She let go of her head and covered her mouth with both hands, trying unsuccessfully to hold back a flood of giggles. "It's not funny, I'm sorry."

Trevor smiled at her, his vision returning even as he could feel his nose swelling to twice its size. It was broken, he knew it. "Is it fuddy?"

"No, I swear! I'm sorry!" she cried between giggles. "I'll get you ice. The bathroom is right there."

She ran for the stairs and Trevor got up quickly, ran to the bathroom and locked the door behind him. He flipped the switch in his mind, hoping she was far enough away that he could shift. She was. His nose lengthened, bone and cartilage popping into its proper place, the bleeding stopping immediately, as he fell onto all fours, stretching his neck forward while his legs popped out of their joints.

Too late, he saw the lock on the door was little more than a decoration, there was no corresponding piece of metal pushed into the frame that would ensure the door stay closed if someone turned the knob and pushed on it from the outside.

Trevor could hear Ella's feet on the stairs over the sound of his body reforming, reshaping itself and he stared hard at the door, too far gone to do anything but continue to his destination.

The door swung open, admitting Ella, naked, with a bag of ice in her hand. Trevor almost stopped mid-shift, but he forced himself to continue. Stopping mid-shift when he'd gotten so far was never a good idea.

Even as his body continued its alterations, he steeled himself for Ella's scream. He would have to shift back before he chased her. Chasing her as a wolf would only scare her more.

But she didn't run. Instead, she dropped to her knees and watched until he was done. Then she held out one trembling hand to him, touching him lightly on the muzzle.

"I knew it," she whispered.

CHAPTER 28

*E*lla stared at the gorgeous and insanely huge wolf in her bathroom and everything clicked into place. A giddiness swept over her, making her realize she'd been waiting for something like this her whole life. Something strange and life-altering, but beautiful and amazing at the same time. Something that would tell her who she was and why she was here, something beyond a dying mom and sick aunt and hateful sister and a life she never felt she belonged in. Something awesome.

She ran her hand over the wolf's ears and fur, not scared of it for a second. It was Trevor, and Trevor would never hurt her. Even as a wolf. She felt that in her bones.

"Can I talk to you?" she whispered. "Can you talk back?"

The black wolf with the beautiful sprays of silver and gray across its front whined and shook its head. Ella laughed and clapped her hands together. It was like Christmas morning, and she got the best present she never knew she wanted.

"Oh!" She stood quickly. "I have to show you something!"

She ran into the bedroom looking for Baron. He was on the floor. She snatched him up and held him in front of her, facing outward as she turned. The wolf had come out of the bathroom and was stalking toward her. "This is Baron," she breathed. "Look at him. He's just like you."

The wolf whined again and sat, cocking its head in a very human way.

"Remember, I told you about him. I got him when I was a very little girl. He was the reason my sister started calling me Queen Ella. I had done something else, before that—" She shook her head and pulled Baron to her chest with one hand as she chopped the air with the other one. "Sorry, that isn't important. But we were at a store, a wildlife store, and I saw this wolf and I wanted it but my mother wouldn't buy it for me. I cried for three days and when that didn't work, I stopped eating. I wouldn't eat or drink anything until my mother took me back to the store and bought me the wolf. I never asked for anything before or since but I had to have him." She looked down at the wolf and kissed it on the nose. "I loved him. I still do."

She walked slowly around Trevor. "I can't believe how much you look like him." She reached out and touched his left shoulder where a white marking on his fur stood out. It looked like a boomerang. "Except here. He doesn't have this marking."

The wolf whined again and Ella heard footsteps on the stairs.

Ella winced at the booming voice that cut through her thoughts. Trevor's voice.

ABSOLUTELY NOT. SHE'S NAKED.

We already saw her, old hoss, when she ran to the refrigerator. Why are you shifted?

Trevor growled deep in his throat and faced the door.

Long story, if you see her again, I'll kill you both.

Nice. Nice. Kill your own brothers.

Listen to him.

The footsteps faded away and Ella stared out the door, then dropped to her knees again, amazed. "They're your brothers?"

Trevor swung around to face her, then stretched his neck out and whimpered. She saw his fur ripple, then pull back into his body as his muzzle shortened and his legs lengthened.

She fell backwards onto her bottom, unable to believe what she was seeing. Here was the transformation from the very beginning, all the way until a naked Trevor knelt on his hands and knees before her.

She touched his skin lightly, tracing the boomerang mark on his left shoulder. He still had it, even as a human. It had the coloring of a birthmark. He arched his back when she touched it, looking into her eyes. "You make it burn when you touch it."

She snatched her hand away. "Sorry."

He sat next to her on the bare floor, taking her hand in his. "Don't be sorry. Not ever. Not with me. It's a good burn. It reminds me who I am and why I am here, and it makes me think you are someone special."

"What is it?" she whispered, watching as he rubbed her hand along the mark on his shoulder and arched his neck, stretching his chin up to the ceiling like it felt good.

"It's called a *renqua*. It's a piece of the deity who created us. All true *shiften* have it."

Ella forgot everything and everyone else in the world. It was as if she had been swallowed into a different dimension, or the pages of a book, but here she was, still in her own world.

"Is that what you are? A *shiften*?"

"I am a *wolfen*, which is the subset of *shiften* who can turn into wolves. We are the protectors of humans."

"Protectors from…?"

He nodded at the sudden fear in her eyes. "Yes. He is called Khain, among other things, and he is a demon. He wants to kill all humans, and the only thing between him and that goal is the *shiften*."

She shrunk back against the bed, a sudden chill making her shiver.

"Come," he said, pulling her onto the bed, stripping the covers and laying her underneath them, then crossing the room to close the door and return to her.

He lay next to her and stared into her eyes. "You don't have to be scared. I'm here. My brothers are here. We would tear him apart. He operates mostly through sickness and subterfuge and scorched earth tactics. He is powerful, but so are we. He is sneaky, but we are united."

Ella's shaking intensified. The *wolven* seemed like a great secret, one that warmed her from the inside out, but the fact that they were fighting a demon no one even knew about scared her more than she could put into words. "No one knows?"

Trevor put his arms around her and pulled her close to him under the blankets. "No humans know. We work very hard to keep it that way, so they can feel safe."

"Why are you telling me?"

"Let me ask you a question first."

She nodded slightly.

"How did you know Trent and Troy were my brothers?"

"I could hear you." She touched her forehead. "Talking inside my head. You said absolutely not, she's naked and then someone else said we've seen her, why are you shifted? And you said you would kill them if they saw me again and that same voice said kill your brothers, nice, but very sarcastically and almost like he thought it was funny. And then a different voice said listen to him."

Trevor grinned so wide she almost swooned at how handsome he was. "That was Trent who said listen to him, and Troy the other times."

"Why are you smiling?"

Trevor sat up in bed, energy coming off of him in waves. "Don't you see? You can't possibly be a human. You have to be at least part-*shiften*, or maybe more, or else you wouldn't be able to hear our messages to each other. Have you heard us from the very beginning?"

Ella held a hand to her head and tried to remember. "I-I'm not sure. I think I could, but it was fainter then, like I've gotten better at it, or stopped fighting it."

Trevor flipped around and knelt over her, kissing her lightly, making her feel lightheaded. "Don't fight it. I think it means something."

"Means something? You really think I could be part shifter?"

He nodded. "*Shiften*. I do. You would be *wolfen*."

"What other kinds of *shiften* are there?"

His eyes shone. "*Bearen*, they are the firefighters. And *felen*. They work by themselves usually. Mercenaries, or doctors sometimes. They also track Khain and do a few other things."

"Felons?"

"No, *felen*. F-e-l-e-n. Big cats, like pumas or mountain lions."

Ella felt her toes go cold again. "How do you know I'm not one of them?"

Trevor laughed, throwing his head back, then he came forward again and kissed her on the end of her nose. "You can't be, I wouldn't be attracted to you if you were."

"So you can tell I'm part wolf? Smell it or something?"

He frowned. "No, I can't. But if that part of you is less than half, it's possible it's so little I wouldn't be able to smell it. If it was your grandpa, or your great-grandpa who was the *shiften*."

Ella tried to think about her family, but her thoughts were scrambled. Too much information, too fast. She wouldn't believe any of it if she couldn't still see Trevor shifting in her mind.

Trevor stared at the wall and bit his lip as if he were trying hard to make a decision. He looked at her. "There's something else you might be."

"What?"

He dropped his head onto the pillow next to her and stared hard at her. "I hesitate to even tell you this, but I'm going to need to have someone touch you tomorrow, tell me for sure, and I want you to be ready for it."

"Touch me?"

Trevor sat up again, like the energy in his body was just too much for him to handle. "I'm not sure if him touching you will tell us anything, but we have to try." He knelt and stared intensely at her. "This is all new to us. We are operating without a map, without a guidebook, and all we have to go on is a twenty-five-year-old prophecy."

A prophecy. Again, that sensation of being swallowed into a book rocked her, making her close her eyes. "Prophecy?"

"I have it memorized. We can double check it later, but this is it."

He sat up straight and his eyes went blank, almost scaring her. His voice fell flat, so just the words were conveyed.

In twenty-five years, half-angel, half-human mates will be discovered living among you.

This is how you will rebuild.

Warriors, all, with names like flora.

Save them from themselves, for they will not know their foreordination.

They will not be bound by shiften law, but their destinies entwine so strongly with their fated mates, that any not mated by their 30th year will be moonstruck. Those who are lost may be dangerous.

A pledged female will have free will that shiften know not. Never forget this or it will cause grave trouble.

Her body may respond to any, until she is mated in a ceremony of her choosing, then she will acknowledge only one male, as he becomes her one true mate, and she, his one true mate. He shall be sworn to her in her life's purpose, to rebuild the shiften race, so that they may fight the evil Matchitehew and protect the humans from him, until the day he draws his last breath.

Ella held her breath, the words washing over her with meaning she barely understood, pushing away every time she'd ever been teased, ever been rejected by her mother, ever felt like she did not belong in this world.

Home.

She was home.

Trevor was her home.

CHAPTER 29

Boe cowered, breathing shallowly. The air in the *Pravus* was poison, and although his Father had done something to him to make him be able to live on it, it still hurt him to draw it into his lungs.

Khain The Destroyer, his father, also known as Matchitehew, stood in front of him, big arms flexed, powerful hands clenched, awful face tense and angry. "We need more *foxen*! You have sons and daughters. Call them to me!"

Boe took a deep breath. He was over three hundred years old, but his Father was as old as time, and not to be disobeyed. "Father, I cannot. You must call them yourself. They believe me to be dust."

Khain paced through the grand palace they lived in, the rounded temples towering over even his head, but his footfalls fell flat and empty in the space, reminding Boe of their lives there. Khain rounded on Boe, his black eyes narrowed, his jagged mouth snarling. "They do not answer. Why would that be?"

Boe tried to make himself as small as possible. "I do not know, father. Maybe the march of time has whittled your connection with them. Perhaps you are still weak from your fight with the angel and they cannot hear you."

Khain whirled, his expensive suit transforming into black robes, then white robes, then a scarlet red bodysuit. This one scared Boe most of all, as it had no place in any space or time. Khain faced the faded metal enclosure in the middle of the room.

"Or perhaps inbreeding has weakened my line. You know that bitch has a power to draw *shiften* to her that I could never pull off. Maybe all my sons and daughters have flocked to her."

Boe said nothing. He would not remind Father that all the daughters were gone, female *foxen* along with the rest of the *shiften*. Only males remained.

Ah, but maybe that would cheer Father up. "Father, if you could just wait another fifty years, a mere moment to you, the *shiften* will have all begun to grow old and crumble, exactly the way you planned it. There is no need for you to try so hard. The females are gone. The *shiften* are dying."

Khain crossed the room with eerie speed, speed that made Boe slightly sick to his stomach. He snatched Boe up by the scruff of his neck and screamed into his face. "Do you not recall the *Promised*? If even one of them is found, the *shiften* can rebuild. No one knows how many young the progeny of an angel can have, or how short their gestation! Or what the childhood of a half-*shiften*, part-angel will look like! We could be facing a new *shiften* army with powers we've never dreamed of in only a few short years."

Boe nodded his head. His memory was failing him in his old age. He should have died a century ago, but Father kept him alive, somehow. He was ready for the comforting draw of The Light, as even *foxen* were allowed to retire there, and his mind was trying to beat him there. "Then consume the angel, Father. Consume the angel and take the energy he gives you."

Khain dropped Boe to the floor, where he landed smartly on hands and feet. "There is nothing in the signs about consuming an angel. True, it will give me energy, but I cannot do it until I've mated with at least one *Promised*, to continue moving the signs forward towards our end goal. That is why I need another *Foxen*."

Boe shook, and tried to work out in his mind what should be done. "What about the first Promised? You know where she is."

Khain turned and shot a stream of fire from his hand out one of the windows, not starting a fire, but putting one out. One that was creeping too close to their home. He paced around the long white balcony that circled the special metal enclosure in the middle of the circular floor. He looked out the windows, shooting fire seemingly randomly, then pausing to walk in close and knock on the enclosure. Boe watched him, thinking him agitated, but then wondering if maybe he was scared of something. Boe had never known his father to be scared of anything, not even his nemesis. Finally Khain spoke and his voice was uncharacteristically soft. "I do not believe I can get to her. She evaded me twice and I know she is with the *wolven* now. I probably led them right to her." He clenched his hands into his palms and Boe saw living blood spill to the floor and seek a body. He scrambled backwards.

"You are right then, Sire, we must find another Promised. Let me go into the *Ula*, I will get you a *foxen*." The *Ula* was their name for the world in which the *shiften* resided. Boe's original world. One he wished he could return to, but no, his father would never release him, at least not permanently.

Khain fixed him with a stare and Boe knew he was going nowhere. "I want the first Promised. The best Promised. The one who is to be queen. Taking her would destroy the *shiften* as surely as the *vahiy* will."

Boe turned the idea over in his mind. "Is there no way to get her away from the *wolven*? No way to control her? Humans have strong bonds to their families, father, and I'm sure half-humans are no different."

Khain stared at him and Boe gathered himself to run. No matter how sure the punishment, he could not stay his instincts to try to escape it.

But Khain was not mad. He did not smile, but his dark hair lifted off his head at the ends and he floated above the floor, flying almost to the ceiling in elation.

"I need another *foxen*," he growled, and then he disappeared from sight.

Boe sighed and started into his room. Things would be quiet for a while.

He hoped.

CHAPTER 30

revor stared at Ella on the pillow next to him, admiring her quiet, relaxed form and the curve her hip made under the sheet. He felt his cock jump and he averted his eyes quickly. This was not the time. But then she reached forward and touched him lightly, her eyes still closed, her hands feeling their way to his center.

She touched him, stroked him, made him hard, but spoke softly, her words ignoring her hands. "Why do you need these one true mates? Aren't there female *shiften*?"

Trevor bucked his hips forward, not wanting her to stop, but unwilling to not answer her. "There were. Khain killed them twenty-eight years ago."

She did stop the bliss she was giving him with her hands then, opening her eyes in alarm to stare at him. "All of them?"

"Yes," he said softly.

Her eyes drifted closed again and she continued to stroke

him, almost thoughtfully. "You believe I am one of them? The mates?"

He bit his lip in an effort to be able to continue to talk to her while she was touching him. "You could be. You're the right age. There's something between us that I can't deny. But you aren't named after a plant and you know who your father is, so unless—"

"If I'm one of these mates, am I your mate, meant for you alone?"

"I don't know," he admitted, the thought that she might not be making him dizzy with fear for the first time since the war camps. She had to be his and his alone. "We don't know how it works since we haven't found any yet."

She opened her eyes again. "None?"

He shook his head, holding his lower lip between his teeth as her palms drug against his sensitive flesh, taking him somewhere good.

She threw her leg over his hip and quietly pushed his cock inside her core, making him gasp and shudder. She felt so good, so right, like she *had* been made just for him. "My first name is Fern," she said quietly, her eyes still closed, as she pressed herself onto him. "My mother always hated it and I knew that, so I thought if I made her call me something else she would hate me less. I wouldn't answer to Fern, even if they spanked me, so finally, they agreed to call me Ella, which is from my middle name, Gabriela."

Trevor's normally iron stomach fluttered and his pulse raised. He thrust into his mate, the only mate he wanted, feeling the strong connection between them solidify, become steel.

She opened her eyes halfway and peeked at him. "Sorry." He tried to tell her not to say that but she rushed on. "I lied to you. I didn't know my father. I don't look like him. I don't think my own mother even knew who he was. In fact, my sister used to tell me that all the time, that I didn't even have a daddy. She didn't have one either, but at least she had a picture. I didn't even have that."

Ella closed her eyes again and Trevor pulled her close to him, slowing his thrusts for just a moment and doing his best to kiss her sadness away, then flipping her around, his stomach to her back, and trying to distract her from everything that was piled atop her at that moment.

No matter what happened, no matter what Wade told him in the morning, she was his mate, if she would have him.

CHAPTER 31

*E*lla woke to the sound of someone's phone buzzing. Trevor's. He was already out of the bed and typing away on it. She pulled herself into a sitting position, noting how sore her lower body was. She'd only had sex one other time in her life, a hurry-up-and-get-rid-of-it bid to lose her virginity that she'd never regretted, but always knew had been lacking. Trevor had made her feel every inch of what she had been missing, making her come until her body gave up.

She watched his strong, lean, muscular body move as he paced across the floor, wondering if she dared try to entice him back to bed.

He turned to her. "That's Wade. He wants us in his office in thirty minutes."

Ella felt a ripple of fear go up her spine. What if she was tested by Wade, and found lacking? Would Trevor leave her?

She pushed the thought to the side and stood, pulling clothes out of the dresser. "Do we have time for breakfast?" Her eyes went wide. "Oh no, the dogs, we didn't let them out last night or anything. And all they have to drink from is the water in the cat bowl."

Trevor chuckled. "Wolves. Don't worry about them, they're very resourceful."

Ella pulled her clothes on quickly. "Wolves? So they are shifters too? Why don't they ever shift?"

"*Shiften*," he said automatically and he looked at the floor.

Ella stepped to him quickly, running her hands up his arms. "What? What's wrong."

"They can't shift. My fault, actually."

Ella peered up into his face. "How could it possibly be your fault?"

He didn't speak for a moment, then pushed the story out in a rush. "We were all part of the same litter. Trent, Troy, me, and our sister Treena. Treena and I were conjoined at the back. It was a big deal for a couple of reasons, one of them being because only one of us could live. We shared certain parts of our circulatory system that one of us had to get most of and the other would almost certainly die during the surgery to separate us, so they had to choose which one. And to make matters worse, there was a prophecy spoken the day we were born that made our parents believe that one of us would be the one to kill Khain, so not only did they have to decide which one of us would live, they had to choose the right one, or the entire race would suffer."

Ella gasped and held her hand over her mouth. "Oh, how awful."

"Yeah, so while our parents were dealing with that, they left newborn Trent and Troy with an uncle. *Wolven* pups learn to shift by imitating the scent of the hormones adult *wolven* release when they shift. Pups can be born in human form or wolf form and the parents shift around them constantly until they shift at least once into the other form. No one thought to tell our unmated uncle that. He hadn't realized it and he never shifted. By the time my parents gathered them up, they were stuck as wolf pups and no amount of shifting in front of them would get them to shift into humans. There's more to it, but that's the basics."

"Oh no," Ella said, and her eyes filled with tears. "They can't ever shift?"

"They never have yet."

Ella buried her face into Trevor's chest, his strangely hairless chest. "Are they sad about it?"

Trevor shrugged. "I don't know."

Ella looked up at him. "You've never asked?"

He looked out the window. "No."

"Because you think it's your fault."

He didn't say anything.

Ella wiped her eyes. "Trevor, you couldn't help any of that."

"I know," he said brusquely and pulled away from her, gathering up his clothes and pulling them on. Ella finished dressing also, lost in her own thoughts. She would try to comfort him later, when he responded to her again.

They made their way quietly down the stairs, to where the dogs—wolves were curled up on the couch. Ella smiled at the sight of Smokey curled up on top of Trent, a perfect imitation if you overlooked the fact that Trent was a dog and about one hundred and fifty pounds heavier than Smokey.

She picked Smokey up and cradled him in her arms. "Where were you last night? We missed you."

Smokey meowed once and pushed off of her body, wanting back down to the couch, wanting back down to Trent.

Time for breakfast, she heard Trevor say in her mind. *Wade wants us in to the station in thirty minutes.*

Taco salad or bacon and eggs? she tried to broadcast from her own mind.

Trent and Troy's heads came up so quickly, identical looks of canine surprise on their faces, that she had to smile. Trevor laughed out loud from behind her and pulled open the refrigerator.

What's the matter, boys, you never spoke to a lady before?

CHAPTER 32

*E*lla held Trevor's hand as he pulled her into the police station and down a long and sterile hallway. Cops were staring at her from everywhere. Trevor sent the dogs—wolves somewhere, then turned in the opposite direction. "Don't be nervous," he told her.

"Sorry, but how can I not be? I'm nervous to be a one true mate and I'm nervous not to be one."

Trevor nodded sagely and she saw something dark behind his eyes. He didn't try to tell her she was wrong.

She clung to him, scared of the time when he would drop her hand and pretend like they hadn't already connected. She knew it had to come. He wouldn't want his boss to think he'd done something stupid. Namely, her.

"It's that door," he said, pointing to an open door in the hallway. She swallowed hard and straightened her spine. Trevor squeezed her hand and pulled her along. In less than a minute, they both stood before Deputy Chief Lombard's desk, hands still clasped.

"Wade, you know Ella."

Wade smiled warmly and motioned towards the chairs. "Sit, please, both of you."

They sat, and still Trevor didn't let go of her hand. Ella wanted to kiss him.

"Do you think if you touched her, you could tell if she was a one true mate?" Trevor asked. "I think she is, but we both know confirmation is important."

Wade sat back and studied Ella, his eyes traveling over their clasped hands and then up to Trevor's face.

"At this point, does it even matter?"

Trevor frowned. "What do you mean?"

"I mean, you've chosen her. She's chosen you. I sense a bond around you that would be unbroken by news to the negative."

Trevor squeezed her hand. Ella felt a warmth spread through her chest. She looked at Trevor, then looked away quickly, down at the floor, not wanting either male to see the tears shining in her eyes.

"Wade—"

"Don't worry, son. Regardless of how it turns out, you won't face any recriminations from me. I understand that we don't choose our mates with our heads, we choose them with our hearts, and our hearts don't understand prophecy."

Ella bit her lip.

Wade went on. "But if it will make you both happy, I will try." He waited expectantly.

"Yes," Trevor said.

Ella blinked hard and looked up. "Yes."

Wade came around the desk and took her free hand with

one of his. She watched him carefully, not sure what she was hoping he would say. He frowned, then took her hand with both of his. Finally, he placed her hand carefully back on the arm of her chair, then sat down again.

"Nothing."

"What?"

"I get nothing from her, which certainly is strange. Normally I can read humans like a book written just for me, seven or eight generations back."

Trevor shook his head. "But that's not a confirmation."

"No, it is not. You know as well as I do, Trevor, that we don't know what to expect with the One True Mates."

"Is there anyone else who could try?"

"Certainly, we could have a few select *Citlali* try. Our most powerful. But you know none of them are more powerful than I am."

Trevor nodded. He knew.

Wade looked out his window and spoke airily, almost as if discussing the idea with himself. "We could try Crew."

"You think he might feel something you don't?"

"Crew is a mystery even to me, Trevor. A *wolfen* with powers almost too great for this world."

Trevor scoffed. "Are we talking about the same Crew here? The male I usually can't find? The one who you just know is in the next room but then he's not and he disappears for a week? The one who barely talks? The one who I'm not even sure why he's on the team? I know he could have been a *Citlali*, but I also know he lost it, he either refuses to or cannot sit in repose for prophecy."

Wade leaned back in his chair and steepled his hands, looking at Ella appraisingly.

"Um, should I leave?" she asked.

Wade dropped his hands to his desk and shook his head. "No, you can hear this. Human or not, part-shifter or not, one true mate or not, you are Trevor's mate and that makes you a part of all of this, no matter what."

Trevor shifted in his chair. "We haven't actually, um."

Wade raised an eyebrow. "A ceremony is just that, son, a ceremony. Your hearts are entwined so surely I'm a little surprised it could have happened in so few days time." He looked at Ella again. "But that fact alone could tell us many things if we chose to listen."

Ella was not sure what any of what this kind man- person- argh, *wolfen*, was saying to her meant, only that it made her feel warm deep in her chest, and like she belonged there.

Wade looked up at the ceiling. "What I'm about to tell you has only been discussed in the great hall before."

Ella didn't know what that meant but a glance at Trevor told her it was something impressive.

"Crew still has great power. But he has gone underground."

"Underground?"

Wade held up a hand. "Just listen. Crew doesn't have to sit in repose for prophecy. He is the only *shiften* that we know about who can catch prophecy at any day or time, and he can open himself up to it with just a thought. He began reciting prophecy the day he first learned to talk, entire sentences coming out of his tiny mouth and frightening his poor mother almost to her death. His family called us, and several of us went to them. It was frightening, watching that young pup babble on as if he were having a private conversation with The Light or Rhen or the angels, especially when the darker things began to come through."

"Darker?"

Wade held up a hand. "I'll get to that. We gathered

around the child and recorded many of the things he said, but the longer he spoke, the more his body seemed to shrink, like he was using up vast reserves of energy he didn't own. He became skin stretched over a skeleton before our eyes, until his mother pleaded with us to stop him. We tried to distract him and that did not work, so I put him under. Every time I would wake him he continued to speak prophecy and would not eat or drink. Some of the things he said sounded like they came from Khain himself. So I put him under again and we took him to Remington."

Trevor looked at Ella. "A doctor," he said, but his eyes were dark and his face drawn in distaste.

Wade nodded. "Remington fed him artificially until his body recovered some of its fat stores, and then we worked with him, waking him and distracting him until he learned to control the speaking." Wade dropped his eyes. "It took many years, and by that time, his mother was dead."

Ella covered her mouth with her hands.

"Crew suffered, and by the time he was able to be a normal boy again, his world had changed. He never did go to the war camps. He came to live with me and Lorna instead. We took care of him as best we could. His father let him stay with us, having four other boys to take care of, and unable to understand Crew. Even though I shared some of his power, I never understood him either. I tried to be a father to him, but I failed. When he was thirteen, he decided to do something dangerous, something I warned him against and asked him not to do."

Ella felt Trevor tense in his chair.

"He sat in repose and specifically sought to contact Khain, something I don't believe any other *shiften* alive can do. Khain was resting, had been resting for eight years, and when Crew created a connection with him, he had a good fifteen minutes or so to poke around in his head. Almost everything that we know to be true about Khain came from that short time. When Khain discovered Crew in his head, he became very angry and began to show Crew things he did not want to see. He showed Crew the death of his mother, which had already happened, then showed him the death of his father, that had not happened yet. Then he showed him my death." Wade shook his head. "I asked not to be told about that one so I don't know when or how. Khain then stood face to face with Crew in his imagination and spoke prophecy to him. He said that when Crew turned thirty-five, he would meet his one true mate, a female of such beauty, grace, and strength of will, that Crew would be lost to her. And when they were mated, Khain himself would find her and kill her in front of him."

Ella rocked in her chair, her heart going out to Crew, a man—*wolfen* she had never met.

Trevor squeezed her hand and she squeezed back. A new fact of her status as Trevor's mate appeared to her. The danger it would bring. Khain didn't seem real to her in this new sense, and she was already dreading the day that he did.

"I did not know." Trevor said simply. "I must submit myself to Crew. I have wronged him. I'm sorry for what I thought about him, and I do want him to see if he can read Ella, if he is willing."

Wade stayed silent for a long time. "I want you to understand that the experience drove Crew *moonstruck*, but we recovered him. He is now whole, but he and his powers are underground. If he still uses his powers, he doesn't share them with anyone, and I do not know if he will do this."

Trevor nodded. "Let's ask."

CHAPTER 33

*E*lla waited in the chair for Crew to arrive, imagining what he would look like. Scary? With an air of mystery around him? Would she be able to feel his power when—if he touched her? Would she know who or what she really was?

They heard footsteps in the hallway and the three of them turned as one. Crew entered, stopping just inside the door, his face carefully blank. No smile or frown there. He was tall, at least a few inches over six foot, and built as much like a warrior as Trevor was. Ella found him pleasant to look at, but not exactly what she would call handsome, not in the way that Trevor was. His hair was dark and thick, his face unshaven, and his work clothes rumpled, as if he'd been working for a few days without a break.

Trevor shot to his feet and crossed the room. Ella thought she heard a whining coming from him. She stared at him curiously as he hung his head and a very animal-like noise came from him.

"Dude," Crew said, "no."

"Yes. We haven't exactly gotten along since I've been here, and most of that is my fault."

Crew didn't say anything for a long time. Then he bobbed his head. "Cool."

The two men—*wolven* clasped hands. Ella felt a strange undercurrent fill the room.

"Thank you for coming, son," Wade said. "We think we've found the first one true mate and we need your reading on her."

Crew locked eyes with her and Ella stared back, her throat tightening.

"I get nothing," he said, almost dismissively and Ella looked around surprised. That was it?

"Do you think you would get something if you touched her?" Wade asked.

Trevor, standing to Crew's right, moved quickly between Ella and Crew and growled deep in his throat.

No one said anything for a moment, then Trevor seemed to come to his senses. "Shit, sorry," he said, moving to sit down on the other side of Ella.

Crew looked at Wade and Ella saw Wade raise both eyebrows and incline his head towards her. Crew took a few steps toward her before Trevor heaved out of his seat, again placing himself between her and him. A loud, terrifying snarl filled the room, causing Ella to pull her feet up off the floor before she realized it was Trevor again.

Wade stood up and approached Trevor, watching him carefully, then waved a hand in front of his tense face. "Trevor, you here?"

Trevor shook himself visibly, but he didn't relax. "Step back," he said. "You don't touch her."

Crew stepped back and leaned against the doorway, a small smile on his face for the first time. Wade got in between them. "Trevor, you asked him to touch her."

"I know." Trevor relaxed again. "Shit, I'm sorry again. I don't know what I'm doing. I—"

Wade appraised him. "You sure you don't know what you're doing? Because I think it's pretty clear."

"I can't help myself."

Wade shook his head. "Not your fault. My guess is there's something stronger in your connection than ordinarily would be there. And The Light help us if it's like this for all of you. Supposedly there are thousands of one true mates. The fighting could get worse before it gets better."

Trevor turned to look at Ella apologetically and take her hand. She smiled at him and brushed her fingers over his arm.

Footsteps sounded in the hallway. Crew looked out then looked back at Wade. "It's Mac."

"Good, bring him in. We'll see if he can touch her."

Trevor's face contracted into a snarl and he whirled around, his body contorting as he shifted right there. Ella watched with fear in her heart as his clothes fell off of him and he bound across the room, his huge leap taking him right to the center of Mac's chest as he stopped in the doorway.

Mac shifted at once, even as he dropped to the ground under Trevor's greater weight, his snout and body lengthening, his leg joints popping, while Trevor tore and bit at him, fastening on his throat. Mac's wolf had gorgeous, glossy white fur that quickly became red with his own blood.

"Get Trevor!" Wade yelled to Crew and jumped toward

the fray. He and Crew both caught Trevor under his front legs, pulling his jaws apart and screaming at him to stop before he killed Mac.

Ella climbed up on her chair and watched the four males roll around on the floor, biting back the scream that was caught in her lungs.

***

Twenty minutes later, the drama was over. Mac was gone. Wade and Crew had shifted to heal their injuries and cleaned the blood off themselves in Wade's bathroom. Trevor sat quietly in the chair next to Ella, the blood cleaned from his face and neck, his demeanor completely tightened down. Ella didn't know what to think or do.

Wade sat in the chair across from them while Crew stayed near the door. Wade cleared his throat until Trevor looked at him. "My guess is that you will calm down a bit once the two of you are mated, but until then, no one will be able to get close to her, except mated males, like myself."

"Good thing we have a lot of them," Trevor said dryly.

"Indeed. I still want Crew to … see if he can get anything from her though. Would you be willing to let me put you under?"

Trevor stiffened. "Why not just bind me?"

"No way. I will not bind you again. You know why. Besides. I have to wonder if your fervor could break the bind, and then you would be very dangerous. I've never seen a male act quite like this over a potential mate."

Trevor did not contradict that. "Why don't I wait in the hall?"

"Because I don't want my door torn in half."

Trevor nodded again. "Ok, do it. Put me under."

Ella watched, eyes wide. She didn't know what half of the words meant, but she was too anxious for it all to be over to interrupt.

Trevor stood up and laid down on the black leather couch along the back wall, his feet sticking over the end. Wade touched him on the arm and as far as Ella could see, did nothing more than that. But when he moved, Trevor was relaxed, eyes closed, seemingly asleep.

Wade nodded at Crew. Crew approached her slowly, not saying a word. She held up her hand, not wanting him to touch her anywhere but there. She kept her eyes on Trevor, afraid he would wake up and the fighting would start again.

Crew's fingers brushed hers, warm and soft. She watched his face but his expression stayed completely blank. He didn't seem to be moving at all, or even breathing. Too late, Ella realized he was tipping, falling.

Wade shot to his feet as Crew fell to the floor. Ella could feel the reverberations of his big body hitting and she jumped out of her chair, tiptoeing to him.

"What in the world?" Wade murmured as he bent over Crew and touched his forehead lightly. He nodded at Ella. "Go see if you can wake Trevor. I wouldn't be surprised if you could."

Ella went to Trevor on the couch and sat next to him, entwining her fingers with his. She bent over him and whispered in his ear, while she watched Wade try to wake Crew.

Trevor blinked his eyes and smiled at her, reaching up to touch her face. "Ella," he whispered. "How did it go?"

She nodded at the *wolfen* on the floor. "Not good."

"Ah damn," he muttered as he pushed into a sitting position.

Crew's eyes opened and he stared at the ceiling. In a strange monotone voice he said,

"Life begins anew. Love brings two, then four, then six more. Khain's downfall lives inside her. She will be queen."

Ella gasped and covered her mouth with her hand as chills rushed up and down her spine. He couldn't be speaking of her? Unconsciously, she curled her hand around her belly.

Trevor pulled her close and they watched as Wade continued to speak softly to Crew, placing his fingers at Crew's temples and jaw line, then chest, then feet, then starting the circuit over again.

It took several minutes, but Crew began to respond. He blinked rapidly and let Wade help him sit up. Ella and Trevor stayed on the couch while Wade sat on the edge of his desk and waited for Crew to be able to speak.

Crew held a hand over his eyes. "I couldn't understand a lot of it. It came so fast. In a glut."

Wade held up his hands. "It's ok, son. Just tell us what you can."

Crew looked at Trevor. "She is a one true mate, and she has powers that I can't even guess at."

Ella felt a strange lightness enter her chest, even though on some level, she'd known it was true since the first time the words one true mate had come out of Trevor's mouth. But powers?

Trevor spoke, his voice hard. "You said *a* one true mate? Is she mine? Made for me alone?"

Crew shook his head. "Not until you mate her."

Trevor growled and Crew shook his head again, holding up one hand. "You asked for the fucking truth. So handle it."

Wade took over. "So she could mate any *shiften*? Or just a *wolfen*?"

Crew tightened his jaw and watched Trevor warily. "She has the seeds inside her to carry any *shiften* young to term. She possibly could even mate Kh—."

Trevor's growling grew so loud, Ella had to cover her ears. He pulled his hand out of hers and stood, and she was afraid he would shift again. "Trevor," she said, grabbing for him and pulling him down. He came easily and quieted a bit, but his body was still tense.

Crew raised his voice to be heard over Trevor's growling. "But once you claim her and you are joined in a proper mating ceremony, she can only have your young, unless you die, and then the claiming is nullified."

Trevor stopped growling. He stood up, shaking free of Ella, and approached Wade. "We mate tonight. I want you to perform the ceremony. We'll have it in the woods, with a proper run afterwards. I want Crew and Harlan and Blake to stand for me, and we'll need to get Ella a dress and flowers. Anything she wants."

Ella stood up, unable to believe what she was hearing. Wade nodded, not even looking at her. He fired questions at Trevor as Crew looked at the door, seeming about to sneak out of the room.

"Wait," Ella said, but neither male heard her. She stood up. "Don't I get a say in this?"

The two males continued to talk over her, not even looking her way. She heard the words *veil, claiming,* and *witnesses* thrown about and with each of them, her anger grew. Ella marched into the middle of the room, her hands clenched. She touched Trevor on the shoulder. He held up a finger and continued to talk to Wade.

Ella side-eyed him, unable to believe that a man—she shook her head—not a man. Unable to believe that some wolf she barely knew and another wolf she had just met were planning a—a shotgun wedding of some sort and not even talking to her about it.

"I will not mate you!" she yelled, and then she turned on her heel and ran out of the room.

CHAPTER 34

revor shot up to his feet, pushed around Wade, and raced out the door, following Ella. "Ella, wait," he called.

She was to his left, not running but walking quickly and with purpose, tension holding her spine straight. His mind whirled, trying to figure out what he had done wrong. He caught up to her, grabbing her around the elbow and spinning her to face him. Her expression was tight and he realized it was the first time he had truly seen her this angry.

"Ella, I'm sorry. Hear me out, I-I should not have done that. I wasn't thinking. It's too much, too soon, right?"

Ella relaxed slightly. "You've got to give me a chance to breathe here, Trevor."

Trevor nodded eagerly. "You're right. I wasn't thinking." He stared into her eyes and an idea came to him, something to take the pressure off. "Here, let me show you something."

She relaxed more and twined her fingers in his, letting him pull her down the hallway. She followed him into a dark alcove off to their right where there were no lights. At the very end of it there was a door, which Trevor stepped up to, bending slightly so the cursed retina scanner could scan his eyeball. He felt her shift her weight from one foot to the other behind him. He turned to her "What? What's wrong?"

A vertical line had appeared between her eyebrows but still she shook her head. "It's nothing."

Trevor could tell she was holding something back, but he wouldn't push her. She had to come to it at her own pace.

He turned back to the door, but it had closed already. He pressed his eye close to the scanner again and pulled her through as soon as the door whooshed open.

The darkness and the coolness of the tunnels soothed him at once, as it always did. They walked slowly on the downward slope, the only sound they could hear was their own footsteps. Several small, dim lights above gave the tunnel a warm ambiance.

"What is this place?" Ella finally asked and her voice was small.

"The tunnels. The police station is connected to every important *wolven's* house in Serenity. Some of these tunnels go on for miles. Our secret meeting places are down here too, and the prophecy room is this way."

She seemed to hesitate before she spoke. "What happens if a *wolfen* dies? Do you die of old age?" Her voice turned little-girl curious.

Trevor stopped walking and turned to face her. "We do, in about the same time as humans do, unless we are mated. Then we live longer."

"How long?"

"Sometimes two hundred years, sometimes slightly more."

"Will I live that long?" she asked and her eyes held fear that Trevor could easily see in the dim light.

"I don't know."

They stared at each other for a long time before Trevor began to walk again, more slowly this time. That would be a cruel fate, for her to be taken from him early. Assuming he could get her to mate him.

"So let's say a *wolfen* dies of old age, or quits police work, what happens to their tunnel?"

"*Wolven* don't quit."

"Never?"

"Never. It's in our blood, protecting humans and being police officers." The door to the prophecy room spilled light out into the hallway in front of them. Trevor stopped and faced her. He leaned against the wall and pulled her into him, kissing her once, twice, three times on her soft lips. "Do you want to hear the creation story?"

Her eyes shone. "Yes."

He pulled her into the prophecy room, one of the places he loved most of all in Serenity, second only to his own home and the woods. He put her in the softest chair in the middle of the room. She barely looked around, her eyes directly on him.

Trevor took a deep breath. "I've told you Khain is a demon—"

She nodded her head, then interrupted him. "Wait, do shifters believe in God?"

"*Shiften.*" He sighed. "I'm not a philosopher, but I do think that humans tell many tales of many gods that all could be the same being. We refer to this being as The Light. Whether or not they truly are the same? That's a question for Wade."

"Is he like a priest?"

"Wade is like a priest, judge, jury, father, and boss all rolled up in one." He watched her carefully to see if she understood or had any more questions. She nodded her head.

Trevor leaned over the arms of the chair and kissed her on her nose. "Back to Khain. He used to walk with The Light, but he chose to break ties and come down to earth. We aren't sure what the original reason was but he ended up killing humans for fun or sport or purpose, not that his reason matters. Rhen was sent to stop him."

Ella shivered. "Rhen. Is she an angel?"

"She is a *deae*. The word roughly translates into little god or goddess."

"In what language?"

Trevor cocked his head and smiled. She was like a detective, or a very good lawyer. "I don't know. We don't have a written history and since all of our mothers were killed, no one did a very good job of sharing the oral history."

"What about your father?"

"He died shortly after my mother."

Ella's eyes grew big. "Trevor, I'm so sorry."

He let himself be gathered into a hug for just a moment before he pulled back and knelt on the rug before her.

"Who took you in?"

"I went to the war camps."

Ella covered her mouth with her hands. "That sounds awful!"

Trevor looked at the wall as memories washed over him. "It was." He had to pull himself back to the little room, back to the present. "Since I've been here, I've been studying the prophecies. They are all we are allowed to record."

"How long have you been here?"

"Two years."

"Same as me. From where?"

"New York."

Ella smiled. "I knew it. I can hear the accent sometimes in certain things you say. I thought you had to be from somewhere on the East Coast."

Trevor did not smile back. "I tried very hard to get rid of it."

Ella looked confused. "But why?"

Trevor rolled his shoulders, not wanting to think about it. "I don't exactly fit in here."

"But you want to," Ella said softly.

Trevor stared at the volumes and volumes of prophecies lining the walls. His mind dredged up the ones that Wade thought pertained to him. Did he even deserve a one true mate if in reality he was the fraud he believed himself to be?

***

Ella watched Trevor slip away from her. She was beginning to recognize some of his complexities, and there were many of them to deal with. She ran her fingers lightly down his arm. "You were telling me about Rhen?"

Trevor pulled himself back to the moment. "Yes. Rhen. She fought with Khain but could not stop him, and one night after a long and hard battle, she asked for the help of some wolves they ran across."

Trevor stood and she could see his spine straighten as he lifted his chin and went on. "The wolves fought Khain for her and together, they were able to drive him away, gravely injured. Rhen was also weak from the fight, so she could not pursue him. Instead she decided to enlist the help of the wolves in all future fights with Khain. She put a small piece of herself in the body of each member of the pack and those became the first *wolven*. The wolves gained the ability to shift into the likeness of Rhen that night. They ran through the forest on a quest to find more animals who Rhen could enlist as a kind of army. She found a bear and her cubs using their paws to put out the fires Khain had started. She gave each of the bears a piece of herself, placing it in their left shoulder, where it became a *renqua*. With the help of the *wolven*, she found several male bears and gave them pieces of herself also. They were the first *bearen*. Again, she ran through the forest with the *wolven*, even in her weakened state. She pulled them away from their territory, so they did not know where they were going. She ran fast and just before she could go head-long over a blind cliff, a mountain lion jumped out in front of her and warned her away with a scream. The *wolven* were ready to tear the lion apart, because they did not know what it was doing. But when Rhen saw the cliff, she stopped them. She put a piece of herself in the mountain lion and they found more and she gave them pieces of herself also."

Trevor's face shone with the effort of telling the story. Ella thought he had never looked so handsome. "These three species of animals became the first *shiften* —and they were essentially given their jobs that night. They evolved with the humans. As the human population grew, so did their number. They integrated with humans, always living with them, always protecting them, but the humans never knew what they really were. They were unable to shift if humans were around unless Khain was near. *Wolven* started the first Police Departments, graduating from lone sheriffs and deputies to full departments, while *bearen* built the fire departments and *felen* did their own thing. Most of them are mercenaries, some are in the human government, some are doctors, some track Khain where he lives, and some watch Rhen's body."

"There are *shiften* in government?"

Trevor chuckled. "They are the ones always involved in the sex scandals. It's good to have them there though, they can sway things our way when we need it."

"Rhen's body is still around? It's close, isn't it?"

Trevor nodded.

"Didn't this all happen a long time ago, though?"

"It did. Before recorded history. But remember, Rhen is a *deae*."

Ella stood. "I can feel her body. It's like a magnet." She turned and walked to the door, glad when Trevor followed her. She didn't want to be in the tunnels without him.

She began to walk towards the right, away from the way they had come, taking another right, and then another, then a left and following a tunnel on a steep incline downwards. Trevor followed, never saying a word. When they had walked for over twenty minutes, he stopped her. "You can't go any farther, but you are right. Rhen is that way."

Ella stared in his face. "Why can't I go any farther?"

"The *felen*. The ones down here are dangerous. We don't mess with them."

Ella turned in a circle. "I can feel her. All I feel is love."

"She is love. And your father loved her."

Ella stumbled. "My–" she shook her head. "I don't want to talk about my father right now. I may be at my limit for weird stuff today."

Trevor pulled her to him with an arm around her waist, then took her hand and kissed it, directly in the center of her palm, sending chills through her body. "Unfortunately, weird is a daily staple around here."

CHAPTER 35

*E*lla put her head back slightly and closed her eyes, soaking up Trevor's nearness. This was what she wanted. Simple, uncomplicated. Just to be together. He nibbled on her fingertips and she smiled. "Mmmm."

"You like that?"

"I like you."

Trevor pulled her closer, walking her towards the wall of the tunnel, pressing her body against it with his own. "You don't think I'm scary?"

She opened her eyes and blinked at him in the dim light. "You are scary, but not to me."

He leaned in and kissed her neck, his voice lowering. "I'm sorry about what happened in Wade's office. That wasn't me acting like that." He rubbed his chin as if remembering Mac's blood there.

"Don't be sorry for something you can't help, Trevor. I

can't say I enjoyed it, but, in a strange way it made me feel safe."

Trevor pressed the hardness of his body into her. She ran her fingers over his biceps and up to his shoulders as he continued to kiss her.

"You are always safe with me."

His soft mouth and scratchy scruff found just the right place behind her ear. She shivered and felt her body respond strongly.

Trevor sniffed her skin. "Ah, you smell so good."

Ella laughed. "What do I smell like?"

"Cinnamon and sugar and when you get aroused, there is a healthy spray of vanilla in there too."

Ella put her hands on his chest. "Seriously?"

He smiled and pulled away from her slightly, covering her hands with his. "Yes, it's a wonderful smell, it's what first attracted me to you."

"My smell?"

"Why do you look upset? That's a good thing, especially to *wolven*. We care a lot what females smell like. I've never smelled anyone who smelled as good as you."

"I don't know. I guess women like to be noticed for their beauty, or their minds, but not so much for their scent." She looked over his shoulder for a moment. "Wait, am I a woman? I'm not a *shiften*, and I'm not quite human, so what am I?"

Trevor leaned in close, his voice soothing. "We're writing this history Ella, and I say you can be anything you want to be."

"I want to be a woman." She caught his eye and smiled. "I've never fit in anywhere, Trevor, not in my family, not at school, not with other kids. I feel like I could fit in here, even if I'm not quite the same."

Trevor nodded solemnly. "You do fit in. You heard Crew. You are to be—"

She stopped him with a finger over his lips. "Sorry. I don't want to think about that right now. It's too much."

Trevor nodded and pressed his lips together, miming locking them and throwing away a key. He closed his eyes and took a big breath through his nose. "Scent is beauty, you know." He opened his eyes and curled a lock of her hair back from her face. "You are also very beautiful to look at." He took another breath and smiled wickedly. "Vanilla."

Ella hit him in the chest and leaned in close, whispering. "Are you saying I'm aroused?"

"Aren't you?"

She dropped the game. If he could smell it, he knew she was. "Yes. I want you. I seem to always want you no matter how much I have you, no matter how much crap we have to go through."

He groaned and leaned into her, kissing her neck again. "I need to take you home."

"You need to take me," she whispered into his ear, reaching down to feel him through his pants. He was hard, huge, and ready against her hand. She loved that she had done that to him with barely a few words.

"Ella, don't touch me like that. Not unless you want me to turn you around and take you right here in the tunnels."

She looked left, then right. "I don't see anybody. Take me, but don't turn me around." She undid her pants and let them fall to the floor, staring into his eyes. "We've been together several times now, and you've always taken me from behind. Is that the only way *wolven* do it?"

"It's the only way I've ever done it."

Ella bit her lip, not wanting to think about him with

others. But she could be his first in this manner. The first to look in his face, kiss his lips, as he shuddered out his release. The thought made her feel powerful and she felt her body respond to it and to him.

She pulled him forward by his pants, undoing them quickly. "Are we safe here?"

"Yes, no one will come this far. There is no reason to."

"Good." She reached into his pants and pulled him out, running her hands up and down his shaft.

He threw his head back. "Oh God, Ella."

She smiled and stroked him faster. "God?"

"It's an expression. You're making me believe in him."

He looked at her and his eyes glowed yellow, making her gasp. A growling came from the back of his throat and he lifted her easily. "You control me, Ella, you know that, right?"

Ella nodded hesitantly, wondering if that really could be true, if the beast inside him really could be fully controlled. She wrapped her legs around him and urged him on, wanting the wildness, needing the connection with him.

He thrust into her and she held on to his shoulders, her body shaking with need that had come on quickly and perilously hard. She was close to orgasm already and the sensations that built quickly as he lifted and lowered her and thrust into her overtook her, making her drop her head against the wall and whimper.

"I believe in heaven too," Trevor growled into her ear. "You take me there every time you let me inside you."

The words swept over Ella and she rocked into him, that one simple movement and his sweet sentiment pushing her over that beautiful edge she had barely had to reach for. Ecstasy flooded through her and she cried out into the darkness, keeping her eyes on him, the echoes coming back to her as Trevor pressed his upper body against hers and moaned out his own release in time with hers.

CHAPTER 36

*T*revor stared hard at Ella for a moment, needing some time to catch his breath. That had been intense. They touched foreheads and he could tell she felt as overwhelmed as he did.

She gathered herself. "Did you mind it?"

"Taking you while being able to watch your face as you came? I loved it. That's how we do it from now on."

Ella laughed. "You think you're in charge of an awful lot, don't you? There's something to be said for doggy style occasionally."

"Doggy?"

"Wolfy? Wolf-style? I don't know, what do you call it?"

Trevor threw back his head and laughed. "We just call it sex. Or mating." He lowered Ella to the floor, looking around apologetically as he tucked himself back into his pants and snapped them. "I don't have anything to clean up with."

"I'll live," she told him, catching his lips for one more kiss. He felt his cock jump and he told it to relax. She pulled back and looked around. "Which tunnel goes to your house?"

"You want to see my house?" he asked eagerly. He wanted to take her there but hadn't quite dared until now.

"Yes."

"Come on." He pulled her back the way they had come, walking more quickly than they had on the way there. His heart was light. She was a one true mate, and even if she hadn't said she would mate him yet, it would happen. He knew it would.

He reached out to Trent and Troy, who agreed to meet them in the truck in an hour, after he got them out of the tunnels and talked to Wade one more time.

An hour and a half later, they slowed to a crawl as Trevor locked eyes with the stone cougar baring its teeth in a perpetual deadly snarl on the country road that led towards his farmhouse.

He could feel Ella's eyes on him and the agitation of the wolves in the back seat, but he couldn't speed up. He had to pay his tribute. After they passed, he noticed a small sign driven into the dirt, but facing the other way. He whipped his head backwards to read it. It hadn't been there the last time he'd headed in to town from his house, but that had been several days ago.

Werewolves aren't always controlled by the moon. Wake up people!

Trevor pulled over quickly and put the truck in park. "Just a sec," he said, then jumped out and ran across the street. He pulled the sign out and threw it in the back of his truck, weighting it down with a rock. He would assign an investigation into it to someone when he had a moment to breathe.

He climbed back in the truck and they were off, pulling down a small dirt road that led only to his house, his thirty acres where he felt most at home.

Ella leaned forward as they drove down his long driveway. "Oh, it's cute. And big. Why do you need so much space?"

"I needed the acreage. The house didn't matter to me." He pointed behind it. "See that tree line there? We run out there every day that we can. It keeps us healthy."

"You and Trent and Troy?"

"Yes."

"You run as a wolf?"

"I do."

The scent of vanilla filled the truck and he chuckled.

"What!" she demanded but by the flush on her cheeks, she knew. He thought it was hot as hell that she was turned on by his true nature. He'd have to shift in front of her as often as possible. Maybe play a few stalking games in the forest, if she was into that kind of thing. He couldn't wait to find out.

He stopped the truck near the house and they got out.

"Why are the windows so big?"

"I ripped out the old ones and widened them. They pop out completely during the summer. I like to let in as much light and air as possible."

She turned toward him. "You did it yourself?"

"I like to work with my hands."

She nodded thoughtfully, then followed him into the house. As soon as she entered, she made a small noise of amazement and turned in a circle, staring up at the ceiling.

The outside of the house looked very similar to the way it had the day he bought it, but the inside he had completely changed. Rough-hewn logs covered every corner, and the ceiling and walls were lined with thin sticks, giving it a very log-cabin look. All of the furniture was handmade, and even the countertops in the kitchen and the shelves on the wall were made of a luminous and matching hard maple.

"You did this?"

Trevor nodded.

"By yourself?"

"It's still a work in progress, but this is what I do if I'm not at work."

"Wow," she breathed. "Can I see the rest of it?"

Trevor took her through the bottom floor, showing her the bathrooms and the guest bedrooms, then taking her to the other side of the house. "This is Trent and Troy's room."

"They sleep on actual beds?" Before he could respond she shook her head. "Don't answer that. Of course they do."

"This way. That's the basement," he said pointing towards a door in the hallway, "but I don't ever go down there."

He led her to the stairway. She ran her hands over his rough banister. "This is gorgeous."

Trevor smiled to himself. She was more perfect every minute. At the top of the stairs, first he went left and showed her another bathroom and three more bedrooms he hadn't done anything with yet, then he pulled her to the master bedroom.

"Oh wow, this is like heaven."

He smiled, remembering saying something similar to her just a couple of hours before. He looked around the room, admiring it with fresh eyes. The entire room was done in dark, rustic oak, the bed left rough and chunky, while the armoire was sleek. A chest covered with deep green pillows sat on one side, and a handmade couch on the other. The walls and ceiling were lined again with twigs, giving the entire room a very outdoor look. On nights when he lay awake, unable to sleep, he could very well imagine he was outside. She crossed to the bed and ran her hands over the detail there. "Careful," he growled. "Don't lay down unless you want to stay up here for a while."

Vanilla flooded the room, thrilling him. He caught movement out the window and crossed to look out. A car had pulled up at the end of the driveway and parked.

Ella looked out with him. "Who's that?"

"Mac maybe. I'm not sure. Wade said he was sending a crew out to watch over us."

"What? Why?"

"Just a precaution. You're very precious to us, all of us."

Ella sat on the bed and her fingers curled around her lower belly. Trevor watched her closely, Crew's words flashing through his mind.

Life begins anew. Love brings two, then four, then six more. Khain's downfall lives inside her. She will be queen.

He bit his lip, trying to contain his excitement. Could anyone really know if she were with young already? It had been what, a day at the most? But those words, *lives inside her,* they struck him hard.

A realization flashed through him, about one of the prophecies that was supposed to apply to him. It was referred to as the *demon death* or sometimes, *Khain's downfall.* He sat on the bed next to Ella as weakness flooded his legs. Had he been right all along? Was this his confirmation that it wasn't about him at all?

Ella interrupted his thoughts. "How long are they going to watch us?"

"I don't know. Until we are properly mated, I'm sure. Maybe longer?"

She turned to him. "But Trevor, that could be years."

Trevor's chest ached. "Years?"

"Yes, I mean, we barely know each other. We should do this properly, don't you think? Date, get to know each other, get engaged, plan a wedding. That all takes time."

"You are thinking of human courtship."

"Isn't that how *shiften* do things?"

"Not normally. Two *shiften* who belong together know it at first scent sometimes. At first mating for sure."

Ella touched her throat, her graceful fingers trembling. "So you don't date?"

"Not much," he admitted.

"But Trevor, I don't—I don't love you. I'm sorry."

"Another human construct," he said, but his voice was weak and unsure, as a spiritual knife cut through his heart, leaving it scarred and unsure of its next beat.

She touched him on the arm. "Do you … love me?"

Trevor swallowed hard, but couldn't find a word to say.

***

Troy watched out the window in the falling darkness as a convention of *shiften* gathered on the front lawn. He counted two *felen*, a *bearen*, most of the KSRT, and someone he didn't recognize. Someone big. He lifted his nose to better sort through the scents.

If I didn't know better, I'd swear there was a dragen out there, he told Trent.

Trent looked away from the documentary *Wolf Battlefield* to see for himself. He scented also.

Trevor, what do you know about a dragen on our front lawn?

Trevor clomped down the stairs heavily, the scent of

despair pushing in front of him. *Wade's idea. He can get into the Pravus.*

Troy lolled his tongue. *Useful ability.*

I thought all the dragen were dead, Trent said.

Ella came down the stairs after Trevor, her scent was indefinable, a mixture of many things, one of them determination. Troy didn't like it, especially if it meant what he thought it meant.

"*Dragen*? Like a Dragon?"

Trevor headed into the kitchen and opened the refrigerator, talking to Ella as he did so. "Yes, exactly."

"I thought you said there were only three *shiften*. Wolves, bears, and the felons."

"*Felen. Dragen* are somewhat of a mystery. There have never been many of them, but most of the ones that did exist worked alongside the *wolven*, just never in this country."

"And you're sure Khain never created them? They breathe fire, right? Didn't you say Khain could make fire from nothing?"

Troy and Trent exchanged a glance. She was smart.

"It has been conjectured over the years that Khain had a hand in making dragons, but most of that stopped when news came from the UK of how fiercely they fought against Khain. How one *dragen* was enough to drive Khain off, when it takes a group of *wolven* to do it."

Ella sat down at the table and accepted the lemonade Trevor brought her with a smile.

Tell her about foxen, Trent sent in his low rumble.

Ella smiled as if she loved to hear his voice in her head, and everyone knew how rarely he spoke. "*Foxen*? Foxes?"

A snarl entered Trevor's voice. "Yes, fox *shiften*. If anyone was created by Khain, it's them. Sneaky, non-working, lie-to-your face fools. Sometimes they don't even have a *renqua*."

"But sometimes they do?"

"Yes. But it's always faint."

"Why don't you ask Rhen? Or have Wade ask Rhen? Then you would know for sure."

Trevor stopped cutting up whatever he was cutting on the counter and went to sit by Ella at the table. "I asked Wade that once and he explained it to me. I'll try to tell it the way he told it. He said that talking to Rhen or the angels is not like this conversation you and I are having. It's a steady stream of consciousness that the *Citlali* can tap into, and the message is always different. No one knows if they are getting a message meant directly for them, or just kind of—eavesdropping on an internal conversation, or some kind of a dream. No one knows if they would have tapped in a minute later or earlier if the message would have been different. None of the *Citlali* can sit in repose for prophecy —that's what they call it —for long. Wade says to do so for more than a few minutes a week is to invite madness. The energy that comes is so different than what they are used to. So what he was saying is, it's very difficult to actually ask Rhen a question. If they get enough *Citlali* together, they sometimes can do so, but still, she rarely will talk directly about Khain. Or the *foxen*. Wade always said it seemed like she had some kind of block from doing so. Like she's not allowed. Her messages always come in prophecy form about what the *shiften* should be doing or not doing, and they always need to be interpreted."

"It's all so complicated," Ella said.

Troy had had enough of the conversation. He got off the couch and headed out his wolf door to the front lawn. Maybe things would be more interesting out there. And he'd get to smell a *dragen* up close. How many *wolven* could say that?

Up close though, the *dragen* didn't look so good. He was big, but he looked sick and closed in on himself, like he'd shrunk recently. His smell had an undercurrent of something rotten in it. Like he was used up, worn out.

Mac was sitting on the hood of his car and the *dragen* was leaning against the side of it. The *felen*, *bearen*, and other *wolven* were congregating in a small group closer to the end of the road. Troy scented the air, separating Mac's smell from the *dragen's*. Mac smelled like fuck-yous and sex, but the *dragen* smelled like a strange mixture of fire and water, gold and scales, wind and royalty.

Mac raised a hand to him, then turned it into a one-finger salute. Troy lifted his leg and shot a stream of piss in the dirt at Mac's feet, then showed Mac his ass.

The *dragen* laughed. "Who's this?"

"That's Troy, Trevor's brother. Non-shifting."

"Nice to meet you Troy, I'm Graeme."

Troy turned back around and showed Graeme his teeth. Mac lifted his chin towards the house. "There really a one true mate in there?"

Troy nodded his head.

"Lucky bastard," Mac breathed, spitting on the grass. "So what, now we all pull sentry duty till fuckwad can get it up?"

"Isn't he your boss?" Graeme asked.

"So? He's still a fuckwad."

Graeme shook his head. "Our meeting was short, but I thought he seemed like a decent fellow. For a *wolven*." He glanced sideways at Mac when he said it, almost a dare.

Troy laughed. He was starting to like this Greeme.

Gray-em, and I'm rather pleased to make your

acquaintance, also. Your brother is no nonsense and all about the mission. I like that.

You speak ruhi, Troy said, sitting down on his haunches.

I do. Dragens rather prefer it. Our throats get cold with speech.

Cool.

Troy saw Mac frowning at the two of them and he grinned and looked at the house. Anything that pissed Mac off was ok with him.

CHAPTER 37

*T*roy walked back into the house. Night had fallen and no one was saying much outside anymore. Just sitting in their cars, quietly scenting the air.

Trevor and Ella were at the kitchen table, eating, seemingly recovered from their earlier fight. Trent was on the couch, his eyes closed, but his ears moving, an empty plate on the coffee table in front of him. Troy's dinner was there. Burgers with a side of salad, not french fries. What the crap? A little splash of mayonnaise was on the corner of his plate and he frowned at it. Disgusting, fatty gel. How Trent ate that crap he didn't know.

Ella's phone buzzed and she looked at it, then an undercurrent of fear and resigned anger filled the room. Like something she'd been dreading had finally happened. She flipped the phone over and didn't say a word.

"I'll get you another burger," Trevor said, standing up.

"I ate two already. I'm stuffed." Her sour smell cleared quickly as she focused on Trevor.

"You don't eat enough. How about some ice cream?"

"Trevor, did you watch me eat? I ate as much as you did. Do you want me fat?"

Trevor stopped mid-stride and turned around. "I want you happy. I want you full. I want you to eat dessert if you want it."

Troy jumped up to the couch, ate his two burgers in two bites, and ignored his salad. He watched the two at the table, interested in the way their smells shifted in response to every word they said and every word the other said. Ella shook her head and gave Trevor a look, but her smell said she was pleased.

"How about coffee? Or tea? Or wine? What do you like after dinner?"

Troy snorted. Trevor was lost completely. Light help him if something ever happened to that woman.

"Tea. With lots of cream."

"Coming up."

Ella's scent changed precipitously and even Trent raised his head to look at her. "I have to tell you something, Trevor. You tell me if it's important or not."

Trevor was the last to know how serious it really was. He moved about in the kitchen like he didn't have a care in the world. Like they were two ordinary beings with no demon at their door.

"Go for it."

"Ah—yeah, well. Ok."

Troy could see her gathering her thoughts and her will and he admired her for it. She looked down at the floor and spoke in a rush, the story that spilled out of her unbelievable, and yet totally believable at the same time.

Trevor had forgotten the tea and come to sit next to her, his hand on her leg. When she finished speaking he stared into her eyes for a few moments as she fidgeted, then spoke.

"How old were you?"

"I'm not totally sure. Ten, I think."

"Was this here, in Serenity?"

"No, down south more. I think we lived in Champaign-Urbana."

"You're certain it was him?"

"Well no, I'm not. Can he do that? Make himself look like a kid?"

"He can make himself look like anything he wants to."

Ella nodded, as if she expected that. "The voice was the same. I'll never forget that my entire life. The way it sounded. Like rocks rubbing against a chalkboard."

"Tell me again, how you repelled him?"

She shook her head, her face tight. "I don't know. I just did. It was nothing I tried to do."

"And last week, when you met him downtown. Was it the same way then?"

"Yes, I didn't try to do anything. I was scared out of my mind. So scared I couldn't even think. He touched me, and just like that, he was flying across the room into the wall. I felt the energy come out of me like a big pulse or something, but I didn't command it."

Trent's voice rumbled through all their heads. *Wade needs to know. Someone needs to contact the felen and wolven down south. See if a report was ever made and if so, what the immediate aftermath was.*

Trevor gathered Ella into his arms, smoothing her hair, massaging the muscles in her back. *I'll call Wade in a minute.*

Troy watched Ella and Trevor, noting how Trevor's scent

mixed with Ella's then transformed it, easing back Ella's fear and upset with an overpowering, all-consuming concern and touching care.

He felt the first stirrings of jealousy in his own chest and he hated it. He hopped off the couch and headed back outside.

***

Mac and Graeme were out of the car, leaning against it and talking softly in the darkness, facing the house. Both had a careful go-along to get-along scent about them, as they talked and learned each other's strength's weaknesses, quirks, likes, and dislikes.

Mac threw his head back and laughed at something Graeme said. Troy heard himself growl involuntarily. If Mac weren't such an asshole he wouldn't be so bad. He had a good sense of humor and was a strong fighter, someone you wanted on your side. But until Mac got over whatever issue he had with Trevor, he would always be enemy number two.

Mac saw him. "What's going on in there? Smells like dinner."

Ella saw Khain as a child. He came after her and she repelled him somehow. Same as she did last week.

Graeme hauled his ass off the car and stared hard at him. "No way—"

Mac took a step forward. "What, what did he say?"

Graeme repeated it and Mac gave a low whistle. "So it's true. Not only do they exist, but they're strong."

Very strong, Troy agreed.

Mac leaned back against the car again and waited for Graeme to look at him. "Do you think there's a one true mate for you, fire-breath?"

Graeme raised an eyebrow. "Thanks for the compliment. And I dinna. *Dragen* sex is rather... complicated. *Dragen* birth and babies even moreso. I am afraid I am destined to remain alone until The Light claims me."

"But ye got yer hand, right mate? Rosy and her five sisters won't never leave ya!" Mac called out boisterously in a passable Scottish accent, his words hanging limply in the air as Graeme ignored them.

Troy smelled a deep layer of sadness coming off Graeme. He tried not to feel pity for the male, but the prospect of never mating made it hard. Until he realized he was in the same situation. That made his jealousy of his brother a triple-edged sword.

Mac broke the silence again, softer this time. "That's hard."

Troy looked up, surprised.

Graeme nodded silently in the night, as did Troy.

The lights in the house went dim. Mac snarled. "Damn slacker, going to bed already while the rest of us pull guard duty."

The light in an upstairs window came on and a female form passed in front of it, then Trevor appeared, pulling the curtains. The light turned off, then a softer one flickered through the curtain, maybe a candle.

Graeme raised his chin. "I'd say he's doing exactly what he's supposed to be doing right about now to ensure the future of the *wolven*. More than any of the rest of us."

Troy chuckled, then outright laughed when he smelled jealousy come off Mac in waves.

If he and Graeme weren't getting any, at least Mac wasn't either. Not at that moment, anyway.

Mac's phone buzzed and he pulled it out and looked at it. "Damn. We gotta go."

"All of us?"

"No, we'll leave one *felen*, the *bearen*, Beckett, Trent and Troy. The *felen* are reporting Khain came through but just for a minute, not long enough for them to pinpoint his exact location, and now there's another disturbance in the *Pravus* near the bluff. It was nothing last time, but we can't take any chances.

Graeme nodded toward the house. "We aren't telling Lieutenant Burbank?"

Mac shook his head. "Like you said, he's busy."

CHAPTER 38

*K*hain paced, fire shooting out of his fingertips, his eyes imploding and reforming in his head. "Boe!" he shouted. "How long do preparations take?"

Boe yelled back something he couldn't hear. Khain let out a string of curses and paced harder. When he'd been in the *Ula*, he could feel the new *shiften* determination, and something like hope. He knew exactly what it was about. The Promised had been discovered and some mangy *shiften* was mounting her all night long. Maybe a hundred mangy *shiften*. The better to ensure her pregnancy took.

Light fuck it all! He hadn't been able to take her. The one he wanted over all others. He hadn't been able to stop the curse of the first Promised.

But maybe there was still time, if Boe would just finish with that *foxen* he had snatched from his evening walk. He'd gotten lucky with that one. Boe had recounted the locations of all the *foxen* houses he'd known when he'd lived in the *Ula*, warning Khain repeatedly that it was different up there now, and there might be nothing to find. But as soon as Khain had popped over to the second location, the air had been rich with the vibration of *foxen*, and he'd found one in a lamb's shake and been able to pop back over to the *Pravus* without alerting any *felen*. He hoped. He hated how the *felen* in the area were able to track him so quickly, but he couldn't move anywhere that they were more lax. This was where Rhen was, and somehow, she gave him strength.

Besides, he had plans along those lines. He hadn't quite perfected his vibrational subterfuge and it hadn't worked when he'd gone into the *Ula* like he thought it would, but he was closer. Maybe someday he'd be able to walk among the humans and the *felen* would be none the wiser.

Khain had marked the area where he'd found the *foxen* for future mining, but now he just wanted to get started.

"Argh!" he screamed, clenching blood from his fists, his eyes shooting all the way across the room and then taking a moment to regrow in his head. "Boe! I want him now! I wait no longer!"

"Yes, Sire," Boe said, pulling an inert *foxen* behind him on a cushion of air. Boe had learned a few tricks over the years.

Boe positioned himself directly in front of the angel's enclosure and Khain did the same. Boe turned to him questioningly and Khain nodded. He was ready.

Boe threw all of the locks on the tiny door at the bottom of the angel's enclosure. Khain stared on. The angel was weak and there would be no fight in him. The *byzant* metal Boe had mined from the inner edges of the *Pravus* did its job well.

Boe opened the door and slid the *foxen* in. Khain could

sense the *foxen's* thoughts and sensations at once, as the extreme light and heat of the angel woke it up as soon as it was inside.

The sight of the angel began to unwittingly destroy the *foxen's* mind and body, and as it disintegrated, Khain was treated to the inner thoughts and knowledge of the angel, as the two beings within the enclosure began to merge. The ground rippled under his feet as the angel woke and began to complain.

Khain had discovered this by accident, when Boe helped him wrestle the angel into the enclosure after they had first caught him, years ago, weakened by his forty nights of debauchery. Khain had no problem touching or looking at the angel, but Boe had done it only under great duress, and whenever he was too near the angel, Khain could hear it's innermost workings. Boe had almost lost his hands and arms that day, but Khain had been able to arrest most of the disintegration.

Still, the angel had put up a great fight, destroying so much of Khain's house that Boe had needed to move them while Khain slept off the damages from the battle.

When he'd woken, years later in human time, but only a few moments for him, he'd tried to make sense of what he'd heard from the angel's mind, but he couldn't. All he could get was a general location in the *Ula*. He'd gone to the *Ula*, in that location, and found a pack of human boys about to molest a human girl in a satisfying fashion. He'd stayed to watch, but something about the girl had called to him. He'd been unable to stay away from her. What had happened then had amazed and destroyed him. The girl had hurt him. Almost as bad as the angel had. A human girl!

He'd retreated back to the *Pravus* to recover, and try to

figure out the great and shameful mystery, which he never had. Until he'd thrown four more *foxen* in with the angel and learned to better interpret what he heard as they were dying. The girl was a Promised, the first Promised, the one with the most of the angel's blood in her, and somehow she had some sort of a power against him. A power he would know if he could. Would destroy if he could. Would harness if he could.

He'd tried again with the girl, a young woman now, more curious than anything, steeling himself beforehand with power, trying to drink from the angel like an emotional vampire stealing good thoughts and strong character.

Then he'd gone after her. The experience had left him shaken and harmed, but not as laid-out as he'd been the first time. Siphoning the angel's energy, her father's energy, before and after had helped greatly.

He hadn't been able to mark her, as she was a curious blank to him, unlike most humans. But he had her address from the angel and had watched her through the eyes of *foxen* in his sleep, until he knew what was going on with her life, and had overheard an appointment she had.

Khain pulled himself back to his home, where the angel rumbled angrily in his cage. He dialed in to the conduit that *foxen* had created, opening himself up to catch any bits of information he could.

An image flashed before him, of the house of the mother on the night the Promised was conceived. A young girl, a toddler maybe, creeping through the house, eating Cheerios out of the box and clutching a stuffed teddy. An older sister.

Khain raked what more he could out of the conduit before the *foxen* disappeared altogether, then began to make his plans.

CHAPTER 39

*E*lla woke up with a start, listening to the old farm-house creak in the early morning wind. Trevor lay beside her, breathing deeply, his naked form under only one sheet, when she'd needed two blankets, even curled up against him. Her eye traced his face and his shoulders, and the cut of his body under the sheet before she crept out of bed and stood, trying to decide what had woken her.

She found her pants and dug out her phone. Accalia had sent her two messages over the last few days but Ella didn't know how to answer them just yet. Accalia wrote fan fiction for all the members of the chat room they'd met in, and one memorable story Ella had read had dealt with almost the exact situation she was in right now. A human woman falling in love with a werewolf. Ella shook her head, for the first time wondering if perhaps she'd gone all the way crazy and what was happening to her was really a dream, or some mental-health-drug-induced nightmare.

Then she realized. She hadn't blacked out or walked in her sleep recently. She wasn't even hearing voices in her head anymore, unless you counted Trent and Troy, and she didn't think they counted, because they were real, weren't they?

She looked at Trevor on the bed again and wondered, remembering the feelings of surety she'd had when they'd first touched. The feeling that everything was right in her life—for the first time.

Before she could follow the line of questioning again, her phone came alive in her hand, the screen showing a crisp picture of the monster she knew as Khain that was so lifelike, she swore she could see his hands moving in space.

She stared, horrified, about to drop the phone and scream for Trevor, when Khain was replaced with her sister, Shay's makeup smeared, her mouth a rictus of terror.

The main selfie camera panned back to Khain and he held a finger to his lips, then said something. Slowly, she moved the phone to her ear, not wanting to let it get too close to her, but knowing she had no choice. When it was within six inches, she heard the man speak.

"Lose the wolf. All the wolves. Or she dies in front of you."

Oh, good God, that voice, it made her physically ill. And what did his words mean? How could she lose any of them? She looked around frantically, realizing if she went down the stairs, Trent and Troy would wake up immediately. They slept a lot lighter than Trevor did.

She tiptoed out the door, not daring to pull it shut behind her, all the way to the room on the other end of the hall. She went into the bathroom there and cowered in the very back corner, then turned the phone to her face again. The man was there. She held the phone up to her ear.

"Very good. Meet me at your house. One hour on the dot. Any *shiften* follow you or even know about it and your sister's blood will forever stain the nice carpet in your entryway."

"Wait!" Ella whispered fiercely. "I have no way to get to my house! I don't drive."

"Tell me where you are. I will come to you."

Ella considered, her throat squeezing off any air she might have been able to pull into her lungs. If he came to this big house, surely Trevor and Troy and Trent were a match for him. And there were more *shiften* in the driveway. But what if they couldn't? What if someone got hurt? Plus he would always know where Trevor lived after that. She bit her lip drawing blood. She had no idea of his limitations. Did he even know where she was? No, he couldn't, or he wouldn't be asking. She couldn't bring him here.

"I can be at the stone cat on the west end of Serenity in twenty minutes," she finally said. "You'll let my sister go?"

"Of course, that's how this works, isn't it?"

The phone went dead.

Ella curled a hand around her lower belly and wondered if she really was going to go to him.

Did she have a choice? Her sister might not treat her well. Her text the night before saying she was back in town had been less than kind, but her sister was still all she had left of the family she had been born into. And Shay was still a human being.

Right?

***

Ella ran down the road in her sneakers as fast as she could. The twenty minute deadline had come and gone. It had taken her almost ten of it to figure out how to get out of the house and off the property without anyone seeing her. Finally she had climbed onto an overhang on the roof and slid down a tree, tearing her pants in two places, then ran through the farmland and woods back towards the main road, skirting far around the *shiften* in the front of the house. Once she found the road, she turned left and ran for her sister's life.

Ahead, she saw the stone statue of the big cat guarding the entrance to Serenity. The three statues on the three major roads into town made more sense to her now. The red wolf, the stone cat, and the growling bear. There was so much she still didn't know about the area though. Were there *shiften* only in Serenity? Or everywhere? Would she live long enough to find out?

She had to believe Trevor would come for her. Somehow. If she could just hold on—

A rip in the world appeared in front of her and before she could even slow her steps, she ran right into it, tumbling down three feet, landing on a cracked, hard ground that hadn't existed a second before. She hit the ground hard, rolling, seeing fire spurt out of the dirt in front of her, and putting her feet out to stop her forward momentum. Her feet slid right into the fire and her pants blazed almost instantly. She stood and beat it out with her hands, then remained bent like that, breathing hard, not daring to look around.

"That's good, Promised. Stay just like that and I'll put all the young you want inside your belly."

Ella shot straight up and ran six or seven paces at a full sprint before she realized there was nowhere to go. She slowed, then stopped, as awful laughter surrounded her from everywhere.

She looked around hesitantly as she turned to face him, her stomach rolling. The terrain was bleak, unforgiving, like a desert made of fire. He stood in the center of it like a paragon of the landscape and his true form made her cower in spite of himself.

He scoffed. "Little girl, this is not what I look like." He clucked his tongue. "It's sad that I cannot be myself, even in my home, but your brain cannot conceive of the reality of my appearance. It would melt, just like it would if you actually saw your father, and we can't have that, can we?"

"My sister." Ella hated hearing her voice shake. She shouldn't have spoken at all.

"Ah yes, your sister. Regrettably, I must hold on to her for just a little longer. Just long enough—well, we'll discuss that in a bit. For now, we walk."

He pointed a finger at her and Ella felt herself be lifted into the air in some sort of a bubble. It skimmed along the ground, just high enough that most of the flames shooting out of the cracks in the ground only grazed the bottom of her feet. Ella didn't even try to get out. She scanned the landscape, caught in a crazy, deadly world that hadn't even existed to her a week before, and tried to think of her next move.

In reality, all she really wanted to do was puke, then have a very noisy breakdown and insist there was no way this could be happening.

CHAPTER 40

*T*revor awoke with a jerk, scrambling out of bed and falling into a defensive stance, the sheet wrapped around his legs, the remnants of his dream of The Destroyer taking Ella falling away. He stood and rubbed his hand over his face, shaking his head. It had been a bad one.

He padded into the bathroom, took care of business, then pulled on some shorts and headed downstairs. "Ella?"

The kitchen was empty and only the wolves were on the couch. Trent hopped to the floor immediately.

She never came down.

She's not upstairs. Panic filled him as he struggled to hold on to anything that was left of the dream.

Trent and Troy pushed past him up the stairs, their noses to the ground. Trevor let himself feel weak for just a moment, then he pulled it together and followed them.

They were in the bedroom at the far end of the hall, looking out the window at the screen that was punched out and laying discarded on the roof.

She went out this way.

"But why," Trevor almost whispered.

Does it matter? Get dressed. We're gone.

The wolves pushed past him again, down the stairs and out the door. Trevor pulled on his clothes, a silent prayer on his lips. He ran out the front door to find Graeme already marshaling Mac and the rest of the team, trying to explain to them that the One True Mate was gone.

Trevor barreled into him without thought, grabbing him around the neck. "How do you know? Tell me before I kill you."

Graeme's face remained neutral. *Troy told me as he ran around the house to the back.*

Trevor shook his head and let go. So help him, if the *dragen* was lying Trevor would carve him up into little pieces. He'd heard Troy say something but hadn't listened in his panic.

Trent's voice, from far away, but still clear in his head: *We've got the scent. Head out to the main road.*

"We've got the scent. Head out to the main road," Graeme repeated. Trevor stared at him for only an instant, then ran for his truck.

Trevor reversed to the end of his driveway, cars scattering in front of him, but Mac's flashy little car was in front of him. Trevor put the gas all the way to the floor, gaining on and then passing Mac and Graeme, only able to do so because the dirt road was rutted and potholed and Mac couldn't gain any real speed while he had to swerve around them. Trevor sailed right over them.

On the main but quiet farm road, he took a left, pressing his truck to ninety mph in a few seconds, and still Mac overtook him, passing him on the left like he was sitting still, whooping like he was at a drag race and not facing the worst event to happen to *wolven*, and Trevor especially, since their females had all been killed.

Trevor growled in the empty cab as he pushed his truck faster. Light help him, he was not a weak pup anymore. If Khain hurt Ella, Trevor would kill him, whether it was possible or not.

A half-mile ahead of him, Mac's brake lights flared and his car spun out as he tried to stop. Trevor slowed down, his eyes searching the side.

Trent and Troy waited, tails out, ears high. Trevor slammed on his brakes and skidded past them, then pulled to the side and got out, running back to his brothers.

The trail stops right here.

Stops?

It's just gone. And we smell him. Khain.

Trevor moaned deep in his throat. *How long ago?*

Thirty, maybe forty minutes.

Mac's car pulled up and Graeme and Mac got out, coming toward them. Trevor faced Graeme. "You have to open a hole to the *Pravus*. Just like you did before. I'm going over."

Graeme looked positively sick as he said, "I can't. Not for at least a day. It's not something that comes easy to one *dragen* alone, and once I do it, I need a week to recover, get my strength back."

Trevor launched himself at Graeme and fastened his fingers around the male's neck for the second time that day.

"You do it now. I'm not asking and I don't give a shit if you're tired or not."

The skin under Trevor's hands changed, grew hot, then scaly, then he was in the air holding on to a dragon's great, burning neck. One he couldn't even get his arms completely around, much less his hands. His brothers and Mac jumped back and Trevor dropped to the ground.

So much for ordering a *dragen* around.

***

Wade held up his hands. "Enough. Everyone calm down. Stop talking." The uproar and arguing in his office didn't quiet at all.

He sighed. He was not a yeller. He bound everyone in the room, except Trevor and Trent, for just a moment, binding the *dragen* too, just to see if he could. He could, but only for a moment. Trevor realized he was the only one still yelling and he stopped, looking around, then sank onto the couch, his head in his hands.

Wade let everyone go, one at a time. Troy first, who'd been barking and howling, just to be in the fray, Beckett second, their transplant from Mississippi, Harlan, the only member of the KSRT to have ever had a mate, Crew, his own personal failing, Canyon and Timber, the computer geniuses who rarely came out of the tunnels, Jaggar, the half-*wolven*, half-*felen* mystery, Sebastian, their ruined half-breed, and Mac last, the resident hothead and playboy. Graeme had already wriggled free and was staring at him, offended. Wade gave him a supplicatory nod.

"Everyone listen to me. Graeme says he can't get us over there for twenty-four hours. I say we use that time to plan our offensive. Nothing like this has ever been done before, and we need to have a strategy."

"She'll be dead in twenty-four hours," Trevor said from the couch, his voice shaking in a way Wade had never heard before.

"She won't," Wade said. "He—" He didn't finish that sentence. Trevor didn't need to hear the rest of it.

Trevor stood up. "Crew, can you get a message to Khain for me?"

Wade swallowed as he watched Crew, afraid he knew where this was going. Crew stared at Trevor for a long time, his eyes turbulent. Finally, he nodded. The other *wolven* in the room only stared, unable to believe what Trevor was asking. Or that Crew could provide it.

"Tell him he can have me. Tell him if he lets her go, I'll give myself to him. I'll hold my head up so he can cut my throat. Be sure to tell him of the two prophecies that involve me."

The room exploded again, while Trent and Troy forced their way into all the minds in the room who could hear them.

No!

Absolutely not!

"You can't do that!"

"You can't trust him!"

As the voices heightened and overlapped, even Mac chimed in. "We can fight him, boss. You don't have to do that."

Trevor only stared until they all stopped and fell silent, a single tear falling down his cheek. "You don't understand. I love her. I can't wait for twenty-four hours. I'll never make it." He ran a hand through his hair. "You don't even need me, just her. She is already kindled with my young."

He held his hands up and out and stared at them each in turn, Crew last. "You are a good team. The best of the best. I know you'll find a way to take Khain down without me. Mac will lead you there. Listen to him, listen to your instincts, run with the moon every chance you get, and never give up." He nodded at Crew. "Please."

Crew nodded back solemnly, then slipped out of the room. The KSRT murmured among themselves.

"*Wolven*, could I have a few minutes alone with Trevor," Wade said, nodding at Trent and Troy and telling them to come back in ten minutes.

Don't let him, Troy said, while Trent only seemed resigned.

The males filed out of the room.

Wade sat down next to Trevor.

"Don't try to talk me out of it."

"I'm not. I won't. But what makes you believe he'll honor his word, if he agrees to such a thing?"

"If he doesn't then I'll fight."

"Let us offer two males. Two have a better chance than one."

Trevor shook his head. "He won't take two. He's not stupid. He'll take me though. I know he is aware of the prophecies."

"Maybe he won't. Maybe he'll be afraid that you could fulfill them both if he lets you into his home."

Trevor didn't say anything for a long time. "All we can do is ask," he finally said.

Trent and Troy pushed their heads back into the room. "Come, come," Wade said, and the two wolves swarmed Trevor, pushing their heads under his big hands, climbing up onto the couch with him. Trevor put his arms around both his brothers and buried his face in Troy's fur. "I'm sorry. I'm sorry for everything. I love you both so much."

The wolves whined deep in their throats and hung their

heads as Trevor's tears bathed their fur. Wade walked across the room, leaving the family alone.

Thirty minutes later, Crew returned, his short hair standing straight up in tufts, his skin yellow and his eyes blazing. He leaned against the doorway, a bit of quiet desperation apparent in his face. His voice was quiet. "It's done. Be at the red wolf statue, alone, in an hour. He says Ella will be returned to the statue an hour after that. Says he's got her sister and we can have her too."

"Sister?" Trevor looked up, his face red, but his eyes dry. He shook his head and stood, the two wolves jumping to the floor.

Trevor walked across the room to Wade, holding out his hand. Wade pulled him into a wolf hug. "The Light will keep you."

Trevor stepped back and nodded, his face constricted. "You have someone take care of Ella. I can't pick. Crew maybe. Or Beckett. Anyone but Mac."

"You come back to us and I won't have to."

Trevor squeezed Wade's arm. "We'll see. Have Trent or Troy send me a message when she's safe. Have Crew send it if they can't reach me. If I'm still—"

Wade could see in his face that Trevor was fully prepared to give his life for his mate.

He only wished it didn't seem to be the only possible way to get her back.

CHAPTER 41

*T*revor stared into the eyes of the statue of the red wolf on the side of the street and wondered what it thought of what he was doing. He'd driven out alone, not knowing what Khain could or couldn't track from his world. Trevor would not be playing games with Ella's life. He'd made Wade swear no *shiften* would come within ten miles of the statue until they knew he was gone. He'd left his keys on the front seat of his truck. It would be Ella's when he was dead.

A car raced by on its way to somewhere else, leaving the scent of exhaust in the air. Trevor ignored it.

The eyes of the red wolf sucked him in to some sort of a communion with it, and Trevor imagined he heard its words in his mind.

Your young will carry your line. You will fulfill your destiny through them.

Trevor tore his eyes away and looked to the sky. His young. He wished that he could see them. Wished that he could be around and teach them to shift, to hunt, to fight, to live, to love. But that was not to be his fate. He wondered if he would be able to see them from the Haven. Watch them grow.

A shimmer in the air to his left, behind the sign that read *Welcome to Serenity* caught his attention and he turned that way slowly.

A perfect oval, as tall as he was, had opened in the air itself. The edges of the oval were green with the forest that was visible behind the sign, but when his eye traveled inward, all he saw was the yellow dust and red fire of Khain's world. This opening between the dimensions was nothing like the one Graeme had forced open. It was controlled. Easy. Simple.

He wondered if Khain would bring his body back to this world for Ella to bury. It didn't matter. He walked toward the hole, lifted his right foot, and stepped inside.

***

Wade watched the *felen* in the chair opposite him arch her back and close her eyes. That meant something, he was sure of it. He fiddled with the pens on his desk, feeling impotent as hell since Trevor was alone, Ella was taken, and nobody could do a thing about it.

"Khain did not come over. He opened a portal only," Kalista said, her eyes still closed. After a moment, she lifted her head and looked at him. "It is shut now."

"Is Trevor through it?"

Kalista shook her head. "I cannot tell that."

Wade took a deep breath. "Ok. We wait thirty minutes,

then we head out there. Thank you for your help." Light help them if they found only Trevor's body and no Ella.

Kalista nodded to him and stood to go. Wade kept his eyes on his desk. As she slid out his door a knock sounded on the doorjamb.

He looked up. "Graeme, come in."

Graeme did so, sitting in the chair Kalista had just vacated. His skin was sallow and his cheeks sunken. "I needed to talk to you."

Wade nodded. "I can feel your confliction. It is not your fault. You cannot work outside the confines of your own biology."

Graeme shook his head. "It's nae that. I wanted to try something."

"What?"

Graeme took a long shuddering breath. "*Dragen* work best in pairs or triplets. When my brothers were around, if we worked together we could open a portal to Khain's world, to any world actually, with ease and precision, and none of us needed to rest for more than an hour after."

Wade tapped his fingers against his chin. "There are other worlds than these?"

Graeme nodded grimly. "There are many, but all are different. *Shiften* do not belong in most."

"Your brothers, they are—?"

Graeme waved a hand and the scent of hot cinnamon filtered over to Wade. He grimaced. He hated cinnamon, but he liked Graeme.

"They are gone. But perhaps I could utilize the help of some of your team. It won't be easy or pretty, but there are many who hold the glimmer of the ability. I would open the portal. I would like to try to find two others to help me strengthen my powers with their minds."

Wade looked out the window, his mind turning it over. "And if you fail?"

"Then we have to wait longer until I can try again."

Wade shifted in his seat. He knew what Graeme wanted to try. A rescue mission. A dangerous one. "How many could you get over there?"

"Six maximum, and that includes me."

"How confident are you that you can do it?"

"It depends on who I have working with me. If I can test a few of your pack first, see what the landscape of their minds looks like, it would help me answer that question. It's risky no matter what, working with someone new to me, new to the concept of crossing over, but I think we have to try. That Lieutenant of yours needs bringing back."

Wade knew it. "Do you have any suggestions?"

Graeme nodded and a smile spread over his face as if he was thinking of a *shiften* he liked. "Troy."

"Troy?" Wade chuckled, surprised. That was the last name he expected to hear.

"He's quick. He's fluent in *Ruhi*, which is a *dragen*'s native tongue. He and I get along and affinity always helps. I think he can do it."

"Good, anyone else?"

Graeme looked less sure about his next suggestion. "Crew?"

Wade put his hands on the desk in front of him. "Crew is strong, but possibly not completely stable after contacting Khain the way he did earlier. He might not be your best choice."

Graeme nodded. "I was already thinking that."

"What about me?"

Graeme shook his head quickly. "*Citlali* are always a bad

idea. They have a hard time not taking over, and if you take over, the portal will be destroyed. I have tried before. No offense to you, it's nae worked before and I dinnae think we should risk it this time."

Wade pressed his lips together, his mind running over everyone he could possibly offer. "Then may I suggest Trent."

"The other brother?"

"Yes. He may not know you, but he and Troy have great affinity for each other. He is also strong in *ruhi*, and smart."

Graeme stood. "Do you know where I can find them?"

Wade stood also. "I'll take you there."

Doing something, even a long shot, was far better than sitting in his chair and waiting to hear that his friend had been killed.

CHAPTER 42

Trevor looked around slowly, expecting an ambush that he would not defend against. But nothing. The entire place reeked of Khain, or maybe Khain reeked of the *Pravus*, but he was nowhere in sight. Trevor turned around, back to the portal he had stepped through, but it was gone. The only way now was forward.

The landscape weighed on him. Not one tree in sight. The dirt under his feet felt hard-packed and dead, nothing like the soft, springy earth of his world. Above him, a flat, sand-tan ceiling that looked so different from the gorgeous blue of his world, that Trevor felt like crying. Khain didn't have to kill him. Just leave him in this empty world for too long and he would take his own life. *Shiften* were not meant to live in a place like the *Pravus*.

A spurt of flame shot through a crack next to him, six

feet in the air and Trevor jumped away from it, fear replacing despair. Don't straddle the cracks, got it.

He began walking, just for something to do. Khain would come get him when he was ready. As long as Ella was released, Khain could do whatever he liked.

On the horizon, slightly to his left, a large shape shimmered and seemed to come into view as he walked. Trevor shifted his direction to head toward it. In another twenty minutes he could tell what it was. A house. Or more accurately, a palace of some sort, stuck in the middle of nowhere, flames surrounding it on all sides, like some sort of backwards moat.

Gray towers and parapets rose above the flames, making Trevor think of a castle, instead of a palace, but then they shifted and a drawbridge appeared. Trevor looked away. Khain was playing tricks on him, but there was no doubt that was where he was to go.

He walked faster, but Khain's home seemed to move farther away. Fuck it. Trevor let loose of the shackles on his wolf in his mind and shifted as he walked, dropping to the hard ground, his clothes, badge, and gun, falling off of him. He would not need them where he was going.

He loped across the harsh landscape, setting a comfortable pace, springing out of the way easily as more fire blasts shot up through the ground. Now Khain's home looked bigger with every passing mile Trevor covered. When he drew close enough to it that the wall of flame around it threatened to singe his whiskers he stopped.

Trevor turned left, then right, his wolf looking for a way in. Trevor had hoped that shifting would make what he was about to do easier, would make saying good-bye to Ella easier. But no, his wolf was just as in love with her as he was. The yearning and sadness hadn't lessened at all.

What had changed was his plan. His wolf was more bloodthirsty than he, willing to wait until Ella was safe, and then he would go for Khain's throat. Better to die with his fangs buried in Khain's jugular—or whatever was under that foul skin—than to sit passively by and let Khain carry out whatever plans he had.

A loud horn blared, startling Trevor, but his wolf held his ground, ears ticked high, hackles raised, tail straight out behind him, moving slowly. A wall of flame approximately three feet wide dropped into the ground, exposing a path for him to follow.

The smells came at him thick and fast, of burnt skin and rotten things, making Trevor realize if he had been in his human form, he would not have been able to continue, but his wolf was made of stronger stuff.

Trevor passed through the very small opening into Khain's home.

The flame shot up again behind him, locking him in. No matter, as long as Ella got out.

Ella. He could smell her.

He turned toward the scent and headed in, ever deeper.

***

Trevor wandered around inside the strangely circular… building for thirty minutes without finding Ella. Her scent never got stronger or weaker, just stayed the same, like he would find her around the next turn, which he never did. He reached out with his mind and was so disheartened when only an empty whooshing sound came back that he almost couldn't try again. But he did, to his brothers. He got nothing from them either. It was like the *Pravus* sucked the communication right out of him and burned it up before it could get where it should go.

The marble-looking floor was hot beneath his feet, but he ignored it, just as he ignored everything else. His mind was completely focused on one thing only: finding Ella.

To his left, as he wound his way ever downward on the seeming marble corkscrew into the ground, a large metal enclosure sat suspended in the air, how Trevor couldn't see, but it did not steal his focus.

He continued to walk quickly, purposefully, until finally he came to a great door. The door was taller than any door had any right to be, stretching up as far as he had walked, to the upper sections of where he had just come from.

Trevor looked up. Sat back on his haunches. Waited for something to happen. When nothing did, he decided to try to contact one more being.

I am not impressed, he sent to the Great Destroyer himself.

Thick laughter filled his head and Trevor knew he was about to finally get what had long been his greatest wish.

A face to face with his species' greatest nemesis.

CHAPTER 43

*E*lla paced back and forth in the large clear enclosure she and her sister were confined in. She shuddered as she looked around. More like a cell, with a bed and a toilet and a sink, but some see-through material surrounding them on four sides and even over the top as a kind of ceiling. It reminded her of Hannibal Lecter's cell in the Silence of the Lambs and the comparison was what made her shudder. She had found that movie to be super creepy and never made it past the part where the guy in the cell next to Lecter had thrown his jizz on Jodie Foster.

Lucky her, she was now living in her own personal horror movie. She stared at her sister, unconscious on the bed, irritated at herself. She was so stupid! Of course Khain wasn't going to release her sister and of course she was now trapped down here, too. If she were in a real horror movie she would have been the first to be killed, the stupid bimbo who says,

"What's that noise?" and goes off to investigate it all by herself, all the while laughing and telling her boyfriend, "knock it off, it's not funny anymore," all the way up until her—

Ella pulled her thoughts away from that line of thinking. Trevor would get her out of here. She had to believe that. And if he or his brothers or his teammates got killed trying to, it would be all her fault. She would carry that guilt for life as the stupid girl who trusted the demon—

"Argh," she said, pounding her fists into her thighs and turning around. She had to quit whatever trips her mind kept trying to take her on and find a way out of this. She wouldn't be able to carry her sister out, but she couldn't just sit there and wait to be rescued, either.

She ran her hands over the wall in front of her again, looking for a crack, a seam, anything. Some part of her mind still drifted as she worked, attracted to the metal cylinder she'd seen in the center of the castle on her way in. The pull of it was strong and she thought she knew why. No, she knew she knew why. Her father was in there.

Her father the angel. Which made her half angel. Which was still incredibly hard for her to believe. She didn't have wings or a halo and she didn't glow in her sleep or anything like that. She seemed 100% human and totally vulnerable.

A horrid, twisted laughing filled her mind, making her freeze and look down towards the rest of the room. Her... cell was perched on a balcony on one side of what was big enough to be a dungeon, although she would call it a laboratory of some sort, with large monitors covering the walls, even though she could see no computers. As she watched, the room shifted with the laughter, losing its light, modern look and becoming something else altogether. A lair of a monster, with cobwebs brushing the walls and a molten pit for a floor. She blinked and the image retreated, showing her the laboratory again.

Queasiness swept over Ella, since she couldn't believe what her eyes were showing her. She felt the floor vibrate under her feet as the colossal door to the far end of the room began to open and Khain appeared in the center of the room as if by magic.

But not the Khain she had seen before, who had walked her there in the bubble with the flames brushing at the soles of her shoes. He had been eight feet tall, max. Taller than any human, tall and wide enough to be terrifying, but what stood before her now was a giant. Fifty feet tall with dark hair that brushed the ceiling and hands that could pick up a semi-truck like a child's toy.

Ella sat backwards on the floor with a thump, unable to keep her footing. If this was the real Khain, they were doomed. *Wolven* did not grow like that. A hundred *wolven* could not hurt that monstrosity.

Her eye was drawn to the door, which had opened fully. On the other side of it, one wolf. Her wolf. He had come, and with a sudden, cold clarity she knew how and for what.

He was sacrificing himself for her.

"Trevor, no!" she screamed, scrambling to her feet and throwing herself against the wall of her enclosure. "Go back! Get the others! I'm fine. I'll be fine. You can't..."

Her wolf twisted his strong, warrior's face towards her, and she swore she could see the love shining out of his eyes, even from so far away. Tears streamed down her face. She'd just found him. She couldn't lose him already. He couldn't be taken from her because of something she did, some horrible decision she'd made under duress. She was nothing without him. Just some awkward girl who always made the wrong choice, did the wrong thing.

Khain raised a hand towards Trevor, making Ella scream at the top of her lungs. A bolt of thick red light shot out of his hand straight at Trevor, lifting him off the floor and crumpling his body in pain.

Ella screamed louder, helpless in the face of her mate's torture and oncoming death, reaching her hands to her head to tear at her hair as her scream raised in crescendo, rebounding off the walls and coming back to her.

Her voice cut off as a thick pulse of invisible energy shot out of her body, knocking the walls of her enclosure flat and pushing the ceiling up into the air where it hit the wall behind them and rebounded toward Khain, the pulse of energy that had come out of her pushing it faster and faster until it and the pulse hit him and his red light, blasting the red light into nothingness as Khain staggered backwards, his skin and clothes pushing in with the invisible shockwave.

He turned toward her, eyes blazing in their sockets, bleeding black blood from a thousand tiny cuts, the ooze dropping to the ground and incinerating instantly in what now looked only like a monster's lair, Khain's feet submerged in the red lava. Surprise showed on his face but he did not waste time verbalizing it.

Khain lifted his hand again, toward Ella, and she knew she had only a second before he struck.

CHAPTER 44

*E*lla tried to force her body to send out the energy again but she didn't know how she had done it. She tried to gather, to send, to defend herself in some way but it was not coming to her.

She looked around wildly for somewhere to hide and her eyes fell upon her mate, still outside the door, his body limp, on its right side. Even from so far away, she could see his *renqua*, a white boomerang against his black fur. She longed to touch it just one more time. Feel the sleek of his fur under her fingers. What she could not see was if he was breathing.

The scent of burnt wolf fur reached her and a hot anger spread through her. She faced Khain, hands clenched into fists, opening her mouth and with a sudden stiff outrage, she screamed out the anger at what he had done. No words, only a primal scream that was a poor substitute for the pulse of energy she had somehow emitted before.

In front of her, Khain's hand pulsed brightly and the energy shot out of him towards her.

With her scream, her own power came, full and powerful, shooting out from her body, meeting Khain's light as it left his fingertips and pushing it backwards towards him, then making him stumble and fall as the full force of her energy hit him.

Ella didn't wait around to see exactly what kind of damage she had done. She had to get to Trevor. Had to protect him anyway she could. She scrambled to the edge of the balcony that now looked like a rocky outcropping, sensing she was seeing the true nature of the room now, and that the laboratory had only been an illusion. Rough, wooden stairs were built into the edge of the rock. She scrambled down them, wanting to run two at a time, but afraid she would fall and tumble all the way to the bottom, breaking her neck.

She chanced a glance at Khain as she ran, pleased to see he had shrunk to almost half his former size, which still put him at twenty-five feet tall, and that he was running his hands over his skin, possibly healing the cuts that covered him.

Ella ran for her life, and for the life of her mate, to the bottom of the stairs. When she got there, she saw a small man cowering in what looked to be a large crack in the wall. She almost stopped, but she just couldn't. Trevor was all that mattered.

She skidded to a stop just outside the door and dropped to her knees next to her mate. His fur, his beautiful black and gray and silver fur was burnt to the skin in places and badly singed in others. His eyes were shut and sunken and his ears were burnt and curled in on themselves. "Oh God, no," she breathed, holding her hands over his body, not daring to touch him, not wanting to hurt him. "I'm so sorry. It's all my fault." Worse, she still couldn't tell if he was breathing. If he was, it was shallow.

Thick, fat anger, hot enough to burn the place down, filled her soul. He'd been so beautiful, so perfect, so strong and noble. And now he was twisted and burnt on the floor. All because he'd wanted to help her.

"I do love you, Trevor, I just didn't know it until now." she whispered, feeling it inside her, strong enough to force the anger aside for just a moment. She placed one chaste kiss on his burnt muzzle, then stood and faced the demon. Time for her to find out exactly what she could do.

Could she kill the demon? Avenge her mate?

Or not?

CHAPTER 45

*T*roy picked his way slowly through the woods over the bluff as night fell and the sun disappeared from the sky, Trent beside him. He couldn't help but feel that they were on a *foxen's* errand, one doomed to fail. But he was willing to try. Graeme had schooled them both for hours on exactly what to do, until Troy had snapped at him and told him if they didn't do it soon, there would be no sense anymore. None of them had been surprised when Ella had never appeared at the appointed time.

Graeme and Kalista walked ahead of them, talking softly, Kalista occasionally pointing to an area of the ground and Graeme always shaking his head.

Choose, Trent rumbled, apparently as ready to be moving as Troy was.

Graeme stopped and looked back at them. *You're right. I choose here. It's as good a place as any.*

He turned to Kalista. "Thank you, Madame, for your help. We must prepare now."

She nodded, all business, no flirtatiousness, which was rare for her. "I would like to come."

Graeme's eyes narrowed. "Come, to the *Pravus*?"

"To the fight. I have fought him before, which is more than you can say for any of the rest of you."

"You have not heard of the battle of Loch Bee, then, Madame?"

"Just Kalista, please." She turned her head to look at him from just one eye. "That was you?"

"Aye, and my brothers."

"But that was, what, six centuries ago?"

"*Dragen* live longer than other *shiften*."

She nodded. "Consider it. I won't be leaving until it's done."

Graeme bowed slightly, looking every bit the Scottish lord, even in his work boots and clothes. "Thank you Kalista of the *felen*, I shall talk to Wade."

Trent and Troy stopped on exactly the spot where Graeme stood. Troy whined and tossed his head.

"Calm, gentle wolf. We will move soon enough."

Troy flashed his teeth at Graeme, but the male was already moving through the underbrush, gathering up the rest of their team.

Within a few minutes, Harlan, Mac, and Beckett stood near them, the three of them stomping their feet and swinging their arms as if warming up for the Olympics.

Wade arrived with Graeme. "Just shift already, you aren't going over there like that and nobody's getting any gold medals." The three males did what they were told, dropping to the earth, their clothes falling off in small, messy piles.

An earthquake shook the area, making the tree limbs rustle and the ground move under their feet. Troy looked around guardedly. Small earthquakes were not entirely rare in Illinois, but there had been no warning, no disturbance that any of them had noticed beforehand, and that was unheard of. Mac sat on his haunches and howled away his agitation.

Wade squared his feet, holding up a hand until Mac stopped, then spoke loud enough for Kalista, waiting twenty feet away in the woods, to hear. "No, you say only six can go, it's going to be this six. All KSRT." He waved Kalista over. "If all six go through the portal and it's still open, you can go through, but be warned, if it shuts on you, you will be cut in half."

Kalista nodded and Troy could almost see her ears twitch.

Graeme stepped in the center of the wolves. "I go first, then Troy, then Trent. I am certain we will be able to open the portal, but there is a chance we won't be able to hold it open long enough for everyone. If it starts closing you get through fast or stay on this side. You don't want half of your body here and half there, believe me. The three of us *must* go together and first or we won't be able to make a big enough portal to get back if one gets stuck over here. Once over there, *ruhi* does not work there, for us anyway. Our communication will be nil. We stick together. We grab Trevor and the one true mate."

Ella, her name is Ella, Trent interrupted.

"Ella, of course. As soon as we have them, we will open the portal. You three, if you have to hold Khain off of us while we are doing that, you do so, but keep an eye on the portal. You three leave first and take Trevor and Ella. If they have to be carried, you'll have to shift. We three will come last. We could be under heavy fire so it will have to be quick."

He stopped talking and looked around for agreement. All the wolves nodded. Mac barked his approval.

Wade stepped forward. "If you can only bring one back, it must be Ella. Is that understood?" he said, his voice apologetic, but firm as he stared at Trent and Troy.

Don't worry about Troy and me, Trent said. *We love Ella like we love Trevor and we understand the stakes.*

Troy shook his head till his ears flew. Trent was eloquent as shit. But damned if he was going to leave anyone. Even Mac.

Another earthquake rattled the bluff, as much of a surprise as the first one.

Graeme squared his shoulders. "I'm afraid that's not good. They're fighting over there."

Mac howled again and Troy couldn't take it anymore. *Now! Let's do it!*

"As you wish." Graeme disappeared and a red and yellow dragon stood in his place, no bigger than Troy.

Troy snorted. *I thought you fellas were bigger.*

Just wait. The dragon's neck stretched out and Troy felt a gathering in the air, like a strong wind, but centered only in front of him. A tiny black spot appeared in his line of sight. He stared into the dragon's eyes, concentrating as hard as he could, doing what the dragon had told him to, thinking of what Graeme had described the *Pravus* as being like, and lending the dragon all the mental energy he had. Next to him, he could hear a deep mental rumble that sounded almost like a cat purring, as his brother did the same.

"Go boys, you're doing it," Wade whispered.

The spot widened, grew, and leaves began to lift from the ground. When the black spot was a foot across, the leaves trembled and flew directly into it, along with some dirt and twigs. Troy watched as a moth whipped in front of his face and into the hole.

Sorry, little flying buddy.

Concentrate! his brother threw at him.

Right, sorry. Troy doubled down, fixing the image of the *Pravus* in his mind and giving it everything he had. The hole grew wide enough to allow him in. He prepared to jump, still straining as hard as he could. Graeme went through first, then Trent, then Troy last. The hole slipped as he was jumping but when he landed hard on the other side, he turned and stared at it, holding the image in his mind still, not daring to look around at reality.

The hole was closing at an alarming rate. It was Graeme. He was flagging. Troy doubled down again, but he couldn't hold it by himself. He felt his mind slipping, ripping free from where it had always been.

Mac's white wolf sailed through the hole, landing between Troy and Trent, even as the hole fell shut and disappeared, clipping a bit of the hair off Mac's tail.

Shit. They hadn't all made it through! Troy whirled around to see Graeme passed out on the pale, dusty ground, a bit of fire coming up from a crack and hitting him on his scaly cheek that was pressed against it.

Troy latched onto the dragon's tail as gently as he could, pulling the dragon away from the fire, though why he bothered he didn't know, dragons couldn't be burnt, right?

That done, he looked around at the bleak and empty landscape to their fronts, and the wall of fire twenty feet to their backs.

What were they going to do now?

CHAPTER 46

*E*lla faced the too-big Khain and watched him grow before her eyes, the cuts her offensive had made on him healing like they'd never been there.

So, your father gave you power to fight me with. Too bad. He should have kept some for himself. Then he wouldn't have been my prisoner for so long.

Ella put a hand to her head. Khain's voice in there was just as awful as what she had heard before, and it made her brain crawl.

She ignored what he was saying. Whether or not he had her father was irrelevant. He was trying to distract her. Trying to make her forget what she was about to do.

She stood in front of Trevor, arms out, and let loose the anger inside her with a scream, just like she had before. But this time, the energy did not come. She tried again, her cry echoing off the walls of the dark chamber as Khain squared his shoulders, waiting for her onslaught.

Curdled laughter entered her head. *Let me just help you out, shall I?*

Khain held out both his hands and Ella could see the power building in them. She was about to be flash-fried. Terror built in her chest and she retreated, throwing her body over Trevor's.

But the pulse came as soon as her body touched Trevor's. It stopped the double-wide flame Khain had sent at her and hit him square in the face and body, knocking him backward against the far wall, but not incapacitating him.

Trevor did not respond in the slightest.

Ella felt a great wind move over her and she looked up to see what could only be a dragon the size of a cow flying at full spccd towards a winded Khain. Ella gaped, watching it as it grew to match Khain's size, then opened its mouth and spit fire at Khain. Fire against fire, although she could tell the dragon's fire was different than Khain's, and it hurt him.

Her attention was drawn by a pounding of feet behind her, almost like a stampede. She turned, never so glad in her life to see Troy and Trent, and another wolf, an all-white one, running at them full speed. The wolves separated, running around her and Trevor like water, all heading for Khain, launching themselves at him. She could see their feet burning as they jumped from rock to rock over the barely cooled lava.

Ella held her breath as all three wolves jumped on Khain, biting and tearing, their mouths and noses filling with that awful black blood, their snarls terrifying her, even from across the room.

With a great bellow, Khain pushed himself away from the fray, swatting the wolves off his knees and running towards her. Ella threw herself over Trevor, knowing she was poor protection.

Khain was shrinking as he ran, his gray face set, his eyes on the door behind her. The dragon shrieked and flew for him, but Khain feinted and shot straight up into the ceiling instead, seeming to disappear completely.

Ella stared after him for a long time. Even when the wolves came to her, whining and pushing Trevor's limp body with their noses, she could not look away. The white wolf transformed. She knew him. Mac. And he was naked. She kept her eyes averted as he lifted her mate from the floor.

She scrambled to her feet, still not looking. "Be careful with him, he's hurt," she said.

"Graeme, let's go!" Mac shouted at the ceiling where Graeme was flying in slow circles. "Get us out of here."

The dragon stared hard at their group, and Ella felt wind pick up around her. Ash began to fly through the air, then in front of her, a small black hole opened. Through it, she could see only darkness, but the smell! It smelled of home. She waited for the hole to grow bigger but it didn't. Trent and Troy were staring at the hole with the same concentration the dragon seemed to have. She held her breath and prayed whatever they were doing would work.

A piece of whirling ash landed on her arm, burning her. She slapped it away. And still the hole did not grow. The dragon dropped to the outcropping she had been held on and stretched out its somehow graceful neck. She could see his eyes glow purple.

"Come on, come on," Mac urged.

Trent barked once, deep and low and Troy whined and sat down, his neck stretched in the same way the dragon's was.

"Yes!" Mac exclaimed and Ella snapped her head to the portal. It was almost the size of a small window.

"You first," Mac said, pushing at her with Trevor's body. Ella was not about to argue. She jumped at it, having to leap through, since it hung four feet above the floor.

She hit the ground rolling, sticks and twigs scratching her skin, leaves gathering in her hair. Above her, the moon shone brightly, welcoming her. She scrambled to her feet, watching Mac jump through, drop Trevor with a thump, then turn and yell through the hole.

Oh no. "My sister!" she screamed, but Mac ignored her, yelling encouragement at the others. A man came next that she'd never seen before, diving like he was going headfirst into water. No, she'd seen him. The man in the wall crack. Next came Trent, who jumped neatly through, then turned and focused on the portal. Then was Troy and he did the same.

Ella waited for the dragon to come, knowing they couldn't risk any more lives for her sister. Tears streamed down her face. She'd always hoped that one day they would reconcile. Now that would never happen.

The dragon's snout was first and she wondered if he was going to make it, the hole was closing already. But then his neck and body came, and in his great claws, he held the limp body of her sister. He pulled his tail close to his body and tumbled to the ground as the hole closed with a deafening snap.

Ella couldn't believe it. She sat in the dirt and underbrush for long enough to pinch herself, then scrambled to her feet and ran to Trevor.

Trent and Troy flopped over on their sides and panted, with almost identical wolfy smiles that she had to ignore. Mac whooped up at the moon, then looked around. "Where are we?"

Troy sat up, pointed his nose at the moon, and howled. "Arooooo."

The sound, long and low, made Ella think of Trevor. She bent over him, placing her head on his chest. "Guys, I don't think he's breathing," she said, her voice hitching.

They all scrambled to her as an answering howl came from their left. Then another, then another.

"Wade will be here soon," Mac said, standing straight and tall, not caring at all that he was naked.

"Can't you heal Trevor?"

"We can take him to a doctor, but that's all. Wolves who can't shift can't heal."

"A doctor..." Ella stared down at him, trying to remember how to do CPR on a canine. Her brain wouldn't work right. Her vision blurred as tears dropped from her eyes.

A voice filled her head, deep, with a thick brogue accent. *Bite me.*

She looked up. It could only be the dragon. *What?* Troy's voice.

Someone has to bite me. I'm too weak. Dragon's blood has healing properties.

Troy looked up, but Ella could tell he hesitated to leave Trevor. "Mac, the dragon says to bite him. Dragon blood has healing properties."

Mac looked at the dragon, laying on its side in the leaves and underbrush, then looked at Trevor. He grabbed Trevor by the haunches and hauled him over to Graeme, then shifted. Ella held her breath, thinking if she could go without breath for that long, so could Trevor. She prayed.

Mac's wolf latched onto a meaty part of the dragon's front arm? paw? claw? and bit, growling as he did so. Fat drops of blood appeared at once, reddening Mac's muzzle. Ella rushed forward and moved the dragon's arm over Trevor's muzzle, trying to drip blood into his mouth. One big drop, then two, then three.

That's enough, the dragon sighed in her mind.

What about you? Do you need some?

My own blood will nae heal me.

Ella stared at Trevor, about to ask how long it would take, when before her eyes, he shifted, his muzzle shortening, becoming a proper nose, his fur pulling into his skin, his ears shortening and moving, his body lengthening.

In the moonlight, though, she still couldn't tell if he was breathing. She dropped to her knees and put her ear to his mouth, looking down his body.

Her eyes went wide as she saw he had an erection, bigger than she had ever seen it. Trent and Troy scrambled backwards.

That's a side effect of dragon's blood. He'll have it for a few hours. But it does mean he'll be fine.

Ella didn't know if she should laugh or cry. So she did both.

Um, Mr. Dragon, sir, can I give some of your blood to my sister? she asked, thinking it awful of her, but unable to help herself.

Of course. Take what you need quickly, before it clots. I'm going to sleep now.

Ella touched him gingerly, not wanting to hurt him. She cupped her hands and gathered a few drops of blood from him, the same as she had for Trevor and walked to her sister, tipping the blood between her lips.

Then she returned to Trevor's side to wait.

CHAPTER 47

*E*lla sat in the chair beside her sister and watched her slack face as the monitors and IV machines beeped mercilessly around them.

She could hear her guard out in the hall, swapping stories. Mac's voice was the loudest.

"You should have seen it. He came to, then breathed this spout of blue fire that totally obliterated Khain's fire. We could run through it. It didn't burn us at all! Then when we got down into the dungeon, he quadrupled in size and flew right at Khain's face. That Graeme, he's an all right guy. I'll be happy when he's up and moving again." His voice lowered a bit, not quite as excited, but not hostile. "Good job adding him to the team, boss."

Ella smiled as she heard the surprise in Trevor's voice. "It was all Wade. I was against it."

"Eh, you had a good reason, I'm sure, but he's staying right?"

"That male can stay as long as he likes. I might even give him your job, Mac."

A wave of laughter greeted that, but then another male spoke. She wasn't sure if he was Harlan or Crew. She didn't have their voices down yet, although she didn't think Crew talked much, so maybe it was Harlan.

"Any word on the *foxen*?"

"Nope, it's been three days and no one has been able to find him. We lost his scent in a stream."

"What's our operating belief? Was he there against his will or not?"

Trevor sighed. "We have no way of knowing. We just need to find him and question him. Oh, hi Doc."

"Gentlemen."

The curtain moved and Shay's doctor moved into the room. "Hello, Miss Carmi, good to see you."

Ella smiled. "Thank you, doctor."

"I have some news about your sister. Unfortunately nothing has changed. Her vital signs remain strong, but her brain is still dormant. No activity at all."

Ella dropped her eyes. How was that news?

"Miss Carmi, did you realize Shay is pregnant?"

Ella sucked in a breath, feeling its coldness as it passed over her teeth. She half-stood, then dropped into the chair again.

She looked towards the door, but heard only happy banter between the males out there.

"I didn't, doctor, and I need you to do me a favor. Don't tell anyone else."

The doctor's eyes narrowed but he nodded. "Of course. We would not. Doctor-patient confidentiality."

Ella nodded. "Good. And you still plan on moving her tomorrow?"

"Yes, to the facility we talked about."

"Thank you, doctor."

He left quietly and Ella took Shay's hand. It was cold. Or Ella was cold. She wondered if there was any place in her new life for her sister, if her sister ever recovered. The dragon blood had not helped and Ella didn't know if anything could. The doctors seemed to think not.

An image flashed through her brain, the pendant she'd found while going through the boxes at her aunt's home with the angel on one side and the wolf on the other. Ella could see it perfectly in her mind. An angel… and a wolf. That was no coincidence. She would give anything to have that item back again. Mrs. White had moved her business to another shop. She would visit and try to buy it back as soon as—well, as soon as she could.

Trevor came in the room. "Sorry to rush you El, but we are out of time."

Ella stood, looking at her sister one last time. "No. I'm ready." She took Trevor's hand and walked out of the room, on her way to be mated, finally.

CHAPTER 48

*S*uch pretty hair," Lorna said, looking at Ella in the mirror as she twisted Ella's black hair up above her head. "And your dress? It's going to be perfect. Worthy of being seen at the first mating ceremony in twenty-eight years."

"I didn't realize your mating ceremonies were so much like human weddings," Ella said, trying to hold still as Lorna pushed bobby pins into her hair. They were at Ella's aunt's house, getting Ella prettied up. She could hear her guards joking and laughing in the living room, but Trevor wasn't there. He was already at the farm property they'd rented one county over to have the ceremony at. He'd calmed down in the days since they'd returned from the *pravus*, letting the KSRT look at her and talk to her and even be her constant guard without him there. Even Mac, as long as Trent and Troy were with him. Ella hoped the guard thing would ease up once they were mated. It was getting tiring.

"Of course, honey, we gotta pass for humans. We can't go doing too much too different."

"What was your mating ceremony to Wade like?"

Lorna laughed. "That was a long time ago. I barely remember. But he was handsome as all get-out in his tuxedo. I couldn't wait to get to our honeymoon suite after."

"Oh, a honeymoon? Do you think we will go on one?"

"Perhaps, though how you are going to drag seven *wolven* and maybe a *dragen* after you, I don't know."

"That's the issue, isn't it?" Ella pushed it out of her mind. She wasn't going to let anything ruin the day. Her day. Her… wedding.

"So is anything different than at a human wedding?" she asked.

Lorna tsked her tongue. "Only if you haven't been claimed yet, but I'm sure Trevor did that long ago, pretty little thing like you, he wouldn't be able to help himself."

"Claimed?" Ella felt tiny tendrils of panic flutter in her belly. She had no idea.

"You know, where he bites you right here." Lorna touched the back of her shoulder. "Right where your *renqua* would be if you had one."

"Bites me? He's going to bite me?"

Lorna stared at her in the mirror for a second, then moved to the front of her and leaned down. "You mean to tell me he hasn't already?"

"No, will it hurt?"

Lorna stood and clasped her hand to her heart. "Wow, that is special then. I haven't seen a claiming in a hundred years."

"Seen? What?" Ella had an image of a dozen *wolven* watching her and Trevor together. She couldn't do that.

"Don't worry, honey, we don't actually watch, but if a female hasn't been claimed by her male yet, the claiming happens right there at the ceremony, in a special room behind the bower, or sometimes right in the woods, depending on the size of the ceremony. But the males who stand for your mate don't let anyone near the couple. Sometimes, Rhen's blessing can be seen in the sky afterwards."

"Rhen's blessing?"

"Oh child, it's beautiful, thick clouds in the shape of the couple's *renqua*s, combining in the sky, with the sun shining behind them like Rhen herself smiling down on the couple."

"Why do you think he hasn't claimed me yet? Do you think there's something wrong with me? What happens if he doesn't? Do we get divorced?"

Lorna laughed and patted her on the shoulder. "Calm down, girl, it just never happened yet. It will. Don't worry. He'll see that spot where your neck meets your shoulder and runs down into your back and he won't be able to help himself. That's why it usually happens before the mating ceremony. But always after."

"Oh," Ella said in a small voice.

"What, honey?"

"That's why he hasn't done it yet. I always want him to… you know, mate facing me." She held her hands up, palms together.

Lorna threw back her head and laughed till tears ran down her cheeks. She patted Ella on the other shoulder. "Why honey, I never heard of such a thing. You just make sure you let him do it from behind at least once." Lorna wiped her eyes, still chuckling softly.

Ella stared at her, blinking hard. "Do you think I'm too strange to be part of his life? I probably do more stuff like that."

Lorna stopped laughing. "Light, honey, no. You are too sweet for words and he loves you more than I've seen a male love a female in a long time. You're perfect just the way you are. The *wolven* need new blood, a little fresh air breathed into us. You fit that bill right perfectly."

"But what if nobody else accepts me but him."

Lorna shook her head. "You're kidding child, they're already calling you Queen Gabriela. The One True Mate who was pulled into the *Pravus* and made it out alive. You're famous honey, they're out at that farmhouse reciting your prophecy to each other right now."

Ella grabbed her hand. "My prophecy?"

"Life begins anew. Love brings two, then four, then six more. Khain's downfall lives inside her. She will be queen."

Ella shook her head. "What does it mean?"

"So much, child, but you don't have to worry about any of that right now. You just worry about getting mated properly. That's all you have to do for now."

"Lorna, I just have one more question."

"Anything, child."

"What's it like being married to a *wolfen*?"

Lorna smiled and grabbed Ella's hand. "It's wonderful. I think Rhen messed around with their instincts and made them unable to be anything but sweet with their mates and their female young, in the same way that she made us all protective of humans. They can get a little hard on their male young, and you'll need to watch that, but you? He'll treat you like gold every day of his life."

Ella took a deep breath and turned to look in the mirror. "Thank you. I'm ready."

CHAPTER 49

*E*lla looked out the window of the helicopter, her bouquet in her hands, her veil thrown back over her hair, white satin spilling around her ankles.

"That's it, up ahead and to your left," their *wolfen* pilot said over the intercom. Behind them, Crew, Harlan, and Mac sat in their tuxedoes, Crew sedate, Harlan almost boisterous, and Mac green and staring straight ahead, a blank but somehow terrified look on his face. Trent and Troy relaxed on the floor.

Lorna turned around and yelled to him. "Macalister Niles, if you are going to puke, you do it away from the dresses! You hear?"

"Yes, ma'am," Mac mouthed, possibly afraid to turn or nod his head. Trent and Troy both looked at him, then stood and flattened themselves against the doors of the helicopter, out of his range.

"Ooh, it sure was nice of that *dragen* to let us use his helicopter," Lorna yelled in Ella's direction. "Funny, a dragon needing a helicopter though."

Ella smiled, but couldn't take her eyes off the ground in front of them. What looked like tens of thousands of *shiften* milled in one large crowd surrounding a large stage. Hundreds of thousands of *shiften*, maybe.

"There are so many of them!" she called over the noise in the cabin.

"They all wanted to come out. Everybody wants to witness history."

Ella swallowed hard as the helicopter banked and headed for the landing pad. They had secured this location for the helicopter pad and the nearby airstrip that could handle even small jets. Now that Ella saw the crowd, she knew why.

The helicopter set down and Lorna whooped as the blades slowly came to a stop. "Wasn't that fun!"

Outside, a male Ella didn't recognize ran up with a step, placed it on the ground, and opened their door.

"Welcome, wedding party, I am Baron, here to take you to the bower."

Ella bit her lip hard to keep from crying and ruining her makeup. Had Trevor found a male with that name or was it a coincidence?

Baron helped Lorna out, then took Ella's hand and helped her make it to the ground without tripping on her dress.

He smiled at her. "Qu—"

"Ella, I'm just Ella, please."

Baron nodded as the three males jumped out behind them, Mac unsteady on his feet. "This way, Ella."

He led them to a horse-drawn carriage that looked straight out of the past. The carriage was wooden and looked handmade, and white and green flowers adorned the outside, almost as thick as a parade float. The horses were huge and thickly muscled, all-white with flowers braided into their manes and tails. Ella wanted to go to them, talk to them, rub their noses. She'd never touched a horse, but she imagined the noses must be soft. They looked soft.

Baron caught her eye. "They are Percherons. Draft horses like Clydesdales. Would you like to see them?"

Ella could only nod. The emotion of the day was too much for her already but she so wanted to see the horses.

Baron led her over and showed her how to hold her hand out, then he produced a bit of carrot from his tuxedo pocket for her to give one of them. It nibbled the carrot from her hand and she laughed softly. The nose was like velvet.

"Her name is Lucy. Now pet her here, and here," Baron told her, indicating her cheek and then her shoulder. The horse watched her silently, its white eyelashes fluttering in the soft breeze.

"Thank you, Baron," she whispered, allowing herself to be led away, back to the carriage where everyone else was already sitting. She stepped in and sat next to Lorna as Baron climbed onto the front and talked to his horses.

They started forward with a small jolt, toward the hum of the crowd. Ella stared at it as Harlan gave Mac a hard time about his fear of flying.

"*Wolven* don't belong in the air," Mac said, still a little green. "We're not *dragens*."

Harlan laughed and clapped him on the back, as their speed increased slightly over the rough dirt track. She could see now that the *shiften* were spread out over a huge hillside, many with blankets and lunches packed as if they were at a picnic, or an outdoor rock concert.

"This has never happened before," Lorna whispered to her.

"What?"

"So many *wolven*, *bearen*, and *felen* together like this."

Ella swallowed hard. The thought made her feel ill. She was nobody.

The carriage pulled up next to a massive stage and stopped. Baron ran around and opened the door, while Crew, Mac, and Harlan boosted themselves over the side, landing hard, laughing and punching each other on the shoulders. Trent and Troy jumped out, looked at each other, and followed the others up the steps. The crowd laughed back and Mac, apparently recovered, held his hands over his head in a champion's pose, which brought more laughter and some applause. Lorna was next and she went up the stairs without Ella. When she reached the top the crowd whistled and stamped their feet. Ella didn't realize why for a second, but then she did. As one of the few female *shiften* left, Lorna had her own notoriety.

Baron held his hand out to her. "Your turn, Ella. They are going to love you." Ella squeezed his hand hard. Why couldn't they have had a small ceremony at some sterile government office? Or better yet, eloped?

She felt her knees weaken and she held on by sheer will, watching the crowd as they craned their necks to see her around the dais. One thing about the crowd bothered her and she couldn't put her finger on it for a moment, but then she did. It was all males. No females and no children anywhere.

She squared her shoulders. She could do this. She lifted her dress and climbed up the steps, blinking in the heavy sunlight, not able to see what was ahead of her for a moment. The crowd was completely silent. Ella swallowed again, hearing a bird cry in the distance. She'd done something wrong. They didn't like her. Her face began to flush.

It started. The applause. The whoops, the calls and chanting. She couldn't tell what they were saying but the noise made their approval obvious. She looked out at them and raised one hand hesitantly into the air and the applause doubled, hitting her almost like a physical thing. She smiled, and then Trevor was there. She pressed into him, but the noise coming from the crowd made it impossible for him to hear her or her to hear him. He took her forearms and smiled down at her. *Beautiful*, he mouthed. *Like an angel.* He touched her bottom lip gently with his thumb and if she knew him at all, which she did, he wanted to place a kiss there.

She beamed at him, kissing his thumb, then letting him pull her over to the wedding bower. It was beautiful, a living thing with pots on each side with what looked like birch trees growing out of them. The birch was bent and twined at the top into an arch like some crazy bonsai tree and flowers grew wildly up the trunks, sprouting color like fireworks.

On the far side of the bower were Trent, Troy, then Blake, Harlan, Beckett, Crew, and Mac. On the near side, stood two females. Lorna and Kalista. Ella had no one else to invite. Her sister was in the hospital and Accalia, Accalia's life outside the conversations they used to have online was a mystery. Ella had never even met her. Trevor had thought it wouldn't be a good idea to invite her and Ella had agreed, even though it had twinged her heart a bit.

Ella held her head up high, knowing her mother and aunt wouldn't have come even if they had still been alive, but that was ok. They had always been right. She *was* different. She *was* strange.

Trevor led her to the bower and she stood under it as the

noise of the crowd finally quieted. Wade faced her, smiling, dressed in a simple dark suit.

Ella faced her mate and he held out his hands to her. She took them, feeling the tears drip down her face already. There was nothing to be done about them. Wade spoke and Ella hoped the event was being recorded. She couldn't focus on his words. Couldn't make anything make sense. All she could see was Trevor, her strong, healthy, handsome *wolfen* who would tear his way between worlds to save her. Who would give up his life to see her well. She couldn't ask anyone for more than that.

I love you, she mouthed to him, seeing only him, hearing only him, like they were the only two people who existed in the world.

I love you back, he mouthed and somehow she kept herself from falling into his arms.

He would know the right moment for that to happen.

He always did.

CHAPTER 50

*Y*ou may kiss your mate," Wade said and Trevor pulled her close. The moment had come. She closed her eyes and waited for his lips upon hers. When his soft touch made her skin tickle, thousands of *shiften* cheered, the massive noise making it seem like they'd been sleeping before.

As the kiss ended, Ella fingered her new ring, the one on her left hand. The one that connected her and Trevor for the rest of their lives.

They faced the crowd together and waved, and even the *shiften* standing on the stage with them laughed and clapped. Wade turned to the crowd and held up his hands. They quieted and turned around as one, each one of them retrieving something white and lacy from the ground behind them. As Ella watched, thousands of males released hundreds of thousands of butterflies into the air.

She gasped and held her hand to her throat. She'd never seen anything so amazing. So many wings beating, flying up, over the crowd, slowly, erratically, in the manner of butterflies. They bumped into each other but didn't seem to mind, just turning direction and lazily flying upward in the sunlight.

A dozen butterflies flew towards her and she felt them land, whisper-soft in her hair and on her dress like she was a Disney princess.

She laughed as the symbols of new life fluttered about, some heading for the trees and bushes, many choosing to light on the males in the crowd as they had landed on her.

A large yellow swallowtail stopped right on her mate's nose, opening and closing its wings and making her laugh again as the good and soft parts of her new reality settled in on her.

If her life was at least tipped a bit more towards butterfly kisses than demon battles, she would be ok.

"It is time," Wade said, nodding his head at Trevor. Trevor gathered her up and pulled her towards the back of the stage, butterflies flying off her. She held up her hand one more time and waved goodbye. Goodbye to Lorna, Kalista, Wade, her brothers-in-law, her mate's pack mates, and all the *shiften* who had come out to wish them well.

She tiptoed down the stairs that led off the stage. "Where are we going?"

"You'll see," he said, and she thought she heard an edge in his voice.

Just to the right and behind the stage stood a cabin. The path to it was marked by white stones. She hadn't noticed it before, but now her eyes were glued to it.

The claiming.

Trevor opened the door and pulled her inside, then closed it and leaned against it, smiling at her. "We did it."

"We did," she said, pressing herself against her mate. "There were so many of them. I can't believe they all came out."

"Of course they did, Ella. You represent hope to all of them. If I found my one true mate, that means they really exist, and if the rest of them are even half as pretty and sweet and strong as you are, every *shiften* who connects with one will be the luckiest male on earth. They will all leave here renewed and eager to find theirs."

Ella flushed and looked down at the ground. Trevor took her chin between his thumb and forefinger. "El, when you turn pink like that, it makes me hopeful."

She smiled up at him. "Hopeful of?"

"That you'll let me touch other parts of you that are pink and soft, that only I get to see."

Ella flushed harder, but her body reacted strongly to his words. "Is that why we're here?"

Trevor looked around at the room that Ella had barely noticed yet. "Yeah, actually, there's—ah, something we have to do." He frowned as if he didn't know how to tell her.

She made her eyes wide, like she was nervous, tickled that he seemed to be. "What? Will it hurt?"

Trevor licked his lips. "Ah, I don't know. It's not supposed to, but…"

Ella laughed merrily at the look on his face. "I know what it is, Mr. Big Bad Wolf. Lorna told me. It makes me hot just thinking about it." Nervous too, but she wouldn't tell him that.

His eyes widened, then lowered with lust. "Really, Little Red Riding Hood, aren't you the bad girl?"

"So bad," she agreed. "Do I get a spanking?"

He cocked an eyebrow. "You're into that?"

She laughed. "I have no idea."

A growling started deep in his throat and his eyes shone for a minute as he dropped his head and stared at her, desire clear on his face. Ella shrieked and gathered her skirts, then turned and ran through the neat little cabin, around the coffee table, towards the only door she could see. She slammed it open and ran inside toward the bed in the middle of the room.

Trevor caught her around the waist and spun her around, planting her on her feet and holding her so she couldn't wriggle free. "You're mine now."

She struggled against him for a moment, then stopped, dropped her hands, and waited. "I am yours, body, mind, and soul."

He lifted his hands towards her face, then above into her hair, pulling off her filmy veil, placing it to the side on a tan leather chair. Then he pulled out each bobby pin, one by one, until her hair fell about her shoulders. Ella reached behind her and undid her dress in the back then stood patiently under his ministrations as he fluffed her hair back over her shoulders.

He moved his fingers down to either side of her neck, spanning it with his big hands, then down to her collarbone and chest. He tugged on her dress and it went down easily to the floor, where she stepped out of it, leaving her in white lacy bra, white satin underwear, thigh-high white stockings, and white low heels.

Trevor stepped back and looked her up and down. "Good night, you're gorgeous. I'll never know how I got so lucky."

"You were sweet and kind and you took care of me."

He shook his head, his eyes still traveling down her body. "Which I pledge to be and do until the day I die."

Ella teared up at that. She knew it, but him saying it was so powerful she couldn't hold back.

Trevor unbuttoned his tuxedo jacket and took it off, laying it on the chair as Ella stood in her panties and bra before him, watching, waiting for her mate, her eyes locked on his.

He shrugged out of the shirt and tie and kicked off his shoes, then dropped the rest of his clothes. She took a moment to admire his body, the strong planes and lines of it, the curves and bumps she would spend the rest of her life memorizing with her hands and her tongue. His erection stood strong, straight out from his body, curving up slightly and she longed to take him into her mouth. She would not, though. Not until the claiming. This was his show. She was his to do with as he wanted.

They came together and her bra disappeared in a flash, then her panties. "We'll leave these on," he said, fingering her stockings, the thickness of his voice making her desire rise. She couldn't wait to have him inside her. She couldn't wait to feel his teeth penetrate her skin.

He kissed her softly, deeply, sweetly, then worshiped her body with his hands and tongue. He lowered her to the bed, staring into her eyes.

Ella kissed him, then flipped over in his arms.

The growling started at once.

***

He was completely out of control, totally unable to help himself. His fangs grew exponentially and he felt them scraping his lower lip. He would take his female, hard and fast. He positioned her how he wanted her, his hands spanning her hips, his fingers digging into the soft flesh there. She moaned and undulated under him, driving his passions into a fast gallop. He positioned himself at her very center, then speared into her, throwing his head back with the pleasure of it, at the slippery bliss she offered him and he took, as was his right.

His eyes traveled up and down her back, her curves, but always returned to that one spot on the back of her left shoulder. The delicateness of her slender neck screamed to him until he could hold back no longer.

He fell on her, biting hard, letting her blood flow down his chin. She screamed when he did and her inner muscles clamped down on him, hard, forcing a monumental release from him, their orgasms merging as they both cried out.

Trevor pulled his teeth from his mate's skin and rode out his own pleasure as he saw something unbelievable. Wings of silver and gold light erupted from her back, no more substantial than spider webs, but still strong enough to envelop them both in a kind of cocoon, lifting them off the bed.

Trevor closed his eyes, his body still pumping into her, the hard release incapacitating him. They rose in the air, then quietly returned to the bed, just as her moans settled and his body relaxed.

He opened his eyes, almost scared of what he would see.

No wings. No break in the sweet, pale skin of her back. Even his bite had healed over already, leaving only a darkened scab there, in the shape of his teeth.

He hoped it would stay forever.

It seemed only fitting that his mate's *renqua* match a part of him.

EPILOGUE

*W*ade walked through the crowd, shaking hands, thanking *shiften* for coming, answering questions as best he could.

He nodded his head at a young *wolfen* from St. Louis who had just asked him something, repeating what he'd already said a dozen times. "We don't know, Phillip. The One True Mates could be anywhere. We will be sending out a memo soon with what to look for, but my guess is looking won't help. There are forces at work here greater than any of us, and we believe couples will be brought together when the time is right."

Kalista ran up to him, resplendent in her body-hugging purple dress and the highest heels he had ever seen. "Wade, we've got a disturbance outside of town. I need a crew."

Wade nodded. "Tell Mac. Take them all except Trevor."

"What about the *dragen*?"

"He's still recovering. I don't know when he'll be back."

"Too bad."

"Yes."

A blinding light flashed out of every window in the small cabin that Trevor and Ella had retired to, making Wade and Kalista both throw their hands up over their eyes. The crowd gasped and looked away as one.

Wade blinked hard, still seeing the imprint of the wall of light as it covered them all. He hesitantly lowered his hand, and saw the light had curved, headed up into the sky. As he watched, another light gathered in the heavens, then reached down to meet the oncoming light. They met in the middle, somewhere around the place of the clouds, and both evaporated into a blazing, soundless fireworks show.

Wade smiled. "It's done. Our future looks bright."

Kalista snorted a throaty laugh that was somehow sexy as hell. Wade looked away from her, trying to meet the eyes of his Lorna if he could find her in the crowd.

Kalista elbowed him and nodded towards the cabin. "What about them. What happens now?"

Wade shook his head. "I have no idea. But the fates are finally on our side. We just need to keep our ears and tails up and our faces towards the wind."

Kalista nodded, looked at him for a long moment, like she wanted to say something else, then she shook her head and ran off to find Mac, not even wobbling in those heels.

Wade did not watch her go.

Notes from Lisa xoxoxo

I have never had as much fun writing a book as I did this one! I am in love with everyone, especially Trent and Troy. I don't even know how I fell in love with two non-shifting *wolven*, but I did. They were meant not to be major characters but, boy, did they bite me on the neck and say, "Sorry! We're here and we're staying and we are going to do some interesting shit!"

I'm sure you noticed there were several threads left open. There is so much story left! The one true mates could be anywhere, and the *shiften* are more determined than ever to find them. <3 thank you for reading!

One True Mate 2, Dragon's Heat is available! Look for it at amazon and createspace <3

Graeme refuses to believe he could have a OTM meant for him, even as it slowly kills him to do so.

Made in the USA
Columbia, SC
01 February 2025